OVERKILL

Baen Books by Robert Buettner

Overkill
Undercurrents (forthcoming)

OVERKILL

ROBERT BUETTNER

OVERKILL

A Baen Books Original

Baen Publishing Enterprises
P.O. Box 1403
Riverdale, NY 10471
www.baen.com

ISBN: 978-1-4391-3420-7

Cover art by Justin Adams

First Baen printing, March 2011

Distributed by Simon & Schuster
1230 Avenue of the Americas
New York, NY 10020

Library of Congress Cataloging-in-Publication Data

Buettner, Robert.
  Overkill / Robert Buettner.
    p. cm.
  ISBN 978-1-4391-3420-7 (trade pbk.)
  I. Title.
  PS3602.U344094 2011
  813'.6—dc22

2011000591

Printed in the United States of America

10 9 8 7 6 5 4 3 2 1

At twenty-three, Jazen Parker has completed his Legion hitch a hero. But in four months, he'll have a price on his head. Worse, he's lost his past, and he can't find his future. Worst of all, he's chosen to search for them on the deadliest planet in the universe.

Lyrics excerpted from *The Green Hills of Earth* by permission of Lux Transcriptions, Ltd. and the Rhysling Trust, whose cooperation is gratefully acknowledged.

In these Worlds if they be inhabited . . . Are we or they Lords of the World?

—Johannes Kepler

One

Orion Parker lowered her head and stared down into her glass when the cop appeared, silhouetted against the pedway glow beyond the open door. Like all cops, he stood a head taller than the crowd, with his helmet and antennae adding another half foot.

The bar crowd was as light as crowds ever got on Yavet, because by the fortieth day of any month paychips had vanished down throats, into veins, or into somebody else's pocket at gunpoint. The cop, shoulders square, plowed through the drinkers and dancers toward the service 'bot. Some cops deigned to snake sideways through the crowds, polite even in a hole like this. Vice didn't.

The cop reached the service 'bot, pressed his ID against its reader, then watched as the list of open tabs in the bar rolled across the 'bot's screen.

"Crap on crust!" Orion slid off her stool and burrowed into a crowd too drunk to smell its own vomit and too stoned to smell her fear.

She hadn't fled fifteen feet when a gauntleted hand clamped her elbow.

The crowd shrank back, made a hole around them. The cop peered down at her through his face shield with eyes like black stones. It was Polian, from Vice. "Must have been a good month, Parker, if you can still afford whiskey."

She stared at the floor, shook her head. "I haven't served a client in six months."

1

He cocked his head, sneered for show. "Really? Let's talk about it." He shoved her toward a vacant Sleeper, and she stumbled against a fat man who smelled like urine.

Polian slammed her through the booth's open door, wedged in alongside her, then pulled the door shut. He took one breath, voiced up the ventilator, then waited. "Okay. What you got for me, Parker?"

"The trade's slow."

"Bullshit."

"I swear." She pointed at the ceiling. "Slow Uplevel." Down at the floor. "Slow Downlevel." She tossed her head left, then right. "Uptown, downtown. Nobody's got clients."

He stared at her, drummed his fingers against the Sleeper's closed door.

She sighed. "Okay. I hear Mouse Bell's taking clients."

He smiled. "Already? The Mouse just got out of the House last month. Where?"

She stared at the gilt CFA scrolled across Polian's breastplate badge. "I dunno."

Polian stared back at her. "Parker, you of all people know it's cold in the House. Wanna go back?"

She sighed again, turned her head toward the Sleeper's stained padding. "Twenty-second and Elysian. Fifteen lower. Kube fourteen."

"Anything else?"

Orion shook her head.

Polian stabbed his armored finger at her face. "I find out you short-decked me, you're back in the House. For good!"

She wormed her hand up between her body and the booth wall, raised her palm, and looked the cop in the eye, without blinking. "I don't know about any other clients. Mother's Blood."

It was the cop's turn to sigh. "Okay. Where you want it?"

"Someplace that won't bleed."

"If you don't bleed, they'll know you're a snitch."

Orion tapped her index finger to her right cheek.

Polian drew his mailed fist back, until it brushed the Sleeper's padding, then slugged Orion so hard that her body sprung the door, and she crumpled onto something sticky that puddled the bar's floor. She lay gasping, while Polian stepped across her and left.

Orion rolled up, onto her knees, and tasted a salty trickle inside her mouth. It hurt when she smiled, and when she touched her tongue to her teeth, two moved. She spat blood onto the bar floor. It was a bargain price for two successful lies, the one her blood told the world, and the one she had just told the cop.

Two

Ten minutes later, Orion left the bar, squeezed past a robbery in progress on the pedway, then climbed four blocks uplevel, walked two across, and four over, until she reached her Kube.

She sanexed, retrieved the tools of her trade from the dug-out hollow behind the padding, then blew the price of a whiskey on the tube to Sixty-eighth and Park, twenty upper. The hotel district was cream, with sixteen-foot ceilings, virtual sunshine, and pedways wide enough for people to glide four abreast in both directions.

Her client was already waiting. Clients, in fact.

The woman's face was porcelain-smooth, with huge, brown almond-shaped eyes. By Yavet standards, the woman was old. By any standards, she was beautiful. Except for her grotesque body, misshapen by her brush with felony. And her lips, stretched tight by pain.

Orion tugged her off the main way, into a side passage. "You trying to get me sent to the House?"

The woman frowned. "What's the problem?"

"You. You don't exactly blend."

The man extended his hand. "I'm—"

"Shut up. What I don't know I can't tell."

He nodded. "But you *are* O'Ryan? And you've brought what she needs?"

Orion looked over her shoulder. A man in the pedway stared at the three of them. She asked the couple, "You got space?"

The two of them led her down the passage, and to a Kube on the second floor of a first-rate, boutique Sleeper. The place measured twelve feet long by six feet wide, with a private sanex, a curtained window slit that overlooked the pedway, even a rear door to a balcony big enough for two people to stand on.

Orion set her bag on a side shelf wide enough to sit on, nodded as she looked around, then whistled. "You definitely got space!"

The man said, "I gather this is illegal, here?" Like the woman, he was old by Yavet standards, stood straight, like a cop did, but had soft eyes.

The man stood a head taller than an average Yavi, the couple's clothes were cut offworld, and he wore in his lapel a button-sized fabric rosette the color of sky in a travel holo, sprinkled with tiny white stars. Veteran of something. Orion snorted to herself. Who wasn't?

"Illegal? It's a capital crime for you two. Life for me if I go down for the third time." Orion pointed at the window slit. "Draw that curtain." A pistol-sized bulge lifted his jacket lapel. "Better yet, you cover the window, Quickdraw."

"Little over the top here, aren't we?" But he stepped alongside the slit.

"You're not from here, are you? Vice doesn't knock, they shoot."

The man raised salt-and-pepper eyebrows. "You're kidding."

Orion held her hand palm-up toward the woman and wiggled fingers. "Cash up front."

The woman handed her a fat plastck envelope and grimaced. "Cash seems melodramatic."

Orion cocked her head and batted her eyes. "When I file my taxes, I can't exactly fill out the "occupation" line "Midwife," can I?"

The man shook his head. "This is nuts. A planet so crowded that people live in a layer cake and sleep standing up. The cops ignore drugs and stickups, but childbirth is a hanging offense."

"Dope and gunplay thin population. Childbirth increases it. If you don't like Yavet, why'd you come?"

The man drew the pistol from the holster beneath his jacket, and Orion raised her eyebrows. A blunt gunpowder automatic, not like the sharky things cops and robbers carried. He stood alongside the curtain, pushed it aside with his pistol's barrel, and peeked out. "We came to Yavet for the culture."

Orion opened the envelope and walked her fingers through the bills, counting. "Yavet has no culture."

"The brochure misled us."

Orion ran her fingers over the raised crest on the envelope, then swore. "Where'd you swap cash?"

The woman said, "At the hotel desk. Why?"

Orion rolled her eyes. "Fuck!" Then she sighed. "Pray the desk clerk's lazy or crooked. That's a push bet." She opened her bag, and pointed the woman to the horizontal bed. "Strip down, honey, and let's see where you're at."

The woman was gravid, and seven centimeters dilated. She panted through a contraction, then said to Orion, as she sat beside the woman on the bed, "This is dangerous for you. Keep the money. Go. My husband's delivered a child before."

Orion's head snapped back, and she pointed at the man as he stood by the window. "You kiss him with that mouth?"

It proved to be brutal, even for a first birth. Seven hours later, Orion dripped sweat as badly as the woman did as she laid the baby on the mother's quivering belly. But the woman never uttered a peep, and the husband—the expression sounded almost nice since the woman had said it aloud—seemed to manage to keep watch, encourage his wife, and assist Orion without stress, like he had endured a lifetime of it.

Orion sat back, took a breath, and smiled at the woman. "Nice job, mama. If this were legal, I'd do it for free."

The woman stared at her newborn son as she stroked the infant's matted hair. "Why *do* you do it?"

Orion rubbed the little one's tiny back. "You just look at this guy and tell me how anyone could—"

"Crap." The man, peeking out the window, snapped back the slide on his pistol.

The woman clutched the baby. "Jason! What's wrong?"

He said to Orion, "Your vice cops wear *armor*? And carry assault rifles?"

"Crap on crust! How many?"

"Eight. So far. They're still piling out of a four-wheel."

"Twatface desk clerk reported your swap!" Orion tugged bloody sheeting out from under the woman, and sluiced water over the woman's loins. "Finish cleaning up! Change into fresh clothes."

She pointed at the man's pistol. "Lose the cannon. It could hurt somebody."

"It has. Trust me. I thought this place was Dodge City."

Orion wadded up the woman's underwear, the sheeting, the afterbirth, her own bag, then vac'd the whole gory mess down the sanex. "You can't shoot *cops*! And if you could, you couldn't shoot a twelve-man, armored shakedown squad!" She turned to the woman. "Is he always stubborn?"

"Usually, he's worse." The woman gritted her teeth as she struggled, hollow-eyed, into a robe.

Voices shouted faintly, down in the lobby.

Orion paused, took a breath, then faced the two of them, palms out. "This is gonna be all right. You tell them you swapped for cash to buy dope. But you got stuck up, so you got no dope and no cash to prove your story."

The man named Jason rolled his eyes. "That's the most—"

"It happens all the time. The worst they'll do is summarily revoke your visas."

The woman clutched the newborn. "What about my baby?"

"The baby can't be here." Orion pointed at the rear balcony. "I'll take it out that way."

A doorway banged in the distance, echoing as though up a stairwell.

The woman shook her head, clutched the baby tighter. It kicked and squalled.

Jason shook his head. "No. Our baby stays. If we have to appeal this, we can do that. We know people—"

"Appeal, my ass! A vice cop's badge legend reads "CFA." For Child First, Always. That doesn't mean equal opportunity. It means being born unauthorized is a summarily judged capital crime, just like giving birth." Orion pointed at the door. "When the goons break down that door, the first thing they'll do is suffocate your child while you watch. Then they'll shoot you."

Boots thundered against metal stair treads.

Jason shook his head again, fingered the pistol beneath his lapel with quivering fingers. "It won't work. They'll cover the back of the building."

Orion shook her head. "*You* would, soldier. Cops get lazy and stupid when crooks have no leverage."

The bootfalls rumbled in the hall, now, mixed with the ring of cocking rifle bolts.

The man called Jason said, "Then we'll all go."

"If you both aren't in the room, they'll assume an unauthorized birth and keep looking. For your baby. 'Til death do you part."

The husband pried his son from his wife's arms, kissed the top of the baby's head, then handed him to Orion.

The wife sobbed.

The husband's eyes glistened, but his jaw was set. "This won't stand. We'll get in touch with you. Get him back."

Orion stepped backward, shook her head. "If they know he exists, they'll hunt him down. Not just the government. There are freelance bounty hunters all over this planet. And every other planet, too. Let the government deport you. Go tour the galaxy, or whatever you're doing, and forget this ever happened. Never tell a soul, anywhere, that the boy was born, if you want him to live."

Something heavy pounded the Kube's front door.

Orion tucked the struggling newborn between her breasts, and buttoned her blouse over it. She said to them, "I'm sorry." Then she ran to the balcony, and swung a leg over the rail.

Craack.

Behind her, plasteel splintered.

She lowered herself until she dangled from the balcony's floor, like a trapezeier, and dropped the last six feet to the passage pavement. Then Orion Parker stood, clutched the mewling infant to her breast, and ran toward the dark.

Twenty-four years later

Three

"Next!" The bald Customs and Immigration clerk on the stool behind the podium had long since sweated through his uniform blouse. He shouted to be heard above the insect drone beyond the terminal's open, steel-cage ceiling. Shuttles landed on DE 476 bang on the planet's equator. Therefore, even at midnight, local, the temperature under roof as well as outside stagnated at an identical, breezeless ninety-eight degrees Fahrenheit. The air was so thick that the flies didn't buzz, they droned.

I held my place behind the yellow line, as I stared to my left, at the adjacent podium with a sign above it: NATIVES RETURNING TO DE 476, ONLY. The podium's stool was empty and dust covered, as was its yellow line. Apparently, returning to DE 476 was an even lower priority for natives lucky enough to leave than visiting DE 476 was for everyone else.

The Human Union preliminarily graded new planets that were warm enough to liquify water, but cool enough to avoid boiling it away, "E," for "Earthlike." If the planet proved too distant, too deadly, or too different, it earned the prefix "D," which officially stood for "Downgraded." Downgraded Earthlike 476 was all three, and known to everyone but its tourism bureau as "Dead End."

The clerk periscoped his thin neck and swiveled his head around the empty arrivals auditorium. "I said next! Anybody here named Next?" He scowled at me over old-fashioned wire and glass spectacles, then waved me forward while he fanned himself with a sheet of folded paper.

11

With my boot toe I nudged my duffle alongside his podium, then bent forward and pressed my eye against the retinal. After a heartbeat, the scanner chimed.

"Gotcha. Stand back." The clerk yawned into his fist. "For the comfort and safety of the next person in line, please use one of the tissues provided to wipe the receptacle. Thank you."

There was no next person in line. I wiped anyway. If a Legion hitch teaches a recruit anything, it's hygiene and following orders.

The clerk eyed his screen. "Parker, Jazen. What the hell kind of name is Jazen?"

I shrugged. "Yavet name."

"Never heard of it."

C-drive and jump technology made the Human Union, all five hundred two planets of it, possible. But barely. Interstellar voyages took as long as sail-powered voyages took on the oceans of a garden-variety pre-industrial. Average citizens of the galaxy knew worlds beyond their own the way average Victorian Englishmen knew Borneo, which is to say as dark places run by savages.

"I suppose. There's bookoo jumps between Dead End and Yavet."

"There's bookoo jumps between Dead End and everywhere. You're twenty-three?"

"Subjective. About twenty-four, in undilated time." They say GI life is boredom punctuated by intervals of sheer terror. But aboard a troop transport moving between jumps at near light speed a month not only *seemed* to pass slower, it did. A Trueborn named Einstein proved it, they said, and that's all the thought I'd ever given it.

"So I see. Legionnaires spend lots of time near light speed." He ran a finger along the screen. "Awarded Star of Marin with Leaves. You get that for doing good or for doing bad?" He frowned.

Worlds apart breed ignorance. Ignorance breeds misunderstanding. Misunderstanding breeds the need to do unto others before they do unto you. If it wasn't for xenophobia, the Legion wouldn't exist.

I shrugged again. "Depends."

He narrowed his eyes. "On what?"

"On which side you were on."

He grunted and frowned deeper. The Legion only broke things and hurt people for the greater good. It had said so right in my oath. But that didn't make hired killers popular.

He sat back. "Purpose of visit? R and R, maybe?"

A Legion honorable discharge earns twelve months amnesty from whatever a legionnaire might have done before. Even a Yavet Illegal like me, who was otherwise dead meat walking for any bounty hunter in the Union who tracked me down. There are two kinds of Yavet Illegals. The kind who cover their tracks, and dead ones.

So I hesitated before I answered. He drummed his fingers while he stared into his screen. Hell, my information was in every 'puter in the Union, anyway. During the four months left on my amnesty, neither this guy nor anybody else in government could rat me out to a bounty hunter for a finder's fee. "I was discharged eight months ago."

He tapped his screen, yawned. "I can see that. It was a joke. Nobody takes R and R on Dead End."

"I'm with the Cutler party."

He periscoped the empty hall again. "You got 'em in your duffle? That's a joke, too."

I stretched a smile. "Got it." I jerked my thumb back up the pedway. "Mr. Cutler and the others are behind me. They have checked luggage to claim. All I have is the duffle." It wasn't much to show for a life.

His keyboard rattled. "Ah. Cutler, Bartram." Then the clerk raised his eyebrows and whistled. "Trueborn Earthman. Wa-di-doo. Purpose of the Cutler Party visit, then?"

"Hunting."

He raised his eyebrows higher. "Hunting what?"

"Grezzen."

He stared, while sweat trickled down his cheek. Then he grinned. "No. Really. I have to type something in this blank."

"Really." I paused. "Is that a problem?"

He swivelled on his stool, and pointed at the terminal wall. A pirate-black flag that hung there bore red script: "Libertarian Republic of Dead End: Live Free or Die."

Not bad. As a Yavi I appreciated physical and behavioral elbow room more than most. Maybe I'd come back.

He shook his head. "Nope. Libertarian republic means do what you want, unless you get in somebody else's way. But most come for the live free, not the die." He jerked his thumb over his shoulder. "Have a pleasant stay. Move along."

I snapped my fingers. "Oh. Since I'm first through, I'm supposed to claim our oversize freight. Where—"

He stared at his screen while he pointed over his left shoulder, at a lighted passage. "For the freight terminal, bear right at the plaque. Bang on the door. There's only two of us here at night and he's a heavy sleeper. The shuttle will taxi over there after the morning shift gets here and pumps out the crappers." He held up the soggy single-paper sheet he had been fanning himself with. "You care for a fine dining brochure?"

I smiled as I hefted my duffle. "I know. A joke."

He stared at me over his spectacles. "I don't get it."

The roofed trench that led away from the arrivals hall stretched four hundred yards, as black beyond its barred ceiling as a tunnel through a coal seam. The open roof that arched above my head was fabricated of steel bars as thick as my thigh, spaced a foot apart. Spherical metal lanterns dangled from the overhead bars, the lantern flames sputtering oily smoke that sank to the passage floor like lead fog.

Dead End's tourist site lauded the yesteryear charm of the local coal oil lamps. In fact, the only export component of Dead End's GPP was boutique kerosene. The fine print said the kerosene fumes discouraged local insects. They didn't discourage many. I swatted as I walked, but replacement squadrons swarmed in between the bars.

A hundred steam-bath yards down the passage, a fork distributed passengers left to ground transport, and straight ahead to freight pickup. I flopped my duffle down at a section where the bars wilted apart like limp spaghetti. Additional steel sections had been welded between the gaps. Freshly wire-brushed, the welds gleamed beneath the lanterns' smoky flicker.

I rested my hands on my knees. Some kind of animal bellow echoed in the distance. Sweat dripped off my nose onto a platter-sized brass plaque bolted to the concrete floor below the repaired bars.

"Thom Webb. Beloved father and husband. Slain by grezzen on this spot, May 4, 2108."

I eyed my 'puter. May 27, 2108.

I shouldered my duffle, double-timed the remaining three hundred yards to the freight terminal, then pounded the locked, armored door so hard that sweat spray exploded off my fists.

Four

I stood with my back pressed against the armored door, scanning the night, for four minutes, while my heart pounded. When the door finally opened, I nearly fell in on my ass.

A stooped man in coarse coveralls, stevedores' medallion pinned to his collar, relocked the door behind us. He faced me, scratching a beard the color of wash water. "This is the freight terminal. Ground transport is—"

"I want the freight terminal."

"Then lucky you." He turned and limped toward a counter flanked by thirty-foot tall crate stacks.

Panting and wide-eyed, I pointed back toward the floor plaque and twisted bars. "You should keep this door unlocked. I could have—"

His back to me, he waved his hand like he was discarding a candy wrapper.

"Modern bars are grezzen-proof. And there hasn't been one grezzen attack inside the Line since the Rover 'bots went operational ten years ago. Tourism bureau updates the plaque, and shines up the welds, every month. Heightens the adventure for visitors."

I rolled my eyes. "The whole thing's a fraud?"

"Oh, that grezz got Thom Webb right out there, alright. Tore him apart, bone from bone, like a wolf on a rotisserie chicken."

I rolled my eyes again. "If it's part fraud, why do you believe any of it?"

He stepped behind his freight counter, and tapped real papers edge-up into a stack. "Thom Webb was my daddy."

I dropped my jaw and my duffle. "I'm sorry."

He shrugged. "S'alright. There's not a person on Dead End hasn't lost family to the grezzen. They got my mother, too. My daddy used to say, if you meet a grezzen and the devil walking down the street together—and on Dead End you might—kill the grezzen first."

The Handtalk in my thigh pocket shivered, and I answered it. "Parker?"

"I'm at the freight terminal, Mr. Cutler."

"Parker? Speak up. Christ! These things are crap."

His crap, though he didn't know it. Handtalk was a wholly owned Cutler Communications subsidiary, but a mere pimple on its colossal corporate ass. There was no gain in pointing that out to Cutler, a self-described big picture guy. "The Handtalks are top-shelf, Sir. But they're line-of-sight, and we're both in a ditch. DE 476 has no satellite net."

"Seriously? Christ. This hole makes the boondocks look like Manhattan."

I covered my mouthpiece with my hand and sighed. Most citizens of the Human Union knew what boondocks looked like. Only a Trueborn few, like Bartram Cutler, knew what Manhattan looked like. In fact, he owned two penthouses there.

"We're going on to the hotel, Parker. That flight was a bitch."

For me down in the cargo bay, too, thanks. I had been hired by Cutler sight unseen and didn't know much about him beyond what anybody could read in the 'zines. But he was easy to dislike.

"Parker, did you *see* those bars and that plaque in the passage?"

"I did."

"You don't really get a sense for the *power* of these things from the holos. I was right to order hand-reloaded brass."

Bartram Cutler, most trailwise bwana in all Manhattan. "We couldn't have bought rounds off the shelf. The gun's too old, sir."

"Which is why the thing cost so much to restore. Make 'em uncrate everything before you sign for it. I don't care how long it takes."

I cared.

Cutler said, "Remember, at their rates even one scratch is unacceptable! Goodnight. Out. Whatever the hell you say. Christ!"

I sat on my duffle and sighed. Legionnaires were scorned everywhere, but on Earth, evidently, this Christ had us beat. I rubbed sleep from my eyes, and wondered how long it would take to pump out the crappers.

The wall behind the orphan clerk's counter was pinned with curled papers, flapped by a lazy ceiling fan. He squinted as he ran his finger across lines on the one fresh sheet. "Two consignments on this shuttle. Seventy-one ton container, declared as prepacked. Six-ton container, declared as replacement Line Rover 'bots. You're waiting for the seventy-one ton."

"I never said that."

"Didn't have to. Only Wrangler that's in off the Line just now squats to pee. You don't. At least not in *my* warehouse."

I frowned. "Is everybody on this planet a comedian?"

The orphan stared at me. " 'Til you got here. Hold still." He drew back his hand, then slapped my forearm.

A life-raft yellow spider as big as a saucer bounced off the floor, flashing fangs as thick as knitting needles. The clerk stomped it with a thick boot. "Goddamn eight-legged rats."

I shuddered, gasped, and pointed at the bright splatter. "Thanks. I take it that's poisonous?" Survival 101: On every planet, creatures who advertised themselves did so for a reason.

He shrugged. "Lemon bug venom'll kill a woog—six-legged water buffalo to you—in thirty seconds. But not you or me. Different planets, different organic chemistry."

"But it would hurt?"

He shook his head. "Nah. Your hand would swell up like a sweet potato for a while. You'd puke for a couple days."

He jerked his thumb at a door behind him. "I sleep in there. It's cramped. But you're welcome to sleep out here in the freight bay 'til the shuttle taxis over from the passenger terminal."

I stared down at the yellow goo on the floor. "Any more of these in here?"

He pointed at the space behind his counter, and rapped on the countertop. "I spread Bugout back here every morning. You can bed down fine. And I keep a shovel under the counter to whack 'em before they get too close."

A ringing testimonial for Bugout.

Ten minutes later the clerk retired to a back room and turned out the lights. The room seemed uncomfortably vast to a Yavet native like me. I wedged behind the clerk's counter, curled on the Bugoff-dusted floor, then laid the shovel close at hand and kneaded my duffle into a pillow. Lemon bug legs tapped, somewhere in the dark. Like a bounty hunter's boots in the corridor outside a down-level Kube's wall back home, when I was four.

With my eyes squeezed shut, I could still hear Orion's voice as I clung to her warmth.

She touched her fingers to my lips and whispered, "It's all right, babe. He'll walk right on past."

The bounty hunter coughed, a squealing wheeze.

Orion said, "It's Jack, alright. I should've killed him the first time he came after you. The smoking will, but not soon enough."

"Why didn't you?"

She sighed. "All life is precious, Jazen. Even a killer's. And especially an Illegal's. That's a thing that should never be forgotten."

"Am I one?"

My fingers rested on her lips, so even in the dark I could feel her smile. "A killer? Never. An Illegal? Sure, but that's just a stupid name thought up by stupid people."

"No. I mean am I a thing that should never be forgotten?"

"What? I'd never forget you. Why would you ever even wonder about a thing like that?"

"They forgot me."

She squeezed me tighter. "Oh, sweetheart, your parents didn't forget you. Never, ever."

I hugged her tighter, and I felt her tears on my fingertips.

She said, "It's complicated. You'll understand, someday."

"Will Jack get me before someday?"

"Never, ever. I persuaded him. Now he won't mess with us."

"What's persuaded?"

"They call him One-eyed Jack, now. We'll leave it at that."

The coughing outside faded, then disappeared.

Like she did every night, Orion rocked me, hummed, and I closed my eyes.

I woke in the warehouse on Dead End to gray daylight, and someone whispering, "Come to momma."

I creaked to my knees, peeked over the counter, out across the warehouse, and Dead End surprised me again.

Five

Twenty feet across the warehouse, the speaker knelt, back to me, silhouetted in an up-angled ramp that ended in an open roll-up door through which showed a sagging gauze of morning fog. She wore dusty khaki bush shorts, a scale-armor tunic, and over-the-knee leather boots that I guessed reached just higher than lemon bugs could jump. The bare limbs that showed were tan and lean. She held her broad-brimmed leather hat at ground level, while she scooped at a lemon bug with it.

The little monster sprang at her. She trapped it in her hat's upturned crown, then flicked it outside, where it landed legs-to-sky, on moist asphalt. The creature righted itself and scurried away.

The woman turned away from the door, re-creasing her hat crown with short-nailed fingers. She moved with the weary economy of an infantry soldier, or at least of someone used to hard work and grit.

I stood, cleared my throat, and she jerked her eyes up toward me.

I sucked a breath. Weary she might be, but her eyes were Caribbean blue. So were Cutler's wife's, however this woman's looked not only luminous but birth-natural.

I rubbed circulation into the repaired leg, then limped up the ramp and joined her at the door. Then I pointed at the spot where the lemon bug had been. "I thought lemon bugs were eight-legged rats."

She turned, unsurprised, and shrugged. "Everything in this universe has its place. I take it you're claiming freight, too." She nodded to me. "I'm Kit Born."

"Jazen Parker. I—" The thunder of chemical engines cut me off, as the shuttle that had brought me down taxied into the thick barred cage that formed the shuttle hangar. The place was big enough that it enclosed two more parked shuttles.

Even at idle, the shuttle's engines shook the floor beneath my boots, and the tang of their kerosene exhaust sank down the ramp into the warehouse.

Interstellar cruisers drifted down to most planets' spaceports quieter than eight-legged rats, because C-drive manipulates gravity. But drift approaches take time, and time is money. Cruisers served downgraded outworlds like Dead End only by dropping off in parking orbit containerized freight, mail, and passenger modules in a constant parade. It was up to the locals to shuttle the modules down to surface. The heat-scorched wedges out on the tarmac were old-tech, but they were the thread that tied Dead End's tiny colony to the rest of mankind.

As the Downshuttle's brakes squealed, a 'bot tug clamped the nose gear of one of the other two, which would become the morning Upshuttle.

The rear cargo ramp of the Downshuttle that had delivered me here whined down.

The first container that skated down the shuttle's ramp was unpainted plasteel the size of a family electrovan, labelled "Danger—'bots contain explosives," and far smaller than the one I was waiting for.

Somewhere beneath Kit Born's armor lurked a female form, which meant . . . When the shuttle's roar died, I displayed my detective skills. "You must be the Line Wrangler I heard about."

She turned to me, hands on hips, and rolled her eyes. "And you must be the fool who's come to hunt grezzen."

"No. I just work for him."

"They say only fools work for fools."

I shrugged. "They might say different if they knew the job I quit."

She flicked her eyes to my bare forearm, nodded at the Legion Graves-registration bar code tatt lasered there, then fingered a carrot-sized cartridge looped in her belt. "Recognize this, merc?"

I blinked past the slur, nodded. "I've seen a Barrett Double Express split a Hovee's engine block, then drop a forty-foot wronk in its tracks."

She frowned when I mentioned the wronk. "You served in the Marin Suppression?"

I frowned back. "Legionnaires don't choose their enemies."

She opened her mouth, closed it, then blinked. She shook her head, pointing through the hangar's open cage walls at the distant tree line. "My Barrett's just for the small fry out there, Mr. Parker. It barely aggravates a grezz. Which is redundant, because you've never encountered a nastier disposition."

Well, there had been Platoon Sergeant Leto at Basic Armor School.

Kit said, "Grezzen are the deadliest game in this universe. Money can't buy enough gun to drop one. Go home, and take your boss with you."

Crackle.

A stevedore lased the plasteel's top and side slabs. They fell to the asphalt, booming spray clouds into the saturated air.

I followed Kit Born across the vast cage. She counted the folded, six-legged 'bots, each cocooned in frothy plastipak like spider prey, then thumbed the manifest that the stevedore held out.

She knelt beside the nearest 'bot, drew a bush knife as long as her forearm from her belt, and de-cocooned the 'bot like she was gutting moonfish.

I peered down at it. "Hell. It's just a mobile limpet antitank mine."

She nodded. "Reprogrammed Rover 'bots home on grezzen just like they would on a Lockheed Kodiak in combat. Scuttling under a grezz is about like scuttling under a hovertank's skirt." She tapped her knife on the upward-firing shaped charge housing. "Shaped charge detonated into the belly disembowels either one."

"Stationary mines would be cheaper."

"That's what the armorers who equipped the second colonial expedition thought."

"Second?"

She opened the 'bot's access panel, punched in a code, and it whined to its six feet like a camo-painted cockroach six feet across. "The first colonial expedition came to DE 476 armed to the teeth, to combat the hostile fauna the initial 'bot surveys found. Even so, all that survived was a distress transmission so ugly that the tourism board still has it sealed from the general public. The second expedition was escorted by a merc battalion. Same result. The third expedition suffered equivalent casualties, until they deployed the limpets. Since then, the grezz avoid the settlers and vice versa."

I toed the mobile mine's camo limb with my boot. "What's magic about the Rover 'bots?"

She stared down at the 'bot's panel, shrugged. "They work. They work cheap. That passes for magic on an outworld. Come on, Parker. Mercs don't usually overthink killing."

My heart sped up and I pointed at her. "Don't judge what you don't—"

Rumble.

A plasteel forty feet long, eight feet high, thirteen feet wide, and stenciled "Cutler Communications" slid down the ramp and thumped to a stop behind us. The shuttle's ramp clamshelled shut, and the stevedore lased the container until its roof and sides toppled. The slabs jostled the ground fog into twists as they thumped the apron.

Silhouetted against mist-obscured jungle, Cutler's weapon of choice squatted in the dank morning.

Kit Born stared at it, and her head shook slowly. "Parker, your boss might not be a fool. But he might be a menace."

Six

I stepped toward our newly un-crated cargo, and began my walk around.

She trailed me. "I thought civilians couldn't own hovertanks."

"They can't. But they can own historical vehicles." I rapped my knuckles on a rubber block of the left track. "Before hovertanks, there were crawlers. General Dynamics M1A2 Abrams main battle tank, manufactured Lima, Ohio, United States, Earth, 1998. Frame-off restored by Gustus & Son Forge, Marinus, Bren, 2081. Fully operational."

She walked around the prow, then stood on tiptoe to touch the main gun tube. "Operational?"

I knelt and peered underneath at the suspension. No visible damage after a nine-jump trip. "My boss the fool had 120 mm ammunition recreated. Should be very annoying to your grezzen."

I clambered across the sponson, peered into the commander's hatch on the turret, then looked down at her, alongside.

She squinted up at me, a hand visored above her eyes. "Why?"

I shrugged. "Because some of the rounds are depleted uranium penetrators. They used to cut through crawler tank armor like blowtorches through ice cream. Trueborns believe in overkill."

"I mean why does your boss want to hunt grezzen?"

"He's Trueborn." I shrugged again. "You can always tell an Earthman, but you can't tell him much. I'm no mind reader."

Kit levered herself up alongside me, and clutched my elbow. "What's that supposed to mean?"

I pushed her hand away. "Look, his people hired me sight unseen a couple months ago. I know Cutler's rich. And used to doing what he pleases, like every other Trueborn."

She narrowed her eyes. "Then he's *the* Cutler? As in Cutler Communications?"

Why did people get excited because somebody had money?

It took me an hour to pry open the plasteels piggybacked above the engine, check the tank's auxiliary machine guns packed inside, and the mechanicals. The three crates of main gun ammunition —practice, canister, armor piercing discarding sabot, and Cutler's mysterious custom jobs—were also intact.

Kit Born disappeared back into the building, then came back and supervised while the stevedores loaded her cargo onto a trailer. Then she wandered back over to me. My work had earned a cosmoline goop streak on my forearm for my trouble.

I pointed alongside the left track. "Could you hand me that rag?"

She passed the rag over, and her fingers touched mine. "You told me about your boss. But why are *you* here, Parker?"

The Tassini say that all a man has is his story, but an Illegal keeps his to himself. "I joined the Legion to see the worlds. Mostly I saw the inside of transports. Now I'm out. I get to look around."

"For your future?"

While I scrubbed cosmoline off the tattoo on my forearm, I straightened up and stared at the tree line. "For my past."

Which was what Orion had told the Legion recruiting sergeant the day she took me to enlist, at sixteen.

The gray-eyed sergeant had locked his office door behind us, then shook his head. "I don't like this, Orion." He pressed my forearm against the laser's platen, with a hand that was regrown clear back past the wrist.

Orion snorted. "Your site says a legionnaire can forget his past and discover his future, Frank. And that the Legion pays bonus to Yavis for armored because we fit in small spaces."

"We do. But this kid's as tall as a Trueborn."

Orion frowned. "That's why I need to get him off Yavet! It's been tough enough raising an Illegal. Now he stands out."

The sergeant sighed, then stared at me. "You sure about this, son? The tatt burns clear down into the bone, because sometimes that's all that's left. It's indelible. Once it's on, so's your obligation. The Legion can get you off Yavet, but you'll still be an Illegal under Yavet law. If you choose out after your hitch, you'll earn a year without a bounty, as long as you're off Yavet. After that any bounty hunter who finds you, anywhere in the Union, can deliver you to any Yavet Consulate, dead or alive, which means dead. And don't even think about coming back here."

Orion rolled her eyes at the Sergeant. "Save the boogie man lecture. He's been dodging bounty hunters all his life. Frank, I've seen Legion recruiters tatt passed-out drunks on bar floors to meet quota. He's clean as green and smart as a Trueborn." Her voice softened. "And you owe me."

The flint in the sergeant's eyes melted, and he took Orion's hand in his natural one. "We haven't forgotten. We never will. It's not him I worry about, Orion. You're asking me to take your son from you."

Orion covered his hand and my forearm with hers, and whispered, "Jazen's not my son, not by blood. But he's someone's son. He needs to find his past, and he can't find it with me. I'm fine." She blinked, then turned away. "Tatt him before I cry."

I patted Orion's arm, then nodded at the sergeant. The laser crackled and my forearm burned so hot that I bit through my lip.

"Parker?" On the Dead End runway, fingers touched my arm, just below my tatt. Kit the Line Wrangler peered up at me, her brow furrowed. "Your arm okay? You were rubbing it."

"S'fine. For a lady who carries a Barrett, you worry a lot about the welfare of strangers and poison spiders. Would anybody on Dead End weep if Cutler managed to kill a grezzen?"

She smirked as she shook her head. "If Cutler carpet bombed the grezzen to extinction, they'd rename the planet after him."

I climbed down off the Abrams, rubbed my eyes, and stretched. "As long as Cutler lets me get a meal and a shower within the next three hours, *I'll* rename the planet after him."

My Handtalk vibrated. I tugged it from my pocket and turned away as I answered.

"Parker?" It was Zhondro. "My darling arrived in good health?"

"Not a scratch. Even Cutler's special rounds."

He sighed. "Good. Maybe that will calm him down."

I rolled my eyes. "Cutler? Now what? Fuel?"

"No. The local kerosene tests quite satisfactorily. Those old turbines were designed to run even on rubbish. The outfitter wishes to discuss the local guide situation."

I gripped the Handtalk tighter. "There's nothing to discuss. Cutler's people vetted Bauer months ago. He knows the ground, he knows these grezzen better than anybody alive, and they prepaid the outfitter for him already."

They had to make arrangements months in advance and sight unseen, and nobody did it better than Cutler's people. Cutler's family built its empire on moving information around the Human Union. Nothing moved through normal space faster than light, and light took decades to move through normal space, even among the inworlds. Human communications, from contracts to Cutlergrams, had to shortcut through jumps. Only C-drive vehicles like cruisers could jump. So information traveled just as slowly as every tourist, legionnaire, or plasti of Coke traveled.

"Apparently that is not what this fellow has just told Cutler. The outfitter has demanded a meeting in person in one hour."

Meeting. I smiled. "Aha!" Outworld cultures, despite their differences, shared one hatred. Well, Outworlders didn't precisely *hate* Earthlings, but they hated Earthlings' wealth, privilege, and attitude. Outworlders lived by the maxim that it's easier to take a Trueborn's money than it is to take a Trueborn. "They're trying to retrade the deal, Zhondro. Tell Cutler to take the board out of his ass and give them five percent more. Arguing will cost us more than that in delay."

"No."

I rolled my eyes. "Okay, leave out the board part. But tell him! Blame me if you want to." I swallowed. Cutler was both blue-nose enough and prick enough to do just that, and fire me on the spot.

"I meant no, he's not meeting the outfitter. Cutler said that is precisely the sort of triviality resolution for which he overpays you."

Crap. I sighed. "I don't even know where the outfitter is. If I knew, we wouldn't need a damn guide in the first place."

"An excellent point. But it will be lost on Mr. Cutler if it delays us, Jazen. I put my faith in you, my friend, only behind God." Zhondro cut the connection, and I turned back, frowning, toward Kit Born.

Kit shook her head. "No meal, no shower?"

I thumbed off on a manifest that a stevedore held out to me, then shook my head at her. "Maybe no paychip, if I can't get to a meeting in town in an hour. What are business meetings like here?"

"If you're here to kill grezzen and pay cash, everybody will love you."

"Does the mag rail to town stop in walking distance of a place called Eden Outfitters?"

She snorted and rolled her eyes. "Mag rail. On Dead End. You said your *boss* was the idiot."

She turned her back on me, then walked, shaking her head, toward the exit gate. Palms out, mouth open, I stood alone on the tarmac.

After ten steps, Kit turned back and waved me toward her. "Move your ass, Parker. With the Cageway closed, Eden's fifty minutes from here. You've already wasted two."

Seven

Three minutes later, Kit Born's caged, open six-wheel diesel careened up a ramp and out into the steaming haze that passed for a nice day on Dead End. The dash display read 104 Fahrenheit, which made the Sixer's unmuffled roar worth the breeze it generated.

I had never seen or heard of Cutler, much less of Dead End, until a couple of months before, so I twisted in my seat to recon a world new to me.

The obvious thing about Spaceport DE 476 was that it wasn't obvious. It was flat land from which the rainforest had been scraped back to clear runway space. The only visible above-ground structure was the hangar cage, the three heat-scorched shuttles sheltered behind its bars.

The briefs I had read, which were Trueborn-authored, pronounced Dead End colony "splendidly noble, redolent of the libertarian sod dugouts of America's sadly past frontier."

To me, Dead End colony, with its hole-in-the-ground non-architecture, was redolent of trench warfare. Trueborns measured the universe against cultural referents meaningless to the rest of us, and expected us to catch up.

Dead End's human habitations weren't cage-roofed dugouts because of a noble connection to The Land. Below grade was cooler and trenching was cheaper than tunneling. And trenches

28

were safer, because everything on Dead End that wasn't monotone moss-green would sting you or eat you.

Except the low, gray clouds, which the briefs said had not dissipated for thirty million standard years, give or take a few eons. The few colonial kids born and raised on Dead End had to take the existence of Earth and its frontier on faith, because they had never seen a moon or a star in the night sky.

Ahead of us as we drove loomed Dead End's most important—in fact, only—commercial artery, the Cageway, which I had also read about. It ran through a slim canyon that connected the planet's two human habitation nodes, the spaceport and the town of Eden. Eden sat fortresslike in the bowl of an extinct volcano's crater. The Cageway was protected by a newsteel bar roof, and vaulted newsteel doors sealed the passage's ends against large animal intrusions. The Cageway had been enclosed in the early days because grezzen had lain in wait there and attacked vehicles channelized in the canyon. On Dead End, humans didn't make road kill, they were road kill.

Kit braked as we approached the Cageway. Its massive doors were closed, and an example of reverse road kill wedged up against the Cageway's closed doors, in the form of a few tons of trampled plasteel that appeared to have once been an electrobus. Moss had begun to grow on the wreck's north side, and its steel bits had rusted.

Kit sighed. "Bus-woog collision. The only paved road on the planet and it's been closed for two months. Welcome to Dead End."

"The Government's slow clearing wrecks?"

"Government on Dead End doesn't clear a bus wreck. It *is* a bus wreck. If anarchy's too structured for you, immigrate to Dead End."

Apparently, the noble libertarian frontier needed fine tuning before Eden lived up to its name.

One hundred yards before the pavement entered the blocked Cageway, Kit spun the wheel. The Sixer leaned left up a dirt ramp, then bellowed as it climbed a switchbacking gravel trail up the hill, parallel to the closed main road.

I smiled at the empty road ahead of us, then realized that beyond the gravel's edge, a foot from my elbow, the hillside dropped away in a hundred-foot cliff. A Sixer's high ground clearance is handy in negotiating swamps, fording streams, and crossing boulder fields. But its top-heavy center of gravity has a literal downside. I glanced at Kit while I gripped the door handle. "Should you slow down?"

She muttered, let the wheel go, and ducked two hands beneath her seat.

I sucked in a whistling breath as the Sixer drifted toward the cliff.

Kit straightened back up, and wrenched the armored car back on course. In her hand shuddered a sawed-off Barrett Double Express. She thrust it toward me, stock-first. "Make yourself useful, Parker."

I broke it at the receiver, peered in. Loaded. I clicked the weapon shut, felt the safety with my thumb, and frowned. "What am I supposed to do with—"

Whump!

The Sixer, all two armored tons of it, shuddered on its suspension like a baby buggy hit by a bowling ball.

I ducked as, inches above my hairline, a fanged, red-eyed, armored bat as big as an anti-ship missile wedged a winged claw between the overhead bars. The beast's other claw thrashed, tangled in the armored cage by the impact when the diving monster had struck us.

"The gun, Parker!"

The shrieking beast's weight rocked the Sixer like a dinghy in a gale, hanging me out over empty space.

Pus-yellow liquid drizzled onto my forearm, and singed the hair off it. "Crap!"

Kit swung the wheel back so hard that the driver's side door screeched against the rock wall. "Gort drool's not fatal, Parker. But the fall will be if you don't get that weight off our roof!"

A sawed Barrett's a close-quarters-battle weapon to a GI, a saloon peacekeeper to a civilian. It fires just two rounds, from side-by-side barrels, like a vintage shotgun.

I thumbed the safety off, swung the saloon gun up between the groaning roof bars, and triggered the left barrel into the gort's armored belly. The Barrett kicked gently, like a cough in church. After all, it's recoil damping that makes a Barrett a Barrett. But the .60 caliber round's impact sprung the monster up off our roof, where the vehicle's slipstream somersaulted it away like wet cardboard.

I broke the breech, ejected the smoking shell, and rummaged splay-fingered under paper maps that littered the Sixer's teetering dash. I panted, craning my neck at the clouds that seemed close enough to touch. "Where's your ammo, Born?"

She wrinkled her nose while she drove. "Why?"

I jerked my thumb skyward. "Where there's one monster, there's more, right?"

She lifted off the throttle and smiled. "Exactly. Look behind us."

I twisted in my seat and peered out through the rear cage. The gort, back flat against the gravel road, thrashed a shattered wing. A second gort fluttered onto its chest like a sparrow onto a birdbath.

The first one screeched while its predator splashed its beak into the downed monster's wound. A third gort, wings back, talons out, dropped into the melee while two, then three, more circled, black shadows in the mist.

"Dead End lesson for today, Parker. You never have to shoot two gorts if you can shoot one."

The road wound up, then over the hill ring that separated the port from town. We crested the crater's barren lip, and, for an instant as we descended, we saw the settlement nestled in the natural bowl below. On my scale of planetary capitals visited, Eden looked to rank above only Weichsel City, which is three igloos.

"Eden." Born snorted as she waved her hand at the criss-cross of mud streets pimpled with hatch domes. The domes led to the below-grade dugouts that passed for buildings. The only visible industry was the tea kettle refinery that made vegetable matter in the local rock into kerosene. "Impressed?"

I smiled. "You read my mind."

Born snapped her eyes away from the road and narrowed her eyes at me. "What?"

I shrugged. "I dunno. I was just thinking the same thing, that—"

She turned her eyes back to the road, and detoured the conversation back to its original path. "Yeah. Ever see an Outworld planetary capital with a name that fit, Parker?"

I shrugged again. "Funhouse. And Jolly. 'Til you wake up hung over and broke."

Born downshifted as the road ramped lower. "Eden's thin on soldierly delights, Parker."

"What isn't it thin on?"

She smiled. "Rainfall. An ecosystem in stable harmony for thirty million years. Native parasites, viruses, and bacteria don't attack downshipped crop stock, or human tissue. Unless you bring a cold with you, you won't catch one here. The local shale's so full of kerogen that a tea kettle refinery exports designer kerosene to Earth. The locals could probably farm successfully if they'd quit self-depopulating in the name of living free."

I slouched back in the passenger's seat, but kept the reloaded Barrett across my thighs. The road hairpinned two hundred feet above the bowl's flat, forested floor. Emplaced within the hairpin was an Oerlikon HU-40 Triple-A 'bot, dish rotating, barrels-to-the-sky. A plaque on its rusted turret read: EDEN OUTFITTERS. As we passed, the 'bot spun, locked, and its gatling spit. Against the gray clouds, a gliding shadow wobbled, then tumbled.

As we wound down the hill, we passed a dozen more emplacements. I pointed at one. "The Legion yard-saled their HU-40s years ago. Upgraded to units that could tell aircraft from birds. I wouldn't recommend flying in this airspace."

She smiled as she drove. "Nobody does. In fact, nothing's flown over Dead End for years except gorts and the orbital shuttles. The early settlers lost so many aircraft to kamikaze gorts, cloud, and storms that aircraft were declared contraband imports. I suppose that's why Cutler brought a tank. He seems like the kind of sportsman who'd just drop fragmentation grenades on game out the door of a tilt wing."

With four minutes to spare Kit pulled her Sixer up in front of a plasteel entry dome that was gray except for the EDEN OUTFITTERS sign above the door. Another read, HIRING TODAY. It looked permanent.

Befitting a libertarian republic, traffic regulation was minimal. But then so was traffic. The only visible signage announced: USE ALTERNATE ROUTE HIGH NOON TO 1 P.M. DAILY. MAIN STREET CLOSED FOR GUNFIGHTS.

Ha-ha.

I hopped from the Sixer. My boots sank in the street's mud, and I looked around.

A half dozen pedestrians walked the plank sidewalks, three of whom wore sidearms. The fourth's right arm was a six-barrel Gatling prosthetic. The other two people on the street were a mother holding a baby on her hip with one hand. In the other she held an assault rifle. The baby appeared to be unarmed.

Maybe all the guns were to ward off gorts, because Triple-A 'bots were less than perfect. But it might be best to adjourn our meeting well before high noon.

I turned back and leaned in the open door. "Thanks for the lift."

It occurred to me that Kit Born had been nicer to me than she had to be. If her eyes were any indication, it was entirely possible that an attractive woman lurked under her armor. A teenaged boy who isn't legally alive doesn't date much. And since enlistment, in the places where my squad mates dragged me on liberty, the girls did the asking. I tried my first pick-up line. "Say, I don't suppose—"

The Sixer's interior was empty.

Across the mud street, one of the pedestrians, a short-barreled Browning slung over one shoulder, paused in mid-limp with his back to me.

He turned and I saw that he was unshaven, with a black moustache that drooped past his chin. My heart skipped and I sucked in a breath. A black patch covered one eye.

After all these years, One-eyed Jack the bounty hunter had found me? He was ready to pounce as soon as my immunity expired? Yavet Illegals fetched the universe's highest bounties. Payoffs compounded the longer an Illegal eluded termination, like uncashed lottery jackpots. So it was too possible that a bounty hunter had stalked a rare adult Illegal like me to the end of the universe.

The man glared in my direction with his remaining eye, then walked away. I exhaled. It wasn't Jack. But Dead End was a bad neighborhood.

Kit stepped around the Sixer's fender, slipped her armored vest up over her base tunic, sweat-molded to her torso, and chucked the vest back into the front seat. I tried not to stare. Kit Born's eyes weren't the only parts of her that were beautiful and natural.

She said, "I'm coming in with you, Parker."

Well, well. Maybe I was the pick-up-ee, not the pick-up-or. Still, I wrinkled my forehead. "Why?"

Eight

Thirty seconds later, Kit was past me and through the front door without answering.

Eden Outfitters' office manager met us at the bottom of the stairs. His belt supported a gunpowder revolver on one side and a Handtalk that looked older than he did on the other. He was gray, stooped, and limped on an old-fashioned prosthetic that replaced his right leg somewhere above the knee.

On Dead End, amputation appeared to be the new black.

He led us down a passage, at the end of which hung an Animap. It showed the sections of the Line, the border that ringed the safe zone centered on Eden; the Triple-A 'bot emplacements, and a field of winking lights intriguingly labeled "Pest Control." Eden Outfitters' primary business was monster management, not one-off vacation safaris for Trueborns with more money than sense.

The office manager frowned at Kit. "Who's minding your section?"

"The adjacent sections are covering. You know that's standard."

He stopped and leaned against the wall, breathing hard. "Of course I know. My sister called. She saw you drive into town, and she wet her pants. I promised I'd ask, to shut her up."

Kit rolled her eyes. "Ben the florist stopped out on Main Street and gave us the look, too, while I was parking."

The old man waved a hand. "What do you expect? Grezz give people the yips."

On this planet, even the florists gave me the yips.

Kit hung her hands on her hips and cocked her head. "Oliver, has a grezz from my section ever killed anyone?"

He paused. "Bauer."

She raised a finger and shook her head. "That doesn't count. He was dead before I replaced him."

My jaw dropped. This meeting wasn't a renegotiation. It was a renege. Bauer, Cutler's prepaid, hand-picked-by-resume guide was dead.

The manager sat us down in a conference room, in heavy wood chairs around a rough table. One rocky wall was hung with black-framed flat images, below a plaque that read: IN MEMORIAM. FORMER VALUED EMPLOYEES. It was a big wall, and it was full.

The old man spread his palms toward Kit. "No. Sorry. You've been a valued employee. We were fortunate you applied when you did."

Despite the generous Wall of Fame employee benefit, Eden Outfitters had an evident problem with personnel turnover.

I stared at Kit. I had assumed she was born here. Nobody sane immigrated to Dead End. Especially to take a job with limited opportunity for survival, much less advancement.

I asked the office manager, "How long ago did Mr. Bauer die?"

"Six months."

"But you've kept Mr. Cutler's prepayment?"

"Cutler's people wanted a cheaper price. I said okay, if it was nonrefundable, and that's the way they wrote it. We sent Cutler a Cutlergram about Bauer. Figured the man himself would prefer that."

Cutlergrams were the cheapest way for the Human Union's general population to send legal notices, and were worth what they cost. The message would have been months in transit. That would have assured that Eden Outfitters had time to spend Cutler's prepayment before Cutler's accountants found out that the prepaid goods were, uh, damaged.

I ran my fingers through my hair. "Now what?"

The old man studied his fingers. "You won't last a week without a guide. Probably not with one, either, but that's not my rice bowl to break. Pack up. Go home. Trueborns are smart. Your boss will understand. Won't he?"

Nine

My heart rattled in my chest. "Cutler" plus "understand" formed an oxymoron. And if I lost this job, I'd be dead in four months, when my immunity lapsed.

Bounty hunters tracked Illegals as zealously as Triple-A 'bots tracked gorts. My plan had been to earn Cutler's bonus for this job, then spend part of it for up-fare to one of the big hubs, like Mousetrap. You can buy anything at a hub for a price, even a squeaky-clean new identity. Before my immunity expired, I would spend the rest of my bonus for a hub scrub. Then I'd start fresh and broke, but clean and legal, somewhere.

Cutler didn't get rich by prepaying unearned bonuses to screw-ups. If he paid me only severance, that wouldn't even cover outbound steerage fare, much less the cost of a black market ID scrub.

My stomach churned. Illegals could survive for years on an over-crowded world like Yavet, like fish hiding in a sea teeming with fourteen billion other fish. I was the living proof. But Dead End's entire population was less than the population of one *level* in a mid-size stack city on Yavet. A single fish can't hide in a fish bowl. One-eyed Jack was only a childhood nightmare now. But even the florists on Dead End looked mean enough and hungry enough to moonlight as bounty hunters.

If I couldn't get off Dead End, and I couldn't hide within its tiny population, could I hide outside it? Bounty "hunters" were really scavenging jackals. Scavengers didn't take risks. This was a huge planet, and the bounty jackals probably wouldn't risk going outside the Line. But in unfamiliar terrain, among lemon bugs, gorts, grezzen and gods-knew-what else, I wouldn't survive a week. I closed my eyes and groaned.

Kit Born cleared her throat.

Ten

Kit said, "I took Bauer's place four months ago. I can do it again."

The old man shook his head. "That means the other sections gotta keep covering yours. That means overtime pay. And half of Eden beating down my doors, scared shitless."

Kit puffed out a breath. "All that's the same whether it's me now, or Bauer when you made your deal."

I shifted in my chair. That explained why Kit Born left her post out in the boondocks, just to take delivery of supplies that were being shipped out to her anyway. She wanted to size up her potential client anonymously before she pimped with her employer to take Bauer's place. I got smiled at, interviewed, then got a lift to town because I was a potential paycheck, not a potential date.

Okay, business was business. Kit seemed mission-capable to me, but when you negotiated "trivialities" for Cutler, you were still obliged to throw coins around like manhole covers.

I raised my palm. "Cutler paid for a grezzen expert, not a trainee."

Kit's boss didn't mind being a dick about a refund, especially to a Trueborn, but he also knew Trueborns had lawyers. Lots of them. He squirmed in his chair.

Kit snorted. "Trainee? Don't you mean Cutler shouldn't have to pay full rate for a chick?" She held up one hand and began ticking things off on its fingers. "I'm a licensed multi-engine pilot. I—"

I rolled my eyes. "Your breasts and your license have nothing to do with it. Cutler paid for—"

The old man coughed, chopped the air with his hand. "Shut up! Both of you! Parker, I may be an Outworld hick to your Mr. Cutler, but my word is good. I'll get you a male guide as experienced as Bauer—"

Kit reached over and grabbed the old man's hand at the wrist. "Wait. I'll do the job on contingency. If Cutler doesn't get his grezzen, I work for free. If he gets his trophy, he pays me the guide share that Bauer would have gotten. I know how generous you aren't with your employees, Oliver. I'm sure the difference Cutler could owe me will be pocket change to a Trueborn."

That was a terrible deal for her, but it would get the old man off the hook. Not to mention me. He turned to me, and raised his eyebrows.

Cutler liked pay-for-performance. My own deal already had a big bonus in escrow that got released to me as soon as we got a grezzen back inside the Line, or got refunded to Cutler if we didn't. I turned to Kit. "Let's go meet Cutler. It's a deal if he likes you."

He would. Cutler was big on free enterprise and pay-for-performance. Maybe more so if the free entrepreneur had Caribbean blue eyes. The eyes worked for me, anyway, especially when she was angry. Kit had been less than candid with me, but I couldn't blame her for sizing up in advance a bunch of offworlders whose incompetence or inadequate equipment could get her killed. And if she hadn't suggested her compromise, her employer might have let me dangle in a situation that could have gotten *me* killed. Besides, maybe she had made her offer because she wanted to get to know me better.

When the two of us got back to her Sixer, I paused with my fingers on the door handle. "Thanks."

She cocked her eyebrow. "For what?"

"For helping me out."

She rolled her eyes, and snorted. "Help *you*, Parker? I'd blow a gort first. And breasts don't affect a guide's job performance. Mention mine again and your testicles won't affect yours any more."

Perhaps I had overestimated her romantic interest in me.

She jerked her thumb at the Sixer. "Get in. Let's find out if I have a new boss. Which won't be you, fortunately."

Eleven

Kit's Sixer bounced down Eden's mud main street while I stared at her. "Born, what did I ever do to you?"

"Not to me, Parker. The Legion served the secessionists in the Marin Suppression on Bren. Torture and genocide don't charm me."

I shook my head. "You don't know—"

Kit raised her fingers from the wheel, and stared straight ahead. "I know soldiers, Parker. I don't need your excuses. I do need to be your guide. Let's leave it at that."

Eden's Main Street is the length of a fixed-wing forward airstrip, and as muddy. Kit stopped in front of another entry domette, this one painted faux brick, which announced over its door,

EDEN HOUSE HOTEL AND RESTAURANT

IN-ROOM GUN LOCKERS

YOUR STAY LEMON BUG FREE, OR BREAKFAST'S ON US

The Eden House lobby would have fit in any closet of any home Cutler owned. A hand-lettered sign flapped slowly beneath the turning ceiling fan. The sign announced that the lobby hosted Libertarian amateur stripper night monthly, "all genders welcome."

It seemed to me that "both" would've been Libertarian enough. First prize was a Claymore mine.

Kit rolled her eyes as she passed beneath the sign. She didn't pick up an entry form.

40

Bartram Cutler stood up from a worn plastek chair when we entered, then laid his Reader back down on the chair seat. Six feet three, square of jaw, clear of eye, as perfect as Earth genetics and plastics could make a man.

He looked Kit up and down from her scuffed boots to her slouch hat, with a quick stop at They Which Must Not Be Mentioned, and frowned.

I said, "Aaron Bauer, the guide you hired through Eden Outfitters, is dead, sir."

Cutler's eyes widened. "Bauer? Dead? How?"

Kit said, "He was a Line Wrangler. Best guess is a grezzen got him, earlier this year." She extended her hand to Cutler. "I replaced him."

Cutler frowned. "As a wrangler or as our guide?"

She said, "Both. If you approve."

He kept frowning. "I hired Mr. Bauer more for his unique knowledge of grezzen than as a guide. Do I even need you, Ms. Born?"

She shrugged. "Only if you want to live through this."

Cutler snorted. "What I want is a grezzen. Can you find me one?"

Kit said, "Your problem won't be finding grezzen. It will be finding grezzen before they find you."

Cutler rolled his eyes. "What're you going to cost me?"

"Nothing, unless you come back with your grezzen. I told Eden Outfitters I'd take the job on that basis."

Cutler rubbed his chin. "My people didn't bargain for a guarantee. Why would you sweeten the deal?"

"Let's say I'm civic minded. A dead Trueborn would hurt the tourist trade."

Cutler eyed the deserted room. "What tourist trade?" Then he sighed. "All right. Parker, see that she doesn't report for work with the smart mouth and the wet T-shirt." He flicked his eyes at the flapping contest sign as he turned away. "This is her new job, not her last one."

Kit snatched Cutler's Reader off his chair, cocked her arm, and aimed the Reader at the back of his head.

I clamped her wrist with my hand, froze it as she wound up, then said, "Mr. Cutler!"

"Yes, Parker?"

As Cutler turned back toward us, I pushed Kit's hand and the Reader down and forward, while I said, "Don't forget your Reader, sir."

He wrinkled his forehead, reached out and took his reader, then turned away again.

I hissed in Kit's ear, "You said you need this job!" I knew *I* did.

Cutler disappeared down the passage to the guest rooms.

She said, "He called me a stripper!"

I shrugged. "Let it go."

Compared to merc'ing, stripping was an honorable profession. I had found strippers as a class to be better spoken than jarheads and less girly than squids.

Slowly, her stiff back softened.

I said, "Welcome to my world. No, he's not always such a prick. Usually, he's worse."

She turned on me with eyes as cold as they were beautiful. "Parker, I don't like Cutler. I'm pretty sure I don't like you. But I always do my job. Here's my first local guide tip: When you're in town, where you can do it safely, do outdoor work at night. It's cooler. Clean up, eat, get started. I'll stop by later."

She turned and walked back to the up stairway that led to the street.

I sighed as I watched her walk away. Well, she was only pretty sure she didn't like me. It was a start.

I checked in, showered, then slept until my Handtalk woke me. Zhondro's voice crackled in my ear. "Shall we dine together, downstairs?"

I checked my 'puter. Six P.M., local.

Zhondro asked, "Did the guide business end well?"

I sighed. "See you in ten."

Twelve

The Dead Grezzen Lounge (Full Bar, Open from Breakfast 'til ???) comprised hewn-rock walls enclosing six empty wood tables, one waitress, and a whiskey bottle on a corner table alongside four shot glasses. Zhondro, leaning on forearms as thin as mahogany twigs, looked up and smiled when I sat down across from him.

A smoldering tobacco cigarette dangled from our waitress' lips and she wore a single-action Ruger in a belt holster. I made a mental note to overtip.

I pointed at my chest. "Whiskey, neat?" Then I pointed at Zhondro. "Cold tea."

She stared at Zhondro. "You'll have to leave."

Tassini mark their caste by indigo dye on the face, the purpler, the nobler. A tribal headman is dyed from hairline to chin. A single indigo line no wider than spider silk crossed Zhondro's forehead, which marked him as a slave.

I stiffened, and pushed back my chair. "You don't serve my friend, you don't serve me! Slavery is—"

She shoved me down in my chair. "Back off, Lincoln. On Dead End we serve slaves. We serve pirates. We serve anybody, except poofs who drink tea at cocktail hour."

"Oh." I pointed at Zhondro again. "Whiskey with a tea chaser?"

She pumped her fist at Zhondro. "Attaboy."

When our drinks arrived, I slammed my first whiskey, then Zhondro slid his across to me. I raised it to meet his tea glass while he toasted, "May Paradise spare you from allies, my friend."

43

I nodded, sipped, and let the whiskey burn down my throat. "It may have. Our guide says you and I should work all night, because it's cooler."

He smiled. "She sounds as charming as our waitress."

I set my glass down. "Bigger gun, though."

After dinner, we drove a rented Sixer, towing a C-lift flatbed floater, back out to the port to pick up the Abrams. Theoretically, we could have driven the tank itself. The old heaps could make seventy miles per hour over pavement. They were governed to forty-two to protect them from their drivers, who drove like, and were, teenaged boys. Cutler had the governor disconnected on his. Trueborns were as realistic about their limitations as prepubescent males.

But the more unnecessary miles with which we wore down the old machine, the more spares we consumed, and the nearest spares in addition to what we had brought with us were jumps away.

The floater was one of two flat bed C-lifts on this planet, the only modern, gravity-manipulating ground transport technology within one hundred trillion cubic light years. Cutler's people had pre-leased both, even though the Abrams could only tow one. The Netionary definition of overkill is a holo of a Trueborn with a wallet.

Zhondro and I chose the higher-capacity unit, which was rated to support seventy tons. Zhondro rode shotgun, literally, and plinked the obligatory gort.

It was midnight before we stopped in the floodlit mud yard of the warehouse I had rented on Eden's south side.

I dropped through the commander's turret hatch of the Abrams, scooted feet-first forward into the Abrams' driver's compartment, then raised the seat so my head poked out through the open driver's hatch in the tank's prow. Zhondro spooled his hand and nodded, I thumbed the starter, and the gas turbine whistled up as smoothly as it had out at the port.

Zhondro gave me a thumb up and smiled. Then he stood in front of me, hand signaling me to adjust left or right while I backed sixty-nine tons of steel off into the yard, blind.

When I thumbed off the turbine, I noticed that Kit Born's Sixer had pulled up and parked in the yard. The person who leaned against its fender was blonde, and wore a businesslike khaki blouse and slacks that still left no doubt about her gender. She was unarmed, by Dead End standards, just a demure gunpowder revolver in a waist holster, and it took me a heartbeat to realize that the lady was Kit.

I waved to Zhondro to replace me in the driver's seat, then crabbed backward, up, and out of the Abrams the way I came in, as Zhondro dropped through the loader's hatch then slid past me, to finish moving the tank.

I smiled when I reached her. "You clean up well."

She didn't look at me, but stood staring, hands on hips, mouth open, at Zhondro's indigo-striped forehead, which poked out of the driver's hatch.

I sighed. Shaved, showered, cleaned and pressed, I expected at least a glance, if not a "you, too."

Zhondro restarted the Abrams, pirouetted it like a sixty-nine-ton ballerina, and I chained the now-empty floater to the Abrams' rear tow mounts. Then Zhondro drove the tank and the floater down the ramp, and through the warehouse's open double doors with six spare inches on each side.

I said, "Zhondro's a Tassini, from Bren. Most people are surprised—"

"To know that his family were slaves? Privileged house domestics by the curve of his caste line, but slaves."

I raised my eyebrows. I had fought almost a full year tour on Bren, and even I didn't know that you could tell a slave's sub-caste by line orientation. "Then what *did* surprise you?"

"Not that he can handle a crawler, either. The post-emancipation rebels survive on obsolete arms that they got under the table from the Marini monarchy."

I wrinkled my forehead. She spent her days in a jungle at the end of the known universe, but she knew more about the realpolitik of an obscure civil war than most of us who had bled in it.

The warehouse was three times larger than necessary to house and work on a tank. But we were cramped. The place was crammed to its ceiling with crates bearing Cutler shipping labels that had apparently arrived before us. Whatever was in that pile, we didn't need it to maintain a tank or hunt a monster. More Trueborn overkill.

Once Zhondro had rumbled the Abrams down the ramp and into the warehouse, I waited while he scuttled back from the driver's compartment up to the commander's seat. An Abrams' interior resembles a Kodiak's.

Zhondro rotated the turret out of opposite lock, so the main gun tube swung from its position pointing aft until it pointed ahead, off the tank's prow. An Abrams' turret hydraulics also whine exactly like a Kodiak's turret hydraulics. The way they had on the day, ten months ago, when I first saw Zhondro.

Thirteen

Hydraulic whine faded, inside the turret of the Kodiak I commanded, as the hovertank slipped laterally along the Tassin Desert dune crest.

My company commander's voice crackled in my helmet earpiece. "For the third time, Red Three, do you copy? Parker!"

"Copy, Red One." I eyed the thermal display on the tank commander's screen in front of me, and stared at the green-enhanced Tassini encampment in the midnight darkness below. "I'm looking at Position Victor, sir. But it's no tank park. Just family flappers." Fifty nomad tents, flap sides rolled up to take advantage of the desert's night breeze, had been pitched around a rude stone water well.

"No mech?"

I shook my head, invisibly to my captain, as I spoke. "No fuel trucks, no soft rollers, nothing but hobbled wobbleheads grazing."

The captain paused, then he whispered across the eight miles that separated my five-tank platoon from him and the rest of our company. "You sure?"

"We got the hatches open, and we're upwind, skipper." Of the three indigenous planetary faunas that Legion Heavy Brigade VI had encountered during my tour, the Brigade Webzine's ask-a-tanker poll voted Bren's dinosaurids foulest-smelling. And the wobbleheads that the Tassini rode won "foulest of the foul."

47

The captain came back. "Well, over here we finally got the purple people eaters in our sights."

The plan of this raid had been for a softside vehicle convoy to drive along a Tassini controlled road, to make a demonstration that would bait the Tassini tank unit in our area of operations away from their support base. There, the captain and our company's other two tank platoons would ambush and destroy them. Yes, the big, bad Legion was reduced to sneaking up on rag-tag rebels.

Theoretically, Kodiaks were a century ahead of the rebels' black market crawlers. So the brass allocated a single brigade to this war, figuring that even one Kodiak per five rebel crawler tanks would be overkill.

But we had no air support, with which the Kodiak was optimized to interface in combined-arms operations. The dune topography limited line-of-sight engagements to a thousand yards or less, which cancelled the Kodiak's main gun range advantage. A hovertank's over-water mobility advantage was worthless in the desert, and the Kodiak's speed was slashed by engine breathing problems unique to the Tassin desert.

Also, Tassini tankers didn't cower like escaped slaves and amechanical nomads, as the brass expected. The Tassini fought so hard and so well that we called them the purple people eaters.

The captain presumably had visual on the Tassini crawlers, approaching the ambush kill zone, as he spoke to me. Meantime, my platoon had looped in behind the Tassini tanks, to destroy their logistic support. The captain understood his operation, and he understood what he was seeing. But he wasn't understanding what I was seeing.

What I was seeing through the thermal wasn't a tank park emptied out of tanks. There were no fuel trucks, no spares vans, no sentries. It was a movable tent cluster occupied by sleeping noncombatant nomads.

Below me, something moved. I leaned forward toward the display again and watched, then I radioed, "Red One, I'm watching a little kid who just wandered out from one tent in his nightshirt. He's taking a leak against some rocks."

"Sergeant, you're brevet Third Platoon commander because Haren let a Tassini kid like that get too close, with a satchel charge under his nightshirt."

I sighed. The captain liked Lieutenant. Haren. We all had.

The captain asked, "No bunkers? No hard-shell vehicles?"

The hardest things in that encampment were fired clay milk jugs. "Uh, no, sir."

"Then load flechette, and stand by."

I swallowed. One 145-mm anti-personnel flechette round from a Kodiak's main gun distributed razor microdarts in an expanding, conical pattern. The pattern spread at this range insured that, within the tent cluster, no object larger in circumference than a child's fist would remain unpenetrated. Five tanks, one round each, to assure overkill. Three seconds after the order to fire, those tents would be confetti on the breeze. Every living thing within that encampment larger than a sand flea would be dead, or hemorrhaging life faster than pee splashing rocks.

I toggled to platoon net. "Red Group, this is Red Three. Load flechette. Then form up, on line with visual on the target, and stand by."

I looked away from the thermal's eyepiece, across at my gunner, who faced me in the turret, separated from me by the recoil path of the main gun breech and its autoload ramp. As assistant tank commander, he had heard my exchange over the Command Net. Beneath his helmet visor his eyes were wide.

"Parker?" In the mud yard of the warehouse on Dead End, Kit Born poked my shoulder.

I blinked, then turned and faced her.

She said, "to answer your question, Parker, no, it wasn't your friend's caste line that surprised me. What surprised me is that a man brave enough to engage hovertanks with crawlers, like horse cavalry against panzers, would have anything to do with a merc like you."

I've never considered slugging a woman before, but when I looked down at my right hand, it had balled into a fist.

Then another Sixer, this one a fresh-washed hired car, with a climate-sealed cabin, bounced into the yard.

Kit and I turned as it stopped, and Kit's new boss, who was already mine, stepped out into the mud. Cutler wore a designer's flap-pocketed idea of battle dress uniform, and a bush hat with one side pinned up. Behind him, his driver unloaded matched luggage. We already had a warehouse full of crap that we didn't need, so it hardly bothered me that Cutler was going to dress for dinner in the jungle.

Cutler tugged one booted foot out of the mud, turned his boot sole up to examine it, then turned his frown on Kit. "Right now, how many obstacles stand between us and a live grezzen?"

She ticked items off on her fingers as she spoke. "A hundred miles of bad road. One river ford. Lots of lesser monsters. That's three." She raised her thumb. "Four would be if you suffer an outbreak of common sense."

He sniffed, ignored her, and faced me while he pointed at the Abrams. "How about the equipment?"

"The C-lift trailer's got to be loaded. Fuel bladders, spares, all three ammunition lockers, Sleeper, repair 'bot. Then we run the checklists on the Abrams, remount the auxiliary guns, and we'll be good to go. We could finish tonight, but three days would make better sense. Unless we need any of that other stuff." I pointed at the equipment mountain.

He pointed at us. "The other stuff doesn't concern you. We leave in the morning, then. Also, none of you leave here in the meantime. Nobody phones or texts anyone."

I did a mental eye roll. Radio silence? For a hunting trip? Really? I spread my palms. "Who would we call? Sir."

Kit stood, arms crossed, brow wrinkled.

Cutler motioned to the hire's driver to carry the luggage into the warehouse, and watched while the man waddled, until he passed out of earshot. Then Cutler stared at Kit and me. "I'll explain when you need to know."

Fourteen

Zhondro and I finished our checklists, and had everything stowed on the C-lift, by midmorning. Cutler wanted to leave Eden for the Line immediately, and drive all night. Kit recommended that, once we cleared Eden's Triple-A umbrella, we only drive during daylight.

The Abrams, with the C-lift in tow, made eighty miles outside the city limits of Eden along the dirt single track road that led out to Kit Born's Line section. That put us twenty miles south of Kit's Line camp, and would give us plenty of daylight the following day in which to travel the remaining distance.

At fifteen minutes before End of Evening Nautical Twilight, we laagered for the night.

The fifteen minutes allowed for the four of us to exit the Abrams, button it up, then get buttoned up inside the Sleeper before full dark. We had electrified nets to set out, but Kit told us not to bother. The good news about the hours of darkness on Dead End was that the gorts didn't fly at night. The bad news was that the reason they didn't was that night on Dead End was too dangerous for them.

To Cutler, the Sleeper was "a Boy Scout camp in an armored box, and a damned cramped one." To a Yavi like me, the Sleeper was a capacious and luxurious portable apartment for four, though Zhondro prayed to his God for dispensation to bunk stacked four-high, separated from a woman not his wife only by a forearm's length and a thin foam hammock.

51

Evidently Zhondro's God returned calls promptly, because thirty minutes after we four finished dinner, he lay snoring in his bunk.

Kit and I sat facing Cutler across the Sleeper's fold-down dining table while we sipped coffee, ours from thermcups, his from private stock he had brought along. Outside, something—several somethings—snorted, then thumped the armor plate hard enough that my coffee sloshed. Cutler's eyes widened. I suppose mine did, too.

Kit waved her hand as she shook her head. "Woogs. Closest thing to grazing vegetarians on Dead End. They actually eat plant matter, which doesn't nourish any animal on Dead End. It's the insects inside that actually nourish the woogs. But that means they move and eat all day and all night, every day and every night, to process enough fodder to survive. A mature female weighs six tons. Think your electric fence would have bothered them, Parker?"

Another woog bellowed as it brushed the Sleeper.

I steadied myself with a hand against the wall. "Something's bothering them."

Kit shrugged. "Would it bother you to crap a pound of sand every time you ate a raisin?"

Cutler asked, "How long will this go on?"

"All night, probably. Herds average twenty thousand inside the Line. Two predator species eat woogs. Grezzen, and stripers, which are kind of six-legged tyrannosaurs. If there's a grezzen around, the stripers look for smaller prey. Beyond the Line, there's no doubt about who's the species-in-charge."

Cutler paused. He cupped his chin in his hand, stared at her, and asked, "Why do you think the grezzen have been so dominant for so long?"

She shrugged, stared down into her cup. "Speed. Power. Size. Durability."

Cutler asked, "You think it's that simple?"

She shrugged again. "Why not? Grezz are perfectly adapted to an ecosystem that's been static for thirty million years. On Earth, sharks have succeeded for even longer."

Cutler asked, "But these robot bombs have upset their applecart. Why do you think that is?"

Kit shifted in her chair, then stared at Cutler. "Why do *you* think the grezz have done so well?"

It was Cutler's turn to shrug and stare into his cup. "I suppose you're right."

Zhondro mumbled in his sleep.

Cutler stretched, then exercised his *droit du seigneur* and claimed first dibs on the sanex.

After Cutler was gone, I turned to Kit. "If either of you actually believed what you were saying just then, I'm a duck."

Kit just stared at me. Then Zhondro muttered in his sleep again, louder. Our company medic had said that Tassini did it because they smoked janga, which superanimated their dreams. Whatever. They all talked in their sleep.

The same night breeze that carried wobblehead stink up the dune to me also carried sleepy female murmurs. One woman seemed to yelp in her sleep, and the kid with his nightshirt pulled up looked away from his business in response.

Third Platoon's engines were in whispermode, softer than cat farts, and the wind blew toward us. But at that moment, Red Four, jockeying forward to come on line with the other four tanks, poked its prow beyond the military crest of the dune.

The kid below leaned toward us. Maybe he couldn't hear us, but he could see Red Four. The thermal's magnified image showed his mouth open as he stared up in the dark. He couldn't see us as clearly as I saw him, but he saw enough. He turned, then ran back to the tents, shouting and pointing back and up at us.

My gunner reached across the turret and tapped my bicep. "Jazen, they may not be combatants, but they're sure as hell combatant dependents. They got a radio down there tied in to their tank column. If you don't take the shot right now—"

Bam.

In the Sleeper, Cutler banged open the sanex door, yawned, and rolled into his bunk. He waved the lights low, pulled out his Reader, and lay bathed in its glow, absorbing bed-time stories.

Kit sidestepped past him, then closed the sanex door behind her.

Somewhere distant, something very large and un-wooglike bellowed so loudly that the Sleeper's wall armor vibrated. Then the ground beneath the Sleeper shook, as thousands of woogs stampeded in response.

In his bunk, Zhondro thrashed beneath his sheet, muttering in Tassini.

Kit slipped out of the sanex like a shadow in the dimmed light, visible for a blink wearing thoroughly utilitarian skivvies that on her looked anything but. She vaulted herself into the rack just below the one that would be mine, like a silent gymnast, and vanished beneath the sheets.

As Cutler lay on his back in his bunk, studying his Reader, he said to me, "Big day tomorrow, Parker. Sleep well."

Fat chance.

Fifteen

In the morning, the woogs were gone but not forgotten. The swath they ate and trampled through the trees that had surrounded us looked like twenty thousand bulldozers had wandered past. And compared to woog dung, wobblehead crap smelled like roses.

Zhondro and I broke down the night laager while Kit sat atop the Abrams' turret with her Barrett at the ready, but after she winged the obligatory gort, nothing bigger than lemon bugs interfered. Before full light, we were rolling north again, to Kit's Line camp.

Every kid has played holos set in a Kodiak crew compartment. However nobody born this century has seen an Abrams' gut except museum curators. But the two vehicles don't look all that different inside.

Neither space welcomes claustrophobes. Most of the crew volume in either tank is the roughly tubular, rotating basket inside of, and extending below, the turret. The Abrams' crew space is larger, because it accommodates an extra, third crew member, who loads the main gun. The loader, gunner, and tank commander sit in the turret, and move with it, like diners in a revolving restaurant. The fourth crew member, the driver, reclines in a fixed, forward-facing, coffin-sized compartment in the prow.

Even a Trueborn with his feet on the Abrams' floor can stand upright in the center of the turret, and can reach out from there with a yardstick and touch most anywhere inside.

Everything except the seating surfaces and controls is steel, white-painted to show fluid leaks, and as forgiving as your first drill instructor. An Abrams will break you before you break it, a lesson rookies learn nose-first. Rolling with the vehicle had become habit for me, but Cutler, and, to a lesser extent Kit, death-gripped one handhold after another and fought every lurch as Zhondro whistled the tank north across the uneven road surface.

Zhondro reclined up front, driving. I occupied the commander's throne, to the right rear and high. Cutler sat in the gunner's seat, below and in front of me. Kit sat on the turret's left side, facing us, at Cutler's level, in the loader's position.

Kit predicted visits from the gorts' less sociable relatives, so we rolled buttoned up, with the driver's, loader's and commander's hatches closed.

Buttoning up makes a tank less like a limo in four ways. First, except for the gun sights, one sees the world only through periscopic prism windows, which is like peeking through cereal boxes with both ends cut out. Second, it's hot. Third, it's hot. Fourth is a corollary of two and three. Hot people sweat buckets, and stink.

So, when we arrived at Kit's Line camp, everybody was ready to dismount, even into a cloudy, humid, one hundred two Fahrenheit afternoon. Cutler made for the air conditioned Sleeper. Cloudy or not, Zhondro scooted beneath the Abrams' shade from habit, for a Tassini siesta.

I sat atop the Abrams' turret, faced sideways with my legs dangling down through the open commander's hatch. Kit mimicked my position, but seated on the loader's hatch edge.

Zhondro had parked us atop a bald, granite plateau, looking out at a rolling green blanket of forest below, and a rolling gray blanket of cloud above, that stretched to the horizon.

Distant shrieks and bellows echoed, then hung in the damp air.

I rested my elbow on the receiver of the commander's .50 caliber. "It's safe to sit out like this?"

Kit pointed at the Triple-A 'bot atop the rock knob beside us. Steel clamshell doors bolted into the rock led into the artificial cave that was the Line Wrangler's station. "The Wrangler's station's on this plateau because the fields of observation and fire are clear. The Triple A 'bot and stationary mines out at the tree line have been emplaced long enough to teach the local predators lessons."

Five hundred yards below and to our left front, where the barren rock surrendered to the encroaching jungle, trees moved.

I scooted on my butt behind the .50, rattled back the charging handle, and sighted down the barrel at the movement. Twenty feet above the ground, a fanged lizard head, tiger-striped black and yellow like an overripe banana, poked out through the branches. The head was as long as a squad mess table, and attached to a six-legged body the size of a forty-passenger bus. The beast stared up at us, a prey item just bigger than an overweight woog. I swallowed, then slid my thumbs toward the gun's butterfly trigger.

The monster snarled, then lunged toward us.

Kit leaned toward me and touched my elbow. "Don't—"

Boom! Where there had been a monster, the mine's explosion left red mist adrift among shivering tree limbs. Bleeding ribs and drumsticks bigger than I was arced away in all directions.

"—Bother." Kit sat back and sighed. "Lessons taught aren't always lessons learned. It's a good thing stripers are dumb, because they're a handful up close."

I shook my head. "Everything here has six legs, not just the bugs. Animals don't eat plants. The sun never shines. This place makes no sense."

She shook her head back at me. "You sound as condescending as Cutler, Parker. Since the War, we're the only intelligent species left in this universe. Therefore, we think everything in this universe has to conform to *our* paradigm of what makes sense. Do you have any idea how arrogant that view is? And on how little of this universe we base it?"

I cleared the 'fifty, slapping the charging handle harder than I needed to. "Apparently *you* have an idea. I find *that* arrogant coming from a backwater gunslinger."

Zhondro rolled out from beneath the tank and called up at us, "What was that?"

The Sleeper's door banged open, and Cutler ran out, his Reader in one hand. He squinted at the smoke that drifted away from the spot where the beast had stood. Then he pointed at my hands on the .50. "Was it a grezzen? Did you just kill a grezzen?"

Kit shook her head. "Just a striper. A big pred. Tried to cross the stationary mine perimeter."

"Oh." Cutler waved a pointed finger at us. "Nobody fires on a grezzen unless I say so. Understood?"

Kit said, "The Rover 'bot perimeter's a mile further out from here. The grezz keep even more distance back than that. But don't worry. You'll get your kill."

Cutler walked to the C-lift, rested his hand on one of the three ammunition crates, then shook his head. "Ms. Born, I have no intention of killing a grezzen."

Sixteen

Two hours later, Zhondro and I dragged the last crate off the C-lift. Kit and Cutler stood back and watched as Zhondro pried the crate lid from Cutler's mystery ammo.

Most tank-gun rounds look like forty-pound hypodermic needles, a shell casing with a depleted uranium arrow's pointed tip sticking out the front. Cutler's specials replaced the arrow tip with an oversized tin can that had a straw sticking out its top center.

Cutler bent over the crate, hands on knees, and pointed. "This ammunition was designed by the best cryptozoologists on Earth. It'll inject a quart of dope that will knock a carbon-12 based organism the size of a grezzen cold for an hour."

Zhondro, Kit, and I turned and looked at one another. We were here to fire off the biggest tranquilizer darts in the universe? He had to be kidding.

Cutler said, "I assure you, I'm quite serious."

I asked him, "Where do we have to hit it?"

"They say anywhere on the body. Just so the agent gets injected into the bloodstream. Just like tranquilizing an elephant. These grezzen may look like ogres, but their circulatory plumbing works like any Terran mammal's."

Zhondro frowned. "What if this drug doesn't work? They say also that these grezzen are the deadliest animals in the universe."

Cutler sighed. "We've got conventional rounds, too."

59

Kit had her arms crossed, and feet planted. "Why do you want to play catch-and-release with the deadliest animal in the universe?"

Cutler said, "I don't. All I want you to do is put me in position to shoot the animal. Then you winch it onto the C-lift trailer and haul it back here. Another team is landing in Eden today. They'll bring another trailer out to this camp, stabilize the animal's sedation, and take it from there."

So the second trailer rental wasn't overkill. Neither was all the equipment in the overlarge warehouse. Cutler just might be smarter than I gave him credit for.

Kit's jaw dropped.

She shook her head. "Are you insane? The people on this planet will lynch you if you try to bring a live grezzen inside the Line."

"Ms. Born, each of my major subsidiaries fires more people in a year than the entire population of this planet. I haven't gotten where I am by knuckling under to the irrational fears of timid people."

Irrational? Cutler hadn't seen the striper. Which grezzen apparently ate for breakfast. Literally.

Cutler said, "But that's why I didn't disclose my plans to the locals. And why you won't, either. You're bound by the confidentiality clause in Bauer's contract, just like Parker and Zhondro are bound to theirs."

I scratched my head. "Mr. Cutler, why? A pet? An advertising stunt?"

He shook his head. "I don't deal in trivialities or stunts, Parker. That's as much as you need to know. Now, if you all don't mind, would you continue with the work for which I pay each of you generously?" Cutler spun on his heel, and returned to the Sleeper.

Kit stalked away, then stood, arms folded with her back to us, gazing out across the jungle beyond the Line.

Zhondro stood beside me, the crowbar he had used to open the crate in one hand. We both stared at Kit.

I said to Zhondro, "Contrary to what our fearless leader just said about our pay, she took this job for practically nothing. You think she took this job because she suspected Cutler was up to something like this?"

He shrugged. "At home we say, 'hold friends close, but enemies closer.'"

"We say that, too."

By the next day, the fearless leader and the gunslinger had each decided to pretend they were friends, not enemies.

Zhondro and I had expected to instruct Cutler and Kit in Tank 101 before we left Eden, but Cutler had accelerated our departure. So we did it out here.

First, we taught each of them to drive. They say a child's first two-wheeler is harder to learn than an Abrams. I wouldn't know, because I'm still waiting for my first bike, but driving an Abrams is cake.

The start sequence isn't much more than a button push. The control yoke is a stubby handlebar. To turn left, turn the bar left. The left track slows relative to the right track. The more you turn the bar, the sharper the tank turns. Twist the right grip to go fast, twist back to go slow. You can't confuse the brake and accelerator pedals, because there's just a centered brake pedal wider than even the biggest GI's boot.

Cutler had originally insisted on the tank commander's seat. VIPs always did. Unbuttoned, the TC rode standing on his chair, waist-high out of the hatch in his cupola, which was wind-in-the-face fun. Also, topside the TC controlled the best toy on the tank, the .50 caliber machine gun. The .50 was enormous for a machine gun, more an ancient rapid-fire cannon. It was wicked fun to shoot, too, since the VIP didn't have to break down and clean the weapon later.

But Dead End didn't even have a navigational satellite network for the Abrams' Earth-oriented old computer to interface with. That meant that any map-and-compass help Kit needed, in which Cutler had zero expertise and less interest, fell to whoever sat in the Commander's seat.

Once Cutler realized we would run buttoned up most of the time, he opted for the gunner's station. Down there he could fiddle with his Reader more privately while we rolled. But he could still play Great White Hunter, because the main gun could be aimed and fired from either the tank commander's or gunner's position.

That left Kit to do the job normally done by the person who occupied her chair, the loader. The loader has an overhead hatch, and time to look around when the tank's not shooting. So it seemed a perfect job for the only person who knew where we were going and what to watch out for.

I stood down in the turret with Kit, facing the main gun ammunition, which was stored in the turret's rear bustle. The rounds' bases faced us, like racked wine bottles.

I waved my spread palm across the rounds. "Some tanks this old loaded the main gun automatically. But autoloaders jam. And manual lets the Tank Commander select ammunition type."

"A slaughter smorgasbord. How nice for you."

I ignored her and laid my palm on the various sections of the ready rack. "Practice rounds here. Armor-piercing discarding sabot here. Cutler's tranquilizers here."

She frowned. "Got any canister?"

Canister was the clumsy grandparent of the modern flechette round. Either round shotgunned soft targets into hamburger, across a broad front. Like troops in the open. Or sleeping children. Hair rose on my neck.

"Why?"

"We might need to turn a woog stampede. Canister would do that."

"Oh." I pointed down and right. "Canister's down here. But listen sharp when I call for ammunition type. From habit I might call for flechette."

"—Flechette, yet? What the hell are you talking about, Parker?" The captain's voice crackled to me across five miles of Tassin desert.

I adjusted my helmet mike. "We haven't fired yet. Autoloader relay won't select flechette, sir."

My gunner covered his own mike with his fingers and hissed, "Jazen, that's bullshit!"

I waved him off with one hand.

The captain said, "Parker, I ordered you to—Goddammit! Something just spooked the Tassini. Their column's turned back, short of the kill zone."

My gunner whispered, "I *told* you they had a radio down there!"

Below, in the thermal's sight picture, Tassin women, robes flapping, dragged children by the hands, or clutched babies as they fled the tents and disappeared over the opposite dune, like green-lit ghosts. Within fifty seconds, nothing moved below us but tent canvas. The camp had emptied out faster than a nightclub on fire. I switched to platoon net. "Fire!"

Whoom. Whoom. Whoom. Whoom. Whoom.

Five rounds of flechette left nothing of the camp below but canvas tatters and shattered pots. But nobody in it was dead that wasn't dead before we fired.

I switched back to command net. "Red One, this is Red Three. We cleared the autoloader malfunction. Target destroyed. Over."

"Outstanding, Parker. Truly outstanding. Five simultaneous malfunctions is incredibly bad luck. And clearing them all within one minute is incredibly fast work. I'll put Third Platoon up for a unit citation. Right after your court martial."

My gunner laid his palm across his visor while he lowered his head and shook it.

The captain said, "Meantime, get your platoon out of there, max mil speed. You got thirty Tassini crawlers inbound full-gas. And if you think *I'm* pissed off . . . "

"Parker?" Kit rapped her knuckles on my helmet. "After you call for a round, what do I do?"

I showed her. The loader's job is female-unfriendly. The rounds weigh as much as fifty-three pounds, and have to be wrestled out of the ready rack tubes, then cradled across the turret rear-to-front, dodging sharp steel corners, then slammed into the main gun breech. Speed and accuracy count, and errors cost fingers.

After an hour of practice reps, Kit's hands and one elbow were bruised and bleeding, her lips stretched tight across her teeth, and I could see spasms in her forearms, but she never complained.

Late that afternoon, Zhondro drove the Abrams out to the east tree line that bordered Kit's camp, and I inflated a threedic target intended to represent a grezzen. It was actually a life-sized pink elephant advertising balloon. Kit pronounced it too small, but adequate.

Then we backed the tank across the plateau to the opposite tree line. That put Cutler a thousand yards from his target. The wooded terrain beyond the Line wouldn't allow a clear shot near that long, but I reasoned that if Cutler could hit a target smaller than a grezzen at a thousand yards, he could certainly hit a full-sized one at five hundred.

Everybody strapped on helmets, so we could converse over the intercom, but really, so the earphone flaps would protect our hearing. Not from engine noise. Abrams' gas turbines are actually so quiet that adversary infantry used to call them "whispering death." But a 120-millimeter fired live doesn't whisper.

Cutler sat hunched forward in the Abrams' gunner well, his eye to the rubber reticle of the standard sight. He waggled the turret, and the gun, left and right with two hands on the gunner's yoke, then slid his thumbs to the two red buttons atop the yoke arms. He depressed both buttons once. "Got it!"

I watched the commander's image screen, which was slaved to Cutler's sight. Cutler had succeeded in centering the grezzen in the rectangular sight reticle, which was easier than playing a holo game. Cutler's button push pulsed a laser beam out that struck, then bounced back off the target. The tank measured the travel time out and back, then calculated range to target.

Now, hitting the target had little to do with Cutler and everything to do with the tank. Once Cutler had ranged the target, the Abrams' fire control system was so good and so durable that the Kodiak's was basically just an update of a century-old design. The tank now adjusted for its own tilt, cross wind, even gun tube droop on a hot day. It did so whether the tank was stationary, like we were, or rumbling across uneven ground. The tank would even lead the target if the target was moving. This one wasn't even doing that.

All Cutler had to do was point and shoot.

If he could hit a target out here in the rain forest as well as his simulator results showed, Kit wouldn't have to move much ammo. These old crawlers delivered first-round kills almost as reliably as a modern Kodiak did.

I said into my mike, "Load, load practice round."

To my left, Kit pressed the knee switch that opened the blast door covering the ready rack, pulled the round, pirouetted and fisted it home in the main gun breech. She snatched her fist back, fingers intact as the breech snapped shut, then said, "Practice round loaded."

I glanced at my 'puter. Practice rounds didn't hit like tacticals, and accordingly weighed less. Still, an experienced loader loaded in three to five seconds. Kit had just done the job in four flat. I nearly said "Good girl!" out loud, then realized that would piss everybody off, all for different reasons.

We took the shot stationary and unbuttoned, with me topside out of the commander's hatch, joined by Kit, out the loader's hatch.

I said, "Fire, fire practice round."

Below, Cutler depressed the red buttons a second time, triggering the gun.

Whoom!

The Abrams lurched as if sucker-punched by God. A fireball the size of a small house lit the main gun's muzzle and kicked up a dust cloud the size of a large house. Two blinks later, the target remained.

Cutler muttered, "What the—?"

Then the target sagged flat, undulating on the breeze like struck regimental colors. The practice round mimicked an armor-killing discarding sabot round. When an armor piercing discarding sabot round left the gun muzzle, most of the "bullet" fell away, leaving a central, sharp, dense penetrator rod howling toward the target at thirty-five hundred feet per second. The penetrator had needled through the unresisting target so cleanly that it took a breath before the balloon deflated.

Cutler scrambled out of his seat, then squirmed up alongside me smiling. "That was great! How soon can we kill something?"

Kit glanced at me and rolled her eyes.

Seventeen

Once we got inside the Wrangler's station, which was a series of chambers blasted out within the granite knob, Kit's first job was to report our safe arrival to Eden Outfitters. Radios didn't work much better on Dead End than Handtalks, but old hard-wired field telephones worked fine.

Kit sat at a stool in front of a camp table, speaking into an ancient pedestal microphone, while the voice of Oliver, her boss, crackled through an analog speaker box alongside the mike.

After the usual unpleasantries, he said, "Tell Mr. Cutler his people downshuttled last night."

I thought *we* were Cutler's people. Surprise!

Oliver continued, "They're moving gear into the warehouse he rented."

Kit glanced at Cutler, and he nodded. "He's got the word, Oliver."

"Kit, people here aren't stupid. Cutler's crew look more like pirates than taxidermists. And it doesn't take thirty ex-Legion psychos to stuff a dead grezzen."

"So what are you saying, Oliver?"

I could almost hear the shrug over the land line. "I dunno. Just that even the prospect of a dead grezzen inside the Line makes people jumpy."

Kit shrugged back. "Okay."

"Kit, you don't take any 'bots off the Line for escort when you go out in the bush, got it? Mr. Cutler doesn't know what a grezz loose in here could do."

She nodded. "The 'bots stay in place. Got it. Oliver, I wasn't planning on pulling them out anyway—" While Kit had been talking, she had been gazing at the glowing Animap that hung on the cave's wall.

Whoop-whoop-whoop!

An alarm echoed in the chamber. Kit pointed to a red dot that inched across the Animap. "Gotta go, Oliver. A 'bot just went live."

She stood while Cutler, Zhondro, and I stood behind her and followed her stare.

Two dozen red dots shone against the map's green background, but only one had begun to move.

Kit said, "That 'bot's sensed a grezz within a half mile of it."

Cutler stood, then stepped to the map and stared at it, hands clasped behind his back. "Are you sure? The 'bot could be chasing one of those buffalos, or a striper that's stalking them."

She shook her head. "The Rover ignores anything as small as a woog or as slow as a striper. And a grezz makes random direction changes. The Rovers are also programmed to respond to that."

Cutler stroked his chin. "Why does it change direction?"

"The grezz didn't used to do it. Even now they only do it near the line. It's probably proactive evasive maneuvering. They've learned that the Rovers can sneak up on them."

Cutler nodded. "Rovers aren't as dumb as these woogs of yours."

The red dot on the map stopped moving.

Cutler leaned forward. "Did the 'bot blow the grezzen up?"

Kit shook her head. "The grezz just moved out of range, so the 'bot shut down again. When a 'bot detonates, its dot flickers out. This dot's still there. This was no big deal. Grezz are solitary hunters. They forage over defined territorial loops. But as they orbit within their territories, their territories rotate. Like planets around a sun, and moons around each planet.

I said, "You mean one grezz knows what the other ones are doing?"

Kit shrugged. "Does one moon know what the other moons are doing? Lots of predators warn peers away by marking territory. The grezz that triggered that 'bot was just foraging its territory, and its loop took it close to the Line, then away from it. So the

Rover activated when the grezzen came close, then shut down when the grezzen moved away."

I said, "Well, at least we know it's here. Fortunately, it doesn't know we're here."

Zhondro nodded. Kit, however, didn't. Neither did Cutler.

The workshop cavern just inside the station's armored doors was big enough not only for the Wrangler's vehicles and the 'bot armory but for us to park the Abrams and the floater. Therefore, after dinner, Kit reprogrammed a Rover, and Cutler disappeared into the living quarters in the adjacent chamber.

Zhondro and I sat on a parts crate, legs dangling, watching while our six-legged maintenance 'bot replaced the third right-side road wheel. The job, if performed by last-century tankers, or by this-century Tassini, was a muddy wrestle that cost a couple of soldiers several square inches of knuckle skin.

I smiled at Zhondro. "How many tankers does it take to change a road wheel?"

There are no comedy clubs in the desert. He frowned, counted on his fingers, scratched his head, then said. "I don't know."

"Ten. Two to change the wheel, and eight to stand around and criticize their technique."

After a heartbeat, he threw back his head, laughed, and slapped my thigh. He hadn't been laughing the first time we met.

"Max mil speed my ass!" I coughed a mud of spit and Tassin powder sand into my glove as the captain's voice vanished from the command net. Tassin powder was four microns finer than Saharan Desert sand on Earth. It was also four microns finer than the sand on every outworld the Legion had operated on before Bren.

Therefore, the geniuses at Lockheed who had designed the filters that protected a Kodiak's moving parts were shocked—shocked—that Kodiaks choked themselves to death in seconds if operated in the Tassin desert at more than half of maximum military speed. Filter redesign was the manufacturer's current top priority. Meaning that in the meantime our enemy could run circles around us with antiques.

I was in command of five nano-'puter guided, composite-armored, gunned-to-the teeth war machines that could outrun any armored land vehicle in the universe, over rock, mud, water, or grass. Except here and now, where they could barely outrun dismounted infantry.

I toggled back to platoon net. "Red Group, this is Red Three. Come about and withdraw echelon left, at one eight zero. Maintain best speed but hold formation. Red Three will take left flank." We couldn't flat outrun the Tassini, so our best chance was to back up, presenting the enemy our heavier, frontal armor, in an orderly withdrawal that allowed us to fire on the bad guys, and protect one another. And hope that help arrived.

"How many, Jazen?" Edwards asked.

"Thirty. Inbound, hot."

"Thirty? Echelon, my ass! Jazen, just turn around and boogie full gas!" The trouble with a brevet command is subordinates still think they're debating over coffee with their buddy. Edwards was a tank commander, like I had been. In fact, by date of rank he was senior. He should've been breveted, not me, when Lieutenant Haren closed his real estate deal.

"Run? Then the people eaters blow your ass off for sure, Edwards!" Suarez was a tank commander, too. Edwards had a point, but Suarez and I had a better one. Kodiaks, like most tanks, had thinner armor on their rear and flanks. They were designed to fight facing their adversaries.

I said, "Stuff it! Echelon. Now. Move."

The chatter died.

My driver slewed Red Three around.

"Jazen?" Edwards again.

I rolled my eyes, though he didn't sound argumentative,

"Jazen, my forward impellers just quit."

Goddamn powder sand.

"What's your best speed, then?"

"Zero."

My gunner pressed his earpiece. "I got purple chatter. I can't make out a word, but there's lots of 'em."

Normally, we didn't pick up Tassini intercom chatter until they were close, minutes away, and so committed to battle that they didn't care who knew it.

The school solution was leave Edwards' tank to the wolves, and save the other four. Pick him and his crew up, if there was time. But there wasn't time. And the school solution didn't say how four tanks could outrun thirty that could move twice as fast as the four, anyway.

Surrender was no option. Intel said the Tassini, purple people eater nickname notwithstanding, didn't actually cannibalize captured legionnaires. But they did burn Legion prisoners alive on the spot, as a favor, so we could enter Paradise as warriors.

I sighed. "Red Group, this is Red Three. Form up on line and blow down."

One thing a hovertank can do that a crawler can't is put itself into hull defilade. In other words, by concentrating all the tank's impeller power, coupled with its weight, a hovertank on loose substrate can blow out a hole beneath itself, and bury itself turret-deep. Blowdown piles the displaced substrate around the tank, and basically turns a tank into a revetted pillbox, protected by the earthworks it throws up around itself. If you've ever seen a nature holo of a flounder flapping itself down into the sand, you've got the idea.

Of course, in the nature holo, once the flounder has immobilized itself a shark swims into the picture and eats it. Like the flounder, we would get eaten. Unlike the flounder, we would bite back first.

My gunner's eyes met mine. "Yes, sir." He raised his thumb as he firewalled the impeller throttles. *Clang.*

Clang.

In the man-blasted cave on Dead End, our maintenance 'bot laid down the dog-bone tool that allowed it to change the road wheel, then sank down on all six legs and whined into sleep mode.

Zhondro stretched, yawned, then tapped my thigh again, smiling. "Tonight we sleep, too. Tomorrow, we find out how many tankers it takes to make a monster sleep."

Across the room Kit stood up from the 'bot she had been working on, and stretched, too. She watched Zhondro walk away from me, shook her head, then dragged off to bed herself.

That left me alone with the Abrams and Kit's sleeping Rover 'bots, in silence so complete that it echoed. I lay back and stared at the pocked granite ceiling for a moment. I didn't think I dozed, and when I sat up and looked around the cavern was as empty as before. But I felt as though a stranger was listening to me breathe.

The next morning, we pushed off for the Line at Break of Morning Nautical Twilight, for a four-hour sightsee beyond the Line, just a risk-free toe-dip along the edge of the big pond that was grezzen land.

We were topped up with diesel, the turbine purred, not a bad light showed on the boards, and I sipped coffee that actually tasted good from the thermcup. Everybody's helmet radios were operating static free, and all hatches were safely buttoned up against avian predators.

I rocked in the commander's cupola, humming. Kit sat in the loader's seat, facing Cutler down in the Gunner's well, and both actually were smiling. I smiled, too. The only downside was that our closed steel box was already an oven and the morning was young. But this was shaping up as a safari after all, not a bus wreck.

Two miles later, Kit raised her palm. "Stop!"

Eighteen

In the hand that she hadn't raised, Kit gripped a handheld Animap that mimicked the one back on the Line station's wall, and she stared down at its screen. She spoke into her mike. "Come right twenty yards."

Zhondro pivoted the tank, and nudged over a barrel-round tree like it was a garden stake.

Kit looked up at me, then poked her thumb up toward the hatches. "Okay. Let's open the hatches."

I pressed my earpiece. "What?"

Kit mopped her cheek with her fleece glove back. "It'll be cooler."

"The birds will get us."

She shook her head. "Not a problem any more. Meet me topside and I'll explain."

The two of us scrambled up and stood, torsos exposed, forearms resting atop the Abrams' turret.

I looked around, my first real view of Dead End *au naturel.* Beneath low, gray clouds, green-leaved trees as big around as drive-up pharmacies rose three hundred feet. They were set far enough apart that the Abrams—or herds of big animals—could navigate among them easily. Clumps of orange, yellow, and red flowered brush carpeted the gently rolling forest floor. "I didn't expect this."

She nodded. "This rainforest surprised me too. I expected triple canopy jungle you had to hack through with a machete, not open forest. And the color surprises everybody. Flowers are supposed to have evolved as food. To attract birds and insects that carry plant pollen. So if the birdlikes and insectlikes here can't digest fruit and flower nectar, why did fruit and flowers evolve?"

"I guess." I hadn't known why it didn't add up. I just knew it didn't. The lovely Ms. Born not only knew answers that I didn't, she knew answers to questions I hadn't even thought of.

"The birdlikes and insectlikes here don't eat fruits or visit flowers to eat the plant, but to eat the insectlikes that live in the plant. The woogs do the same thing. It doesn't fit our idea of a natural scheme, but that doesn't make it less true."

I fingered my helmet chin strap while I craned my neck at dragon shapes silhouetted against the clouds. "I dunno. I know the birdlikes will eat *us*. I saw them. That's part of the natural scheme, too."

"Not really. The scheme you experienced inside the Line's no longer natural. Grezzen can jump forty feet straight up. They swat gorts down, like flies." She pointed at the dragons carving figure eights overhead. "The gorts learned thirty million years ago to nest in the trees, up there, and fly above a floor of plus-fifty feet. Out here, you're seeing Dead End in its natural balance."

She said, "Inside the Line, grezzen were killing us. So we got rid of the grezzen. But then the gorts that the grezzen kept at bay modified their behavior, and started killing us. Planetologists call it the conundrum of unforseen ecological consequence. I call it the whack-a-mole rule of human meddling." She clasped both hands, like a child hammering. "Whack! We change something *here*. Oops. That makes another problem pop up *there*, where we didn't expect it. Whack! So we whack *that* mole. Oops. We're so smart that we're a menace."

My heart skipped. "You're saying that the gorts are staying away because there's a grezzen around here?" I laid my hand on the .50's receiver and scanned the distant treeline.

She shook her head. "Nope." She pointed at the ground ten feet beyond our right track. One of her camouflaged Rover 'bots lay powered down in green stuff that looked like weeds. "That's the 'bot that moved last night, because a grezz *was* in the area at that time."

I moved my palm to the .50's charging handle as I swiveled my head.

She sighed and shook her head again. "Parker, relax. A shutdown Rover 'bot's the perfect grezz alarm. If a grezz moves within eight hundred yards of us, that 'bot will wake up. As long as the 'bot's still, we couldn't be safer."

Cutler shouldered his way up alongside me. "Then I'll switch places with you, Parker."

I frowned at Kit. There were roughly sixty things Cutler could reach from the tank commander's station with which he could inadvertently strand or kill us. But it was his tank.

Twenty minutes later, we were headed toward the next of Kit's 'bots, rocking along at sixteen miles per hour across rolling terrain when Cutler, torso out of the cupola, whooped.

Down in the gunner's well, I peeked through the optical sight, to see what he saw. Sixty yards to our front, four tapioca-colored, fanged, bug-eyed, featherless ostriches loped through the trees in a nose to tail line, from our right to our left, like shooting gallery ducks.

Blam-blam-blam-blam.

One .50 round is bigger than a cigar. The four-round burst that Cutler had just fired would kill an elephant wearing a flak jacket. Still, after his first shots, Cutler ripped off three more bursts, sixty rounds, total.

Cutler insisted that Zhondro roll us up close, so Cutler could climb down and be holoed kneeling alongside his first trophies. But after he got close he saw the only thing left of what had been a family was a dumpsterful of guts. Cutler decided to wait on making a holo until he murdered a victim that could be recognized.

While Cutler was off the tank, I bent a link in the .50's ammo belt with my trench knife, so the gun would jam after Cutler fired his next round. When the gun jammed, I explained that the .50 was an ancient design, prone to require frequent head space resetting, which was true. I also explained that meant the gun was out of service for the day, which was crap.

At noon we arrived at Kit's outermost Rover 'bot, hunkered down asleep in the weeds. Cutler, deprived of his toy, had tired of eating bugs and dust topside, so he swapped back into the gunner's well.

Kit and I stood again in the turret, side-by-side, surveying the open forest.

Alongside the tank, hydraulics whined. Kit's 'bot levered up on six legs, skittered forward ten yards, then paused, anterior sensors twitching like roach antennae.

Hair stood on my neck.

Kit whispered, "Uh-oh."

Nineteen

We buttoned up, then followed the Rover 'bot, Zhondro dancing the tank between monstrous trees, over a series of shallow rises. The wind was coming toward us, stiff enough to cover the turbine's whisper.

We topped a rise and movement flickered four hundred yards ahead. I goosed my magnification, and my heart skipped. Cutler was seeing exactly the picture through his gunner's sight that I saw through mine. Zhondro must've seen it too, through his hatch periscope. He stopped us clean and silent without a word from me.

The grezzen stood facing away from us, a shaggy, six-legged grizzly of a beast, bigger than an elephant. Its head seemed to be buried in something hidden by a fallen log. Maybe what Kit would call a prey item. Cutler's whisper rasped in my ear. "Perfect. Absolutely perfect." He ranged the target.

I whispered into my mike to Kit. "Load, load trank round."

The grezzen was a stationary target the size of a truck, four hundred yards away, and we were stationary, too. A potshot for Cutler. The round that Kit loaded rang against the breech, but the animal didn't react.

Kit whispered back, "Trank round loaded."

I said, "Fire, fire trank round." Then I held my breath.

Below me, Cutler's thumb depressed the the firing button.

Whoom!

In the nanosecond before the round flashed downrange, it seemed the animal moved. But it also seemed to me that the grezzen was dead center in the sight reticle when the round would have struck.

Still, an eye blink later, the beast was gone.

We chased, and so did the 'Rover 'bot, but within the seconds it took us to reach the fallen log where the animal had stood, the Rover had shut down. There was no grezzen anywhere in the vicinity, dead, alive, or doped. Kit dismounted, knelt with an elbow on a knee, and pronounced a series of six divots, deep enough to have been backhoe trenches, to be grezz tracks. There were just the six prints, then nothing until a bus-sized, beaten down tunnel through brush, thirty yards away.

I whistled. An elephant that could standing broad jump thirty yards.

Kit said. "Might as well stand down. It's gone."

"Gone? I hit it! I know I hit it!" Cutler pounded his fist against the turret wall.

Kit said, "A grezz can make seventy miles an hour in this country. The 'bot's shut down. That means there's no grezz within a half mile. More likely, it's already three miles away and moving faster than we can. Tomorrow's another day."

At Cutler's insistence, we located the grezzen's tracks, then followed them, bulldozing through the brush, until they disappeared at the edge of a granite patch. Then we traversed the area for two hours, in case the animal was sleeping off the round's tranquilizer juice someplace.

We returned to Line camp before dark. Cutler was half exhilarated, half frustrated, and turned in early with his Reader after a couple whiskeys. Zhondro and Kit likewise, except for the Reader and the whiskey.

On a hunch, I climbed back in to the Abrams, powered up the engine and electricals, and ran the fire control system diagnostics. Then I kneed open the blast door and eyeballed the ready rack.

Hands on hips, I nodded to myself. "Well, well."

Twenty

The next day, Dead End surprised us again. The planet lacked the weather satellites that even second-class worlds had taken for granted for a century, so Dead End's storms arrived without warning and hung around until they left just as unexpectedly. They blew at hurricane force, dumped lakes of rain, and blasted down enough lightning to fry tank circuits.

Not that weather bothered the Abrams. It won the final, great, running tank battle of the twentieth century, on Earth, in rain and sandstorms. On the last day, at a place called Medina Ridge, the score was Abrams, one hundred eighty-six, other guys' tanks, zero.

But it would have been pointless to trank Cutler's grezzen, then be unable to pack it home because of the weather. So we hunkered down in Kit's cave until the storm blew itself out.

That suited Zhondro and me. Armored vehicle preventive maintenance is not performed by the Tank Fairy. One in four subdivisions of any armored unit, whether ancient tracks or modern floaters, was a maintenance outfit. So, for this one tank, Zhondro, the maintenance 'bot and I were covering not only the tank crew's normal work, but the jobs of easily a half dozen mechs.

The two of us knelt alongside the Abrams in the maintenance cavern inspecting the treads. Beyond the cavern's plasteel doors, thunder rumbled like an armored column.

Zhondro rapped his knuckles on a rubber tread block. "This environment doesn't abrade the mechanical components so badly as the desert." He pointed a wrench at the turret. "Cutler is a better shot than his apparent miss yesterday suggested. Were I you, I would run the ballistics computer diagnostic."

I had, last night, but I didn't care to tell him. I shook my head. "I'm too tired. The diagnostic takes two hours."

Zhondro stood, laid the wrench on the fender, and burbled something in Tassini.

I wrinkled my forehead at him.

He said, "It's a proverb. The lazy man pays twice for his arrogance."

I shrugged. "Does it sound better in Tassini?"

"Most definitely. I recall one young man who didn't speak Tassini. He nearly paid for his arrogance with his life." He smiled as he left me, and walked back to the living quarters to say his morning prayers.

I called after him, "I recall, too."

The five tanks of Third Platoon had been blown down into the sand for three minutes when the lead element of the Tassini column showed itself in the magnified green of the night sight's picture. Tiny dots floated along a dune crest, a thousand yards from us.

Platoon net crackled. "I got wobbleheads!"

Another advantage the Tassini armor had over us was cavalry. While our armored units fought "pure," without associated infantry, the Tassini had scouts, who rode web-footed, two-legged dinosaurids with floppy crests on their skulls.

"Targets! One o'clock. One thousand yards. Engaging."

"Don't waste main gun rounds on the little fuckers." Suarez.

"Hold fire!" Even as I said it, the coaxial turret machine guns of two of my tanks rattled.

The range was so long for the coaxial machine guns that their tracers had started to burn out before the rounds arrived at their targets. Still, in the distance, sand spouted, one wobblehead and rider writhed, fell, and slid down the dune face. The others scampered to cover.

"Hooyah!"

"Shut up, you fuckin' idiots." Suarez was right again.

I sighed. The rebel commander had exposed a low value target to learn more about our location and strength. Thanks to itchy trigger fingers that I had failed to control, he had succeeded.

Ten seconds later, thirty degrees left of the spot where the wobbleheads had disappeared, a half dozen Abramses popped up far enough above a ridge line that they could fire main gun rounds at us, then they scooted back out of sight before we could traverse our turrets and engage them. The range between them and us was a thousand yards, easy shooting for either tank's gun.

Three of their rounds whistled high. The turret of a hull-down Kodiak isn't much of a target. Two rounds burrowed harmlessly into the sand revetments in front of two of our tanks. One round struck the glacis, the thick prow, of Edwards' disabled Kodiak, which hadn't been able to blow down properly. The round sparked away into the night.

"That rang our bell!" Edwards' voice quavered. Taking a 120-millimeter round on the nose was like sitting in a washtub sledge-hammered by Godzilla. But a Kodiak's next-generation armor enabled it to absorb an Abrams' punches, at least head on.

I spoke to the platoon. "Load, load sabot. Guess at where they're gonna pop up next. Pre-sight on a spot. Gunners fire as soon as you identify a target, before it can scoot."

The next pop up came thirty seconds later, another half dozen tanks, twenty degrees left of the first.

My gunner twitched our turret and fired without waiting for a fire command. He called, "On the way!" I watched the red tracer on the penetrator's tail flash toward an Abrams that was already reversing after its shot.

Flash. *Foom!*

In its day, an Abrams' forward turret armor could stop any direct-fire round on Earth. But this wasn't its day, and it wasn't on Earth. The Kodiak's 145-millimeter smooth bore was the most powerful tank gun ever built.

Our round spit through the Abrams' skin, liquefying itself and the armor it penetrated, then exploding molten metal rain into the tank's interior. The crew probably never felt a thing, and a fireball erupted up into the night. The ammo in the Abrams' bustle, isolated behind a blast door that couldn't withstand the heat and overpressure our shot injected into the crew compartment, detonated. The thin steel ammunition compartment roof disintegrated like kitchen foil.

I kept the sight on the hulk as it burned. Not because I doubted the kill. All tankers share the nightmare of burning alive in the steel shroud that was supposed to protect us. So I hoped some-body, even somebody who had been trying to kill us, would make it out of that oven alive. Nobody did.

"Tanks. Ten o'clock!"

Our turret, and others, spun. More rounds sped downrange.

One minute later, nothing moved downrange but undulating, bright smudges in the thermal that marked five enemy tanks aflame.

Suarez screamed at the burning hulks, "Ha! You like our silver bullets, amigos?"

Somebody else whooped.

I asked the platoon, "Damage?"

"We got nicked, sir. But we're still good to go." That was Pine.

Somebody in Arcuno's tank said, "I think Muto broke his wrist, skipper."

Now I was the skipper. But I didn't feel like it. I just felt sick. The turret stunk of burned propellant, sweat, and fear. The odds against us were still five to one, we weren't going anywhere, and we would run out of silver bullets before the bad guys ran out of tanks.

In the cavern, Kit touched my shoulder. "The storm's moving off. Tomorrow we can go deeper beyond the Line."

I cocked my head at the diminishing thunder, and kept it cocked as I looked around the cavern. We were alone for the first time since the grezz got away. "Why should we bother?"

She wrinkled her forehead. "What do you mean?"

"You loaded a practice round when I called for a trank. Cutler didn't miss. That pissant penetrator either glanced off that grezzen or just poked it like a sewing pin."

She stared at me, then looked away, then down at the cavern floor and scuffed it with her boot toe.

I waited. "Well?"

"It's no different than your little charade with Cutler and the .50 caliber. Head space adjustment my ass."

It was my turn to stare. Then I shook my head. "No. What I did stopped a gratuitous slaughter that I didn't sign up for. You agreed to help Cutler do exactly what he was trying to do, then sabotaged him. In fact, he was doing less than you agreed to. It turns out he doesn't even want to kill the animal."

She pointed toward the living quarters, while she fixed me with the coldest stare I had ever seen. "Parker, that man can't be allowed to take a grezzen alive."

I narrowed my eyes. "Why not?"

She folded her arms across her chest. "I can't tell you right now."

I wanted to believe her. And I didn't like Cutler's paranoid foolishness any better than I liked hers. But earning Cutler's bonus was the only way I could buy a life. That meant we needed her as a guide. "If you screw this up for Cutler, he'll just hire somebody else. Help him get his live grezzen. When the time comes, tell him whatever it is that's bothering you. I'll back you up."

She cocked her head, and fixed me with those blue eyes. "And if he won't budge?"

I took a deep breath. "If it comes to that, I'll make him budge. Out here, he's no tycoon. There are two of us and one of him." I could stop short of crossing the mutiny bridge later, if I didn't buy whatever she had to say. But first I had to get us to the bridge.

She asked, "What about Zhondro?"

"Zhondro will be fine with what I tell him. We know each other."

"I gathered that. Though I don't understand it." She nodded. "Okay. I'll play, for now." She turned and walked away, then she turned back, and stared at me with the blue eyes again. "What you did, Parker? With the .50? You surprised me. And I liked it. I liked it a lot."

She turned again, and I swallowed. I had just hatched a conspiracy that could cost me my life, or save it, with a woman about whom I knew only that she wasn't what she seemed to be.

But as I watched her walk away, all I could think about was the way she had looked the previous night, when she slipped into her bunk in her skivvies.

I didn't get over it until first thing the next morning.

Twenty-one

In the gray dawn we rolled across the Line like a wagon train in a Trueborn western. We towed the floater laden with gear to deal with a presumably passive grezzen, fuel, the Sleeper, spares, and the maintenance 'bot. I didn't like that the floater reduced the Abrams' mobility to that of a fifteen hundred horsepower oxcart. But there were no convenience stores beyond the Line, and we were going far enough for long enough that, if we broke down, walking back would be no option.

Rover 'bots were programmed to rove no farther than eight hundred yards out beyond the Line. Once we got more than eight hundred yards out, they would provide no warning, much less kill any grezzen we might encounter, until and unless we returned to their protective umbrella. I had lobbied to take along a couple of Rovers as early-warning outriders, in spite of the ban I had heard Eden Outfitters impose on Kit. But Cutler vetoed my suggestion. And, in fact, it made no sense to take along something programmed to automatically kill the very animal we were trying to take alive.

So we kept the machine guns loaded. The main gun, too. With a real bullet, this time. I checked.

We had even loaded up handheld anti tank tubes. Even the Legion, which was even less concerned than Eden Outfitters about protecting its valued employees, hadn't forced us legionnaires to go into battle equipped with HATTs. HATTs were junk against tanks, inaccurate beyond even twenty-five yards, prone to dud, and therefore every arms merchant's loss leader.

Which was probably why Eden Outfitters had cases of them, which it shipped out to its Line Section stations. Kit assured us that, while a HATT wouldn't drop a grezzen, it was a dandy noise-maker to scare off anything else we might encounter.

The first obstacle we encountered was a broad river imaginatively named Broad River. Kit charted our course so that we could cross the river at the point where it tumbled over a thirty-foot-high rock bench that she called Broad Falls. She said that we had to ford there because the river was too deep elsewhere. Also, elsewhere the river was infested with things that Kit said were big enough and mean enough to drag even an Abrams under like a crocodile poaching a wallaby.

I didn't want to die like a poached wallaby, whatever it was, so I was glad to learn that the river rose and fell in multi-day cycles with the rains. So great was the fluctuation that the falls could be driven across on the dry rock bench if we were patient.

Patience and Cutler were strangers, and an Abrams can ford a stream four feet deep. So we blew across the falls' half-mile-long lip while the river still covered it, rooster tailing spray like a speedboat.

Four hours beyond Broad Falls, the ground shook so hard that we felt it even through the Abrams' tracks.

Kit halted us, while woogs stampeded around us like a dusty tsunami. They thundered past us, so thick that every few seconds little, dog-sized, blue-skinned creatures would skitter up and across our prow, then down the other side. Kit said they were symbiotes, who lived scurrying around, protected within the herd from medium-sized predators, living on parasites they nipped off the woog's bellies.

Rather than wait for the herd to pass, Cutler insisted that we disperse the rabble with a whiff of grapeshot. Kit loaded, and Cutler fired, a canister round that left a dozen woogs, and even a handful of the harmless little blue things, dead but parted the herd.

Before we could resume progress, a lone bull woog stumbled across our path. He had a corkscrew rack as wide as a four seat electric is long. Kit said the bull had probably fallen behind its herd because it was so old that it was blind. It would be striper kill within a day. Reasonable, indeed humane, to let Cutler shoot it with the .50, right?

Guess again. Cutler was no woodsman, but he was a quick study. He remembered the trophies he had ruined on the first day, so he poured rounds into the old animal's hind quarters.

Then Cutler held fire, and let the beast bleat and writhe, dragging its ruined two legs behind it with its remaining four, while it bled to death.

At Cutler's insistence, we idled along behind the suffering bull for six minutes. Finally, Kit, topside in the loader's hatch, swore under her breath, unslung her Barrett, and aimed at the suffering animal. If she hadn't, I would have.

Before she fired, a crested mature male striper thundered out of the brush. Presumably attracted by the woog's agony, the striper bowled the wounded woog over like a runaway mag rail and finished it.

We set Cutler up on the turret in seated firing position, gave him a HATT to use on the feeding striper, then retreated below to await a dud or a miss. HATTs were supposed to be recoilless, but in fact kicked hard enough to bruise most shooters. I suppose a part of me hoped the HATT would blow up in Cutler's face.

Amazingly, the blunderbuss took the monster down. Its shaped-charge warhead carved a survivable-looking entry wound, but an exit wound that I could have duck-walked into without bumping my head on a rib. The striper enjoyed his last meal, and never knew what hit him. Cutler got a black eye where the HATT's sight got driven back against his eye socket, which made my day. A good time was had by all.

Except for Zhondro and me, and the maintenance 'bot, who had to spend two hours uncoupling the floater from the Abrams, severing and cryoing the two animals' unspoiled trophy heads, and tying them down to the floater's decking.

We left the carcasses for Mother Nature to police up, but I made sure that we packed up and carried out all the rest of our trash. A legionnaire is a guest on the worlds he serves. It said so right in my oath. When I told Kit that, she rolled her eyes and said that was the only way in which I resembled a "Boy Scout." I couldn't tell whether it was an insult or a compliment.

Then Zhondro and I sat, legs dangling over the floater's deck. We let the warm, clockwork-regular afternoon rain sluice blood off our hands and forearms, while we scrubbed at them.

Kit manned the Commander's .50, watching for unwanted visitors, wearing an earpiece that connected to a handheld sensor, which was supposed to duplicate a Rover 'bot's grezzen detection capabilities.

I realized that Cutler had used the woog's struggles as bait to attract a bigger trophy.

I shook my head. These animals were capable of crushing Cutler like a bug. But given his intellect, cunning, and firepower, it had scarcely been a fair fight. The only animal capable of giving man a fair fight is man. Actually, among ourselves, we fight unfairest of all. And the more we practice, the nastier we get.

Foom. Foom. Foom.

Three Kodiak main gun blasts echoed through the Tassin night.

Barroom!

One Kodiak shot found an enemy crawler, and detonated its ammunition.

Suarez reported. "We picked one off in the wadi, skipper. Hardly seems like a fair fight."

The last thing a good commander wants is a fair fight. I had deployed Suarez' tank to cover the wadi that wound past our left flank. Suarez was a drug pusher from Mousetrap who joined the Legion to duck jail. But he was my best tank commander, not to mention the closest thing to a trustworthy friend I had made in the Legion. The twenty-foot-deep dry streambed, in places just one tank wide, offered the Tassini a covered, concealed avenue to approach us, then pass around behind us. It was our worst weakness, but that made it our best bait.

Any enemy tank that moved up that wadi toward our line would, for a few seconds, be channelized, exposed, and unable to maneuver. A sitting duck to be mercilessly slaughtered. And the wreck might clog that avenue of covered approach for the duration of the fight.

Maybe deploying Suarez like that made me good. But the Tassini commander was good, too. He knew that his tanks outnumbered ours, but he also knew that we outgunned his tanks, one-on-one. We could rotate our turrets to fire our guns in any hour-designated direction on the clock, but we couldn't shoot in all directions at once.

Therefore, fighting his way up that wadi offered him the chance to envelop us, to make an unfair fight for his side. Far better than throwing his superior numbers at our strength, head-on. The enemy would, as Suarez put it, try to hold us by the nose while he shot us in the ass.

I asked Suarez, "Did the wreck block the wadi? Can they get around it?"

"Prob'ly. I know at least a couple got through, already. But they gonna have to slow down, now. We gonna get some for you, Jazen."

Ten minutes later the rumble of traded tank gunnery on our flank slowed. The wadi scrap heap had grown by three additional Tassini tanks unwise enough to test the gunnery skills of Suarez' crew.

Foom. A Kodiak round.

There was no responsive explosion from the wadi. Smoke boiled across the thermal's view plate punctuated by intermittent crackles, as the flaming tanks that Suarez had already destroyed cooked off machine gun rounds.

Suarez said in my ear. "Ready rack empty, skipper." Like the Abrams before it, the Kodiak carried additional main gun ammunition in an outboard locker in the sponson above the impeller skirt, but transferring ammunition to the turret ready rack during combat required the crew to expose themselves. In this case it didn't matter. There hadn't been time to transfer the ammunition into the turrets' ready racks before we blew down. Sand now buried all of our outboard lockers. Suarez was out of silver bullets.

I told him, "Set the scuttle timer and bail. The smoke from the wadi will cover you."

"But—"

Without a usable main gun, immobile, with his position known, Suarez' tank was no longer fightable against opposing tanks. At the moment, the wind direction was blowing smoke, thrown by Suarez' burning victim tanks, between the Tassini and us. The Tassini had thermal sights, too, but every bit of cover helped. Now Suarez' tank was the sitting duck, not the Tassini tanks in the wadi. The enemy commander would concentrate on making that reversal of fortune permanent.

"But nothing. Don't sit there until they open your can. Arcuno, prepare to take Suarez' crew aboard. Suarez, move out!"

One minute later I saw Suarez' turret hatches pop, and he, his gunner and loader spilled out and stumbled through calf-deep sand, detached commo wires dangling from their helmets, stubby personal carbines in hand.

Our nearest tank, Arcuno's, lit the night with covering sprays of green tracer from its coaxial and cupola machine guns. Machine gun rounds wouldn't faze a main battle tank, but would at least discourage the enemy from popping out of his own hatches to take target practice on our guys with his topside machine guns.

I eyed my 'puter, counting down seconds. The abandoned Kodiak's thermite scuttle charge should burn it into scrap, useless to the enemy. If the charge malfunctioned, then, as soon as the crew got clear, I'd have to expend a main gun round to destroy one of our own.

Before Suarez' tank could self-incinerate, a Tassini tank popped up over a dune at seven o'clock behind us. So some of their tanks had made it around to our rear already.

Foom.

The Tassini tank sent an avenging round toward the tank that had killed four of its buddies.

My gunner was already spinning our turret to engage the tank behind us when the Abrams' round struck Suarez' tank. The round was a golden beebe. It burrowed into the sand revetting the abandoned Kodiak's flank, then found the main gun ammunition in the outboard sponson locker. The explosion blinked my thermal plate black for a heartbeat, while the flash lit the cupola prism windows around me.

Suarez' crew had gotten twenty-five yards away from their tank when the round blew it apart. When my thermal cleared, I saw nothing but sand and a scatter of flaming wreckage. My heart sank.

Then one man struggled to his feet, followed by another. The second lifted a third, and laid him in a fireman's carry across the first man's back. Silhouetted against the flames of the burning tank, the man carrying the wounded soldier staggered toward the shelter of Arcuno's tank.

The third man paused, knelt to pick up his carbine, then chased after the other two. The carbine appeared to be wrapped in cloth that flapped in the wind, and he held it in front of him, two-handed, like the ring-bearer at a wedding.

The wrapped carbine seemed to have something dangling from its muzzle. I upped magnification on it.

My head snapped back from the view plate and I sucked in a breath. The cloth was a uniform sleeve, bearing three chevrons. The dangling objects were the fingers of a hand. It was no carbine. It was Suarez' arm, severed at the shoulder.

"Tanks! Four o'clock. Eight hundred yards. Engaging."

Another voice. "Tanks! Nine o'clock. Engaging."

My tank rocked. My gunner fired at the tank that had just destroyed Suarez' tank, without waiting on my fire command. He said, "On the way."

Clang.

The ejected, spent shell casing hit the turret floor, and rolled, clattering, among others already there. Our Driver, who would have been useless, and possibly trapped, in his compartment up front, bent down in the well of the turret and policed up the casings.

Boom.

The tank we had targeted, the one that had blown off Suarez' arm, exploded.

For the next four minutes I lurched left, then right, as our turret spun, we identified targets, engaged, then moved on to others. Outside, muzzle blasts and exploding tanks lightning-flashed through the cupola prism windows. The blasts and explosions rumbled in a constant, rolling thunderclap that drowned the chatter and screams that fed into my ear from Platoon Net.

The Autoloader pistoned rounds from the ready rack into the main gun breech, across the turret with force that could amputate a carelessly extended limb. Red cabin light glowed off acidic smoke that overloaded the turret ventilators. Sweat stung my eyes and blurred my view through the gunsights. Strobing crimson fog made my gunner's and driver's movements jerk like the spastic struggles of hanged men. If hell is a theme park to amuse the devil, tank-on-tank battles are the bumper cars of the damned.

Then a silence so loud that it rang filled our turret.

My driver stood calf-deep in spent brass so hot that his uniform trousers smoldered. "Ready rack empty, skipper." The autoloader paused, dumb and useless.

My gunner continued to slew the turret, trying to keep its thicker, frontal armor presented to the enemy that surrounded us.

Beyond us, the thunderclaps and the flashes ebbed, as our ene-my's guns were silenced by our fire, while ours went mute. I hoped the silence was for want of ammunition, not for want of live crews. I felt for my mike with numb fingers, swiveled it in front of my lips. "Report!"

Edwards' tank didn't respond. I could see it aflame in the dis-tance.

Arcuno said, "We're still here, skipper. We picked up Suarez' crew, but he—"

I nodded at the air. "I saw." Modern battlefield first aid could preserve life through everything from hypothermia to third degree burns. And if life could be preserved until a GI got back to hospital, the surgeons could even regrow an arm. But not on a man who had bled to death in the field.

Two more Kodiak hulls burned beyond Edwards'.

I stared down at my hands. They shook. And they would forever be covered in the blood that coursed from Suarez' severed arm, and the blood of all the others who had died because I was not a skipper, but just a man.

In that instant, the world slowed. Something struck our hull, a single hammer tap. But it was no hammer, it was the cone of an incoming shaped-charge anti-tank round, crumpling as it hit. I knew in that nanosecond that the round had found our sponson ammunition locker, just as another round had found the locker on Suarez' tank. I thought, "Uh-oh."

Then I seemed to be floating.

Blam-blam-blam.

Kit, topside on the Abrams' turret, one hand on the smoking .50, one hand cupped to her mouth, shouted at Zhondro and me. "Get in here! I got a grezz inbound!"

Cutler was already safely inside the tank, presumably burrowed into the gunner's well. Waiting.

I clambered up the tank's front fender toward the commander's hatch, slipped on the wet steel, and skinned a knee so badly that it bled. I wondered whether a grezz was attracted to the smell of human blood, and if so, from how far away.

And then I realized why Cutler, who normally made for the comfort of the Sleeper at every opportunity, was waiting in the gunner's well with an itchy trigger finger.

He had not only used the carcasses of the animals he had slaughtered as grezzen chum, he had dangled Zhondro and me as live bait. As I dropped down into the Commander's hatch, and pulled it closed against the rain, I muttered, "Cutler, you bastard."

I looked around the turret. Kit peered intently through the loader's movable periscope, hands on its grips like a U-boat commander in a Trueborn war holo. Below me, Cutler hunched forward, hands on the gunner's yoke, face pressed against his sight. Zhondro had scrambled forward, and was levering his scat into driving position. But, as I had the night before, I felt like someone was listening to me breathe. I peered into my screen. Dead ahead, obscured by the rain, something moved.

Twenty-two

The grezzen felt them before it saw or heard or scented them. The strongest presence that the grezzen felt was so assured, so—the grezzen did not comprehend the concept of arrogance—so like itself that the grezzen at first assumed it had invaded the territory of another.

But there was in this other the strangeness of viewpoint common to humans. Also, the grezzen felt three more intellects in physical proximity to the strong one, and adult grezzen found physical proximity not merely superfluous but noxious. So the intruders were not its kind.

In that moment, the grezzen heard the distant bellow and scented the stench excreted by a human shell, the peculiar communal skin they fabricated, and in which they sheltered their frailty, when they moved about.

"There! Step on it, Zhondro!" The strong one evidently had observed the grezzen, though the grezzen still did not see the humans or their shell.

Grezzenkind, perfectly adapted to the world that it dominated for thirty million years, had no need of tools, least of all translational computers. But throughout the thirty years since Grezzenkind had first noticed Mankind, grezzen had felt humans' thoughts. Grezzen had compared those thoughts with the coordinated images and sounds that stimulated and followed human spoken language.

And so the collective grezzen intellect had functioned like a transla-tional computer. The grezzen could eavesdrop on human conversa-tion and understand the words. But he seldom grasped the communicative nuances.

The grezzen sorted through the other humans' identities. One, it recognized. The female who called itself Kit.

The other two remained indistinct. Male, clever, dangerous in the way that a lemon bug, though puny, was dangerous if one was careless. But the males were subservient, most probably to the strong one.

The grezzen had no need to measure the speed at which its six great legs carried it, as it leapt and dodged among primeval tree boles, nor any concept of its own bulk.

So it didn't care when it felt the female, Kit, say, "Cutler, don't chase it! You've got no clue what a carbon-12–based organism's capable of. Its skeletal architecture is so dense that it supports eleven tons of muscle. It can double back on you at seventy miles an hour, and it's mean enough to do it."

Indeed. These humans had ventured beyond the protection of their ghosts-that-could-not-be-felt. They had invaded his domain. And so he would kill them.

Twenty-three

I clutched a handhold as I rocked in the commander's cupola, while Zhondro gunned the Abrams forward like a thoroughbred on a track it had been bred for. The old warhorse had been designed to rule tree-studded, rainy, rolling plains a century and a galaxy away. But this was not Earth, much less northern Europe, and a carbon-12 based monster was not a Warsaw Pact crawler tank.

The old tank's ride wasn't a Kodiak's silk float, but with the fire control stabilization engaged, Cutler had no trouble keeping the sight reticle on the grezzen's retreating backside. We were making thirty-five miles per hour, and the beast wasn't pulling away, which didn't match Kit's predictions about its speed.

Ahead, the grezzen dove left, into brush taller than it was. And was gone.

"Stop!" Kit shouted into her mike.

Zhondro slammed the single brake pedal and the Abrams skidded from thirty to zero in ten feet.

Cutler turned to her, snarling. "Goddamit! Now we've lost it!"

She shook her head. "If we'd followed it into the brush, we'd all be dead."

I turned to her and wrinkled my brow. A loaded Abrams weighed sixty-nine tons. Half of that weight was the most sophisticated armor plate that last century's Trueborns could devise. I didn't want to meet a grezzen outside this tank, but in here we were—

Blam!

The tank rocked on its suspension, and torn metal screeched above my head. I stared up at the hatch above my helmet. It was creased as though it had been struck by a giant's battleaxe. Through the cracked left prism I glimpsed an ochre flash that was gone before I could blink.

I shuddered. The grezzen had doubled back behind us, swinging so wide that we didn't detect it in the rain. Then it had leapt across us, swiped our less-armored roof with a paw, and had gotten away clean. A dumb animal had nearly cracked a main battle tank open like a walnut.

I reached up and ran my fingers down the dent in the commander's hatch.

Kit said, "Grezzen integument and skeletal elements have a Moh's scale hardness of nine point nine. That's just less than diamond. Steel's five and a half. But steel can shatter diamond. It can't shatter grezz claws."

I rotated the turret and scanned the mist through the forward-looking sight while my heart hammered. "Is it done with us yet?"

The question about two minutes earlier had been whether we were done with it.

Cutler, his face pale beneath his helmet, stared over his shoulder at Kit, pointing at her handheld. "I thought that damn thing told you where it was?"

Kit raised her palm at Cutler. "A grezz moves too fast for us to react to anything this sensor can pass on to us. I can tell you it's still out there. And it's dead ahead."

Cutler hunched over and peered into his sight. "Then we wait."

We sat there listening to the turbine whine while rain drummed on the turret roof.

Kit raised her hand. "It's moving! It's off to our right."

Cutler tweaked the controls, the turret hydraulics whined, and the main gun breech shifted as the gun adjusted.

This time, the grezzen came at us from two o'clock. I happened to be looking that way, so I saw it flash toward us from a thousand yards away, springing in great, six-legged bounds.

The computer, now slaved to Kit's 'bot, twitched the turret.

The grezzen sprang toward us, a blur, landed its leap fifty yards from us, and raised its six-clawed forelimbs.

The beast flexed its massive legs to absorb the shock of its landing, then sprang toward us again.

Foom.

Cutler fired the main gun.

The trank round passed forty yards, armed, then struck the grezzen in midair, between its outspread paws.

The great beast's kinetic energy carried it forward, but it landed three yards in front of the Abrams, and its clawed forearms ripped at the tank's prow.

The animal roared, then flailed at the tank. The left front fender peeled back like paper. The topside loader's machine gun spun away, snapped off its armored skate mount like a twig.

The tank rocked under the onslaught. Which was impossible. Nothing alive can rock a sixty-nine-ton tank. I thought.

Then the beast slowed its assault. It sagged back on four legs, while one paw scrabbled at its great face. Saliva the color of old mushrooms dribbled from its jaws, and the grezzen staggered side to side. It meandered in a circle ten yards in front of us, like a dog searching a rug for a spot to nap.

The animal's legs quivered, then it collapsed in the weeds, and lay still, its enormous torso rising and falling as it breathed.

Cutler whooped, then pounded his fist against the turret wall.

I exhaled. I hadn't realized that I was holding my breath.

Cutler scrambled out of his seat as he shouted into his mike, "Zhondro, go back and hook us up to the floater. We need to get that thing loaded, strapped down and hooked up to sedation before it wakes up."

I looked over at Kit, and she held my eyes. It was almost time for me to decide whether to cross the mutiny bridge. And for her to answer my questions.

I pointed beyond the tank, toward the great beast. "First, we make sure that thing can't kill us."

She nodded. "No argument."

Zhondro apparently felt the same way. He had already pivoted the tank around, and headed back so he and I could reattach the floater and get the beast up aboard it.

Ten minutes later, Zhondro maneuvered the floater alongside the grezzen, sprawled belly-down in the weeds, and half the size of the tank. The beast's torso rose and fell, and its great eyes, each the size of a grapefruit, were hidden behind opaque lids.

Unconscious or not, beasts like this one had slaughtered the ancestors of just about every colonist on this planet.

Cutler was anxious to claim credit for the kill but less anxious to come out from behind the Abrams' imperfect but formidable armor. So he stayed aboard the tank and covered Kit, Zhondro, and me while we dismounted to restrain the beast.

When I got alongside it, the first thing I noticed was the smell. The next things were the monster's massive foreclaws and jowl tusks. Six per paw, and one tusk per jaw, each was triangular in cross section, curved like a scimitar, and as thick and long as a grenade launcher's barrel.

Zhondro tapped my shoulder, and when I turned to him, he pointed at the Abrams' prow. A tank's glacis, or front plate, is the heavy-armored, outthrust jaw that it dares the world to slug. I had seen an Abrams' glacis absorb direct hits from shoulder-fired tank killer missiles like love pats.

The glacis was carved with a dozen inch-deep furrows, where the weakened grezzen had pummeled the tank when it attacked.

I whistled.

Kit turned her back on Cutler, then whispered to me. "Well?"

I glanced at my 'puter. Sixteen minutes had passed since the round had struck the grezzen. Cutler's geniuses had correctly predicted that their trank round would put the grezzen to sleep. But I wasn't prepared to bet my life on their estimate that the animal was now going to nap for two hours. "We both agree. First we restrain this thing, and get it on a tranquilizer diet. Then we confront Cutler."

She nodded.

The rain stopped, and the ground fog thickened and swirled around our knees as we worked. It took an hour to offload the Sleeper, fuel, and spares from the floater, then winch the grezzen onto the floater in their place. We lashed it down with restraining cuffs as thick as my thigh, then juiced the beast according to the programs on Cutler's machinery. The floater's scale weighed Cutler's prize in at eight tons.

I fingered the IV tube that connected the tranquilizer dispenser to the grezzen while I watched Cutler up in the commander's hatch. He stood with his back to us, while he held a personal assistant at arm's length, taking Two-D of himself with a prize he was still afraid to get to close to.

She shook her head at him, arms folded, while she muttered, "Mighty hunter."

I stared at the beast. "This thing scared the crap out of me. It really is the most dangerous animal in the universe."

"This?" She threw her head back and laughed, then pointed at the grezzen's ochre-furred face. Gray ran in two jagged streaks from the crest of the head to the jowl tusks. "This is a female. And old. She's a more frail example of her species than that blind, stumbling woog was of his."

I stared again at the Abrams. Its glacis was shredded. The turret roof wrinkled like an unpressed uniform blouse. The commander's hatch canted on twisted hinges. All that remained of the loader's machine gun was the stub of its steel mount, twisted like a bent paper clip. One fender cocked skyward like a broken finger.

I cocked an eyebrow at Kit. "Frail?"

She smiled. "Never underestimate the power of a woman, Parker."

A sound like an out-of-tune diesel ripped the mist as the grezzen snored. I cocked my head. "But we got Cutler his grezzen. If it's a less dangerous one, that's the best possible outcome."

She sighed. "For a while, I was starting to think you might not be a dumb hired gun, after all. I just told you this is a female."

I shrugged. "So?"

"Parker, Grezzen mate once in a lifetime, then part company. The female gestates for three years, then delivers one offspring. If it's male, she bonds with her son and he becomes her life work, even after he matures, when they establish separate territories. A robust male weighs half again more than this petite lady. He's disproportionately faster and stronger, too. And disproportionately more aggressive."

"Then it's a good thing we ran across her, not him."

She pointed at the mist, then tapped the handheld, which she had disconnected before we turned Cutler loose in the Commander's cupola. "He's out there, somewhere. And he won't like us picking on his mom."

"If he knows." I stared at our captive, then out at the mist, as hair rose on my neck. "He doesn't. Does he?"

Twenty-four

"Mother?" The grezzen cantered through the rain, sweeping back and forth in sixty-jump arcs as it searched for the humans in their moving shell. He cocked his great head when she did not respond.

The grezzen neither needed or understood communication tools nor, for that matter, tools of any sort. So he did not understand the concept of background noise. He simply and reflexively filtered out the low, ubiquitous buzz generated by the consciousness of uncountable trillions of dumb organisms, and by the distant clamor of billions of irrelevantly distant intelligent ones. The filtering behavior had served his species well for thirty million perfectly adapted years.

There. He felt his mother, but she ignored him. Asleep. That was normal enough. But during the daily rain? When prey that relied solely on what it saw and smelled and heard was disadvantaged?

He had no idiom for putting one plus one together, though he manipulated numeric concepts in a base-six system when he counted herds, estimated distance, or established new territory.

But he deduced that one vaguely troubling thing had happened, followed quickly by another. The human intrusion had been followed by his mother's unresponsiveness. His mother had taught him that, in such cases, the first thing had often caused the second.

Within the vastness of eternal background noise, he sifted until he again felt the consciousness of the dominant human, the one that called itself Cutler. Then the grezzen brought that consciousness forward.

The grezzen froze, two legs up, four down, like a woog at the first scent of a striper. The grezzen felt what the human felt. More importantly, he saw what the human saw, and heard what the human said to its subservients.

Then the grezzen growled, a low rumble so powerful that tree leaves a body length away trembled. He shifted from a canter to great, six legged bounds. As he searched, he splintered trees with his forepaws. Not because they blocked his passage, but because he was angry.

Twenty-five

I cocked my head, pressed one hand on Kit's arm, and the other on Zhondro's as we stood along side the floater and its alien cargo. "Did you hear that?"

Kit had her handheld's earphones on. She looked up, eyes wide. "Incoming!"

I shouted, "Cutler! There's another grezzen coming! We're moving out as soon as we get inside the tank!"

Kit and Zhondro were already running for the Abrams. We would mount over the front fender, and I looked up to give Cutler, atop the cupola, the signal to spool up the idling engine.

He wasn't up there, and the turret hatches were already closed.

A sound like twigs snapping echoed, too distant to be mere twigs.

I sprinted past Kit and Zhondro, and was the first of the three of us to pass the turret, where I could see the driver's hatch, below the main gun.

Cutler's head poked out through the hatch, and he glanced over at me, wild-eyed.

I screamed at him, "Let Zhondro drive! Get out of that seat! And open the top hatches for Kit and me!"

Cutler stared at me. Then he pulled the driver's hatch shut, gunned the engine, and the Abrams lurched at me.

I leapt aside, but the crumpled fender caught my sleeve as the tank sped past, then dragged me like a combat-med practice dummy, until the sleeve tore away and I splashed face down in mud.

I got to my knees and wiped my eyes, as Kit and Zhondro, one on each side of me, grabbed an arm and pulled me upright.

I flung a handful of mud at the Abrams and the floater as they bounced away from us, then disappeared into the mist. "Goddamn you, Cutler!"

The turbine's whine faded as Cutler ran for his life, abandoning us but taking his prize with him. I kicked the ground and exploded mud clods. And I had worried about mutinying against him.

Zhondro muttered something, then spat. I didn't speak much Tassini, but I think it had something to do with feeding Cutler his own genitals.

Crash.

The twig crunches that weren't twig crunches grew louder.

The three of us stood, naked inside our clothes, while an angry monster bore down on us.

Kit pointed. Unloaded supplies, the maintenance 'bot, and the Sleeper lay alongside the fat plastretch fuel bladders, and our trash containers.

My eyes bugged. "An old grezzen just made scrap out of a main battle tank. That Sleeper's armor isn't worth—"

She raised her palm. "I know. But there's stuff we can use over there. Including a couple more Barretts."

I ran with her toward the supplies, panting. "I thought a Barrett wouldn't stop a grezzen."

"It won't. But if the grezz bypasses us, we'll need more than trench knives to make it back to the Line alive on foot."

I asked her, "Bypass? How do we make it do that?"

Twenty-six

*The grezzen broke out of brush and saw in the distance a rectangu-
lar human shell, surrounded by scattered, smaller bits and pieces.
The grezzen reached out and felt three intellects near. The female
Kit, and the two male subservients. He could not see them easily,
but, like all weak species, humans hid well.*

His mother was not among them, nor was the male, Cutler.

*The minds of the grezzen's mother and cousins, and of any of
his race, were transparent to the grezzen, but he couldn't rummage
through the memories of other species, like humans. He could,
however, skim the sensory inputs of human conscious thought,
eavesdropping on what individual human intellects saw, heard,
felt, and spoke.*

He brought forward Cutler, the dominant male.

*"Cutler calling Cutler Xenobiology team two. Christ! Where are
you people?"*

*"This is team two. We've arrived at the Line Wrangler's station.
Sir, are all of you okay? You sound—"*

*"I have the animal, alive, sedated, and restrained. I'm inbound
toward you in the tank. Christ, it was horrible!"*

"Sir?"

*"Another one attacked us. It slaughtered the others. I'm the
only survivor."*

*The grezzen paused, cocked its head. Slaughter? At this moment
he could feel the other humans. His mother had not even scratched*

them. Humans often described the way things were in a way that things were not. The grezzen found this incomprehensible.

Grezzen didn't know that the seamless transparency of their race's consciousness made them the universe's sole perfect telepaths. They could not keep secrets from one another, or lie to one another, and so could not comprehend that other species could.

The grezzen saw what Cutler saw. Through tiny openings in the shell within which Cutler traveled, Cutler, and so the grezzen, saw a copse of four trees. One was distinctively lightning-split into a blackened fork. The grezzen recognized the place. Within his current territory, the spot was close enough to reach easily. The grezzen had enough time to reach his mother. First, he would transform the slaughter of the three other humans from that which was not into fact.

The logical hiding place for the three subservients was in their rectangular shell. He could split the object as easily as he split fruit, to get at the worms inside.

The grezzen trotted toward the shell.

Twenty-seven

Kit and I lay belly down beneath overhanging brush, motionless and barely daring to breathe, while we peered out at the Sleeper, fifty yards away. Fifty yards to our left, Zhondro hunkered down the same way, where the grezzen couldn't see us or, with the wind in our faces, smell us. Our trash now littered the ground in a belt that arced twenty five yards in front of Zhondro's hiding place, and in another arc twenty-five yards in front of Kit and me.

I fingered the HATT at my side, a twin to the one Zhondro carried. We had jury-rigged the business end of a trank round onto the projectiles in each HATT. A HATT's normal warhead couldn't kill a grezzen, but we might be able to use one to put this grezzen to sleep long enough that we could get away from it.

All we had to do was get close enough. That meant distracting the grezzen from hunting us, and channeling it close to Zhondro or to me so that one of us could take a shot.

I whispered to Kit, "You mind telling me how this is going to work?"

"When the time comes, do what I say."

"That's what you always say. When the time comes, how are you gonna tell Zhondro?"

"I already did. He's not like you."

I felt blood surge in my cheeks. "Goddammit! What's your problem with me?"

She sighed. "You mean besides what your Legion did on Bren?"

"*My* Legion?" I jerked my thumb at my chest. "You don't know—"

105

"Shh!" Kit clamped my forearm with one hand while she pointed with the other.

The grezzen emerged from the mist and bounded toward us.

The female had weighed in at eight and a half tons. I raised my eyebrows as this one approached. Mama's boy had grown up to eleven tons, give or take a woogburger.

His ochre integument—Kit had corrected me when I called it fur—hung off him like a shaggy rug, but couldn't obscure muscle rippling beneath. The curved, ebony claws on each of his forelimbs protruded from six digits—two of which, Kit advised, were opposable. They were longer than the claws on the four rear limbs—AKA posterior locomotor appendages.

The animal's flat-faced, hirsute head swung side to side as it moved. Three ruby eyes, lined in a row beneath a brooding brow and above jaws rowed with pointed ebony teeth, surveyed the world. Where a mammal had its canine teeth, great fangs walrused down from the grezzen's upper jaw, as long as scimitars and as thick as human thighs. The fangs gave the beast a permanent scowl, an intimidation display that was overkill.

Kit fingered the remote that deployed our maintenance 'bot.

The 'bot raised up behind the Sleeper and began running the program she had reset it to perform.

The 'bot skittered out into the open, across the grezzen's field of vision.

The belt of trash, shell casings, ration containers, fuel empties, anything noisy, lay visible on the ground. The 'bot shuffled through the belt, and tin clatters echoed.

The beast froze and stared at the 'bot. Distraction mission accomplished.

Kit whispered, "The 'bot looks like a Rover, as far as the grezz can tell. Grezz have learned to avoid Rovers, if they're lucky enough to spot them."

Kit fingered the controls, and the flat, six-legged 'bot charged the grezzen like a cockroach sprinting for a baseboard.

She said to me, "Close your eyes."

"What?"

"Do it or we're all dead. And shut up."

I did both.

The grezzen's roar shook the ground so hard that I felt it in my chest. Then I felt each thud of its footfalls, as eleven tons moved. I was blind, but they seemed to be getting stronger.

I tried to swallow, but I had no spit.

Twenty-eight

The grezzen saw the six-legged thing that ran across the clearing toward him, but he felt its intellect no more than he felt a stone. It was a ghost-that-could-not-be-felt, and the first one he had actually seen. The ghosts resembled lemon bugs, but with harder shells, and were almost as large as humans. Like the stings of lemon bugs and humans, a ghost's sting could kill him. Unlike lemon bugs and humans, a ghost could get close enough to do it before he knew it.

So the grezzen stopped, blinked all three eyes, then backed away in fear.

Grezzen had not known fear, at least of any other animate species, since they ascended to the apex of Dead End's animal pyramid thirty million years earlier. Grezzen were bigger, faster, stronger, and smarter than the competing species that had challenged them over those years, to be sure. But more critical to their race's dominance was their ability to sense the presence, and to know the intent and the fear within, lesser, nontelepathic species.

Humans puzzled the grezzen enough. But these unconscious, animate fellow travelers of humans mystified the grezzen completely. The grezzen could feel no warning of their approach. Unaccustomed to relying on only five senses, the grezzen found themselves vulnerable. And afraid.

If this particular six-legged thing had not showed itself, the grezzen would have been totally unaware of its presence. Conversely, the grezzen was entirely aware that three humans were close by.

Their stings also endangered him. Normally, he could precisely locate hidden prey or threats by seeing what they saw, and then determining where they were. But today when he brought these humans' consciousness forward he saw nothing. But he could feel what they said to one another.

"When can I open my eyes?"

The grezzen felt not only what the male felt and spoke, but its fear.

"Just listen!"

The female was frightened, too, but confident.

The ghost, which the grezzen understood as its most immediate threat, advanced. The grezzen sidled left, out of the ghost's path.

The ghost seemed to move aimlessly, but toward the grezzen, so the grezzen sidestepped, then moved forward.

The grezzen's left center leg crushed tubular bits of human refuse that rattled and clanked.

The female shouted, "Zhondro! It's in the debris field on your side! Open your eyes and shoot!"

Suddenly, the grezzen saw what the humans saw. Two were concealed to his left. Another was concealed just ahead, closer than he should have allowed. The little vermin had closed their eyes, then opened them!

Telepaths couldn't deceive one another. Therefore, they were easily deceived by a species that excelled at deception. The tactic caused the grezzen to hesitate for just one heartbeat. But he hesitated.

Crack!

The grezzen saw the sting's flash, leapt, and nearly dodged it entirely. Something pricked his right forepaw, weakly.

"Zhondro, get outta there!"

The grezzen turned toward the dual human cry that he both heard and felt. The grezzen felt anxiety in those two humans, and felt their anxiety that they were too far away from him to sting him. So the grezzen whirled away from those non-threats.

The ghost-that-could-not-be-felt crouched, now immobile, and so no longer immediately threatening, to the grezzen's left. Ahead, one human fled, far too slowly, from the smoky residue left behind by its sting. The grezzen pounced.

Twenty-nine

Now standing side-by-side in the brush, Kit and I stared across the clearing as Zhondro ran for his life, away from the firing signature that the HATT had left behind.

The grezzen caught up with him in a single bound, but as its forelimbs landed, the right one gave way, and the beast rolled in the brush like an elektruk that took an offramp too fast.

The left paw of the grezzen seemed to nick Zhondro, and the Tassini cartwheeled through the mist and crashed down in brush twenty yards from the grezzen.

The grezzen righted itself as nimbly as an eight-pound housecat, though it favored its right forepaw. Zhondro's round might have hit and injured the grezzen, after all.

Even on five legs, the monster would kill Zhondro within seconds, if he even remained alive.

I leapt out of the brush with my HATT at port arms, screaming like a basic trainee running the combat skills course.

Kit grabbed for my arm. "Parker! Stop!"

The grezzen remained focused on Zhondro.

I got within twenty yards of the beast, then knelt. I shouldered the HATT, sighted on the grezzen's gargantuan center of mass, and thought to myself, "Adios, big boy."

For some reason, the grezzen turned its face to me.

I depressed the firing detente, and tried not to cringe away from the impending impact, which would come when recoil thrust the sight cup against my eye socket.

Nothing happened.

The grezzen stared at me with three red eyes.

With trembling hands, I executed the weapon's troubleshoot sequence, which was stenciled on the barrel. First, I slapped the firing slide smartly with my palm. I depressed the battery reset button, assuring that an audible click resulted. I waited while the sequence light array in the sight display winked from red to amber to green.

The grezzen rumbled from deep inside itself, a bass so low that I felt it through my boots. He was hungry. Or it could have been a laugh.

I gulped, and depressed the firing detente again.

Nothing.

The grezzen just stared down at me, while saliva oozed down its fangs like cream of mushroom soup, then plopped into the weeds.

The next step in the troubleshoot sequence read, "Taking care not to damage the sight mechanism, refold stock. Promptly return weapon to unit armorer for battery replacement."

"Aarrgh!" I reversed the weapon so that I held it two handed by the muzzle, spun like a hammer thrower, and slung it at the beast. I didn't even refold the stock. It bounced off his flank like a toothpick off a watermelon.

The grezzen crouched to spring.

I ran like my hair was on fire.

Thirty

The grezzen crouched in the clearing, his numb right paw elevated.

He swung his head in one direction, then another, and considered conflicting options.

The ghost remained immobile, but the grezzen kept it within his field of physical vision. The grezzen could no longer feel the human that had stung him. He had no need to feel the rabid, squealing one that had tried to sting him, because it was now fleeing. The female remained near, but was again denying him her location. All he could feel from her was her sorrow for the male that had stung him, coupled with abnormally high anxiety for the rabid one. Perhaps that one was her offspring.

He probed for the fourth human from this pack, Cutler, and saw that the human shell had carried him, and the grezzen's mother, closer to the territory that the ghosts had stolen, into which the grezzen dared not go.

The lethargy that impaired his forepaw seemed to have infected his decisiveness, as well. He rocked his head and blinked each eye in succession, but felt no better.

He reached out again. "Mother?"

"I am here."

"What happened?"

"I felt the female, Kit, enter my territory, outside the protection of the ghosts. Like the male, Bauer, she knew. Like Bauer, she had to be eliminated."

Three decades before, the first humans had sprung from nowhere, or at least from nowhere credible to the grezzen, who had never seen the stars that sparkled above their eternal cloud ceiling. It astonished the grezzen to find intelligence not in their own image but in a puny, hairless, bipedal package. Also astonishing was the new species' capacity to inflict efficient, wholesale violence. However incredible their genesis, humans posed the first credible threat to the natural balance to evolve since the grezzen had inherited the world thirty million years before.

The grezzen pursued an eradication strategy, but humans proved pernicious and persistent. Containment and coexistence was determined to be repugnant, but preferable.

What the grezzen felt from, and saw of, humans shaped their strategy. Bloody-minded though many humans were, some strains displayed a grezzen-like appreciation of natural balance. So, overall, the human species tolerated dangers in nature.

What humans did not tolerate were rivals. Like the grezzen, humans expected rival intelligence to arrive in their own image. So the grezzen had simply presented their race not as co-intelligent rivals, but as the dumb brutes that the humans expected. The humans believed that their ghosts kept the grezzen out. The grezzen knew that the ghosts kept the humans in. For thirty years the system had worked. But the survival of the grezzen race depended on continued human ignorance.

The grezzen limped along the edge of the clearing, probing to feel or see or smell the human female. The males didn't know the truth, so they didn't matter. While he walked, he reached out. "But something went wrong, Mother?"

There was no response.

He rumbled a growl that a human would have called a sigh. Lately, he had to prompt her to respond. But this hesitation was more than just a function of her advancing age. The humans must have stung her as they had stung him.

"Yes and no. I was careless. These humans have a new sting that makes one sleep."

"I know. They just wounded me with it, too." He felt her anxiety. "Only a scratch. You seem out-of-sorts."

She said, "A human is attempting to take me in beyond the ghosts. I am . . . restrained."

Restrained! The grezzen howled, leapt, swatted drunkenly at a gort, and missed. In a society of free-roaming individuals, where even proximity to one another was an insult, involuntary restraint was an atrocity that required redress.

"I will free you, Mother. Then I will kill the female."

"No."

"But she is the one who knows who we are!"

"There is another."

The grezzen again unconsciously put one plus one together. "Cutler."

"Yes. I am close to him. He suspects our capabilities. But he believes he has rendered me incapable. When I have regained my strength, I will strike him as I struck Bauer. You will remain there and regain your strength. Then you will kill the female."

"It will be better if I free you, first. Then I will kill the one who restrained you myself."

"No. You will follow my way."

The grezzen did not know that his race was organized as a libertarian anarchy of intertwined, absolute matriarchies. He did know that there was no arguing with his mother.

Thirty-one

I crashed through brush and into thicker trees while I unslung the Barrett from my shoulder, then loaded it on the fly with rounds from the bandolier. Kit said a Barrett might annoy a grezzen, and it had to be more effective than throwing a dud bazooka at one.

I sprinted until I was reduced to a panting stagger, and my hands and face bled from the scratches of unheeded thorns. Finally, I stumbled over a root, fell face-down in something green and slimy, and waited for a grezzen fang to skewer me.

Instead I heard flies buzz and, up beyond the tree canopy, gorts screech.

The only thing crashing through the brush had been me.

I levered myself up on my knees, looked around at the silent forest, and pumped a fist. "Hah!"

Then my heart sank. As I ran, I had indulged the heroic notion that I had drawn the grezzen away from Kit and Zhondro. Apparently not.

I stood, hands on knees, sucking air. Then I checked the Barrett's safety, brought it to port arms, and began retracing my staggers, back to help my friends. I made fifty yards.

Chirr.

A big-eyed, elongate head, covered in skin that looked like a raw, plucked chicken's, poked out from behind a tree trunk, chest high. It was one of those running, featherless ostriches that Cutler had mangled with the .50.

114

It cocked its head at me, opened a mouth filled with fangs like knitting needles, and hissed. Branches crackled to my left and right. From the corners of my eyes, I saw the other two in the pack creep toward me from my left and right, like shadows in the deepening twilight.

According to Kit, I was empty calories to carbon-12 based predators, but these three hadn't taken xenobiology. To them I looked like a duck and quacked like a duck, so duck soup was on.

I swung the Barrett, in one hand, aiming from one to the other as they inched closer to me. At the same time, I backed up slowly, feeling behind me for a tree trunk and hoping I wouldn't find out the hard way that they were a foursome.

My heart rattled in my chest. I couldn't miss them at this range, and a Barrett round would stop something no bigger than these like a sidewalk stops a suicide jumper. But two rounds and three targets added up poorly.

The one directly ahead of me screeched, then leapt at me, hind feet raised, claws out.

Boom.

I dodged left, the ostrich from hell splattered me with its guts as it tumbled by, and the other two straightened up and looked at one another.

The one on the right must not have been the sharpest knife in the carbon-12 based drawer. He leapt and I shot him.

The third one crept forward while I broke the Barrett to reload, then tugged a round from my bandolier. I fumbled the round as I backed up. But when my adversary got to it, he just dropped his head, sniffed at it, and returned his attention to me.

I had chambered another round, and was about to snap the breech closed when something roared. Ostrich number three straightened up and swung his head around to peer into the half-lit brush. Branches snapped like a Sixer was driving toward me. From another heading, two more somethings roared, louder and louder as they crashed closer.

If you're ever lonely in a rainforest full of monsters, drop a half ton of dead meat on the ground, make lots of noise, then sit back and wait for the phone to ring.

Ostrich number three squealed, chose a direction from which no crashing or roaring came, and ran like hell.

So did I.

I'll never know whether whatever was inbound stopped to feed on the two dead ostriches, caught up with the third one, or just lost interest.

I know that fifteen minutes later the forest was quiet again and nothing had eaten me yet. I also knew that I was lost. Dead End had no GPS net with which my 'puter could interface. Because a legionnaire is always prepared, the commander's locker aboard the Abrams contained hard-copy maps of the area and a lensatic compass, which helped me now like pants helped pigs. Even if I had known where to go, there was little chance that whatever came out at night on Dead End would let me go there.

I stumbled around in the blackness until I found a hollow log, and a stone nearby big enough to block the end with. I used my trench knife to evict a half dozen lemon bugs and two centipedes the size of boot socks, then crawled inside the log and pulled the rock across the opening. Then I lay on my back, and listened as things in the distance ate other things. I laced my fingers behind my head and closed my eyes. Confinement in a tube three feet in diameter was like home to a Yavi like me.

Behind my closed eyelids, I saw Zhondro pinwheel through the air again, after the grezzen had struck him. I suppose Zhondro would have hated it in here, because the open desert was home to a Tassini like him. Maybe that was why Tassini didn't bury their dead in coffins, they burned them in the open. They burned a lot of them the night I met Zhondro.

Thirty-two

The next thing I knew after the Tassini round struck our sponson ammunition locker was that my arms throbbed, my right leg hurt worse, and someone was crying. I opened my eyes and saw the smoldering remains of our Kodiak, black against the sand, ten yards away from me. The only way I recognized it was the red platoon commander's pennant, which still writhed in the night wind at the tip of the turret whip antenna.

Four bodies lay like cordwood in a row between it and me, and while I watched, two Tassini tankers in faded coveralls and native scarves laid two more corpses alongside the four.

I couldn't tell if the charred human logs were theirs or ours. The Tassinis' faces were orange. In fact, everything that wasn't black was luminous orange, lit by the flames of the wrecked tanks scattered across the dunes, most still burning, bright against the night sky.

I was seated in the sand with my legs sprawled in front of me, and my arms tied above my head at the wrists, which was why they throbbed. I twisted around and saw that my back rested against a Tassini Abrams' left rear drive sprocket wheel. The ropes that bound my hands were looped up and over the sprocket, and the steel teeth dug into my shoulders. My right leg screamed, and its boot lay flat against the sand, compared to the left boot, which pointed toes to the sky.

Whoever was crying screamed, "Medic! For chrissake, medic!"

I didn't need a medic to tell me my leg was fractured below the knee, most probably a torsional fracture of both the tibia and fibula. I had field splinted too many.

Jelal, Suarez' Gunner, sat propped alongside me, his feet hobbled together and his chubby hands bound and resting in his lap. His helmet was off, exposing his bald head, and a string of dried blood snaked down his neck from one ear, which dangled, half severed.

I turned my head toward him. "What's the count, Jelly?"

He turned his head toward me, to hear me with his good ear. "You, me, Arcuno's crew."

My tears welled up, I swallowed, then turned my face away.

I had killed them all. My first and last command had been a catastrophic failure.

I sobbed, not for my failure but for my friends.

Jelly said, "No. You did good, skipper. I counted twenty-one Abramses lit. We broke the people eaters' back."

I blinked, then stared past the wreck of my tank, at a boiling, opaque wall of oily smoke, part burned fuel and part burned flesh. The smoke obscured our view of the depression where the dependents' camp that had precipitated this slaughterhouse had been.

A Tassini emerged from the smoke, running, one hand holding his scarf across his face against the stench. Something dangled from his free hand.

He ran to us, released his scarf, and I saw that tears streaked his face. He bent down, thrust his bearded face next to Jelly's, and snarled in Tassini. Another Tassini, a corporal, grabbed the man by the shoulder, but the man pushed the corporal away. The screamer was a sergeant by his scarf, and the outranked corporal drifted away, his eyes wide.

The screamer held up a tattered strip of tent canvas, and a shark-tooth shaped flechette, and screamed at Jelly again. Then he pointed at me and repeated himself.

I shook my head. "We didn't hurt them. They all ran away. We *let* them run away."

He stared at me. He understood as much Standard as I understood Tassini, which was none.

I made a walking motion with two numb fingers of one bound hand. "Ran away. All fine. Got it?"

Blank stare.

Jelly rolled his eyes at the screamer. "You dumb fuck. Untie me and I got next. You understand next?"

Jelly was pugnacious, even for a legionnaire. He had enlisted to escape a bar brawl murder charge. Legionnaires weren't *all* psychopaths, but the Legion was a tough enough hitch that if somebody had joined up to dodge a crime, the crime probably wasn't misdemeanor shoplifting.

The screamer howled, then cuffed Jelly with the back of his hand so hard that Jelly's lip split. Then the man held another object in front of Jelly's eyes. It was a coarse cloth stuffed doll, made in the image of a wobblehead. The man's hand shook as tears streamed down his cheeks. He pointed again, first at Jelly, then at me, and he spat in the sand.

Again I shook my head. "Your child is fine. They're all fine. You didn't find any bodies. That should tell you something."

Jelly spat blood alongside the man's sputum, then he raised his hands and pointed a finger at my mouth. "Do you understand the words that are comin' outta of this man's mouth, dumb ass? Do you?"

I wagged my head at Jelly. "Shut up, Jelly! You'll just piss him off worse."

The Tassini sergeant narrowed his eyes, and the stuffed doll quivered in his hand. Then he nodded. "Understand. Mouth." He lunged at Jelly, pressed his weight down on the bound soldier, and rammed the cloth wad into Jelly's mouth with one hand until Jelly gagged. With the other hand, he pinched Jelly's nostrils shut.

Jelly screamed, a muffled moan. His eyes bulged, and he thrashed.

I screamed, "You'll kill him! Stop it!"

The Tassini bore down, and Jelly's movements became spastic.

I twisted my body and kicked at the man with my good leg. "You stupid fucker! The reason we're dead and your kid's alive is me! Don't kill him, kill me!"

The fires burned on. Jelly's struggles weakened. So did mine.

Finally, he lay still.

The Tassini sergeant sat back, gasping. Then he stood, hands on hips, and stared down at Jelly's body. The eyes stared up, and the cloth toy protruded obscenely from Jelly's mouth.

The man had spent his rage, and I had spent mine. I stared up at him and whispered. "You don't understand. You don't understand."

He stepped over Jelly's legs and stood above me, silhouetted against smoke and flame. His eyes stared down, black and empty as he pointed at me, then jerked his thumb at his own chest. "Understand." He shifted his finger to point at Jelly's corpse, then back at me. "Next, you."

Then he raised his boot, and stomped on my broken leg so hard that I felt the cracking sound, like an electric shock through my bones, more than I heard it.

I screamed.

I woke inside the dark log in the rainforest, sat up, and banged my forehead so hard that it bled. Sweat soaked my jungle fatigues, but I shivered inside them so hard that my teeth chattered.

Outside, something snarled, scraped across the log, then shuffled away.

I didn't sleep the rest of the night. Better the nightmare you don't know than the nightmare you know.

Thirty-three

The moment gray light slivered in between the log and my rock doorway, I kicked the rock aside, then inched out on hands and knees with the loaded Barrett in one hand and my trench knife in the other. Nothing pounced.

I was hungry, a condition to which childhood as an Illegal had accustomed me.

But I was also so thirsty that my upper lip had cracked overnight. The leaves on some of the low growth were as large and concave as dinner plates, and rainwater filled them like they were green teaspoons. I've been places where drinking rainwater unleashed bacteria that turned your anus into a storm drain outflow valve. But Kit had said that the bugs here were so different that I couldn't even catch a cold. And dehydration could kill me in days, either directly or by weakening me until I became an easy snack.

I crawled toward a leaf bouquet, dragging my stiff leg. Since that night in the desert the right one took longer to wake up than the left.

After the Tassini sergeant who murdered Jelal stomped my leg, I lost consciousness. I was roused by the turbine whistle and track clatter of an approaching Abrams.

The Abrams screamed through the wall of smoke through which Jelal's murderer had run at us, then the tank bore down on me at twenty miles per hour. I shuddered. Had the Tassini sergeant fetched his tank to crush my legs and pelvis so that I would die as painfully as possible?

Then the tank tilted forward, as it braked and stopped with its left track four feet from my boots.

Through the red fog of pain, I realized that the track hadn't crushed Jelly's body, because it was gone. Probably field-cremated by throwing it into a burning wreck.

The Abrams' commander's hatch opened, and a head-dressed Tassini swung up and out. It wasn't the sergeant. The corporal who the sergeant had chased away offered the man his hand, but the guy slid off the fender on his own, like a pro.

Then he stared down at me, hands on hips. He looked forty, lighter bronze than nomad Tassini, and a thin indigo line wound across his forehead. By his scarf, he was a full-bird colonel, no less. He frowned.

I clenched my teeth. "You must be the good cop. The bad cop was a doozie."

Staring down at my leg, the colonel said something in Tassini to the corporal, and the subordinate turned and walked away. The colonel spoke again, and made a shooing motion with one hand. The corporal double timed.

The colonel turned back to me. "I'm not a cop. I'm Zhondro."

I raised my eyebrows. Zhondro. The Spooks said the dashing tank commander Zhondro was propaganda, a composite myth combined out of the best moments of several lesser commanders. Or Zhondro was the hallucinogenic product of a janga blow. But this guy wasn't smoke. Not only did he speak standard, he spoke it with a diplomat's accent. Or, with that slave line on his forehead, more likely a butler's accent.

He peered at the red patch on my sleeve, then flicked his eyes up to the red commander's pennant on the Kodiak behind him. "You're the commander of this unit?"

God, my leg hurt. "Parker, Jazen. Brevet lieutenant. Service number—"

He raised his palm. "This isn't an interrogation. I already know what you did."

I coughed and my chest hurt. "Kicked the great Zhondro's ass, apparently."

He nodded. "More a product of my carelessness than your skill, I think. But my wife told me that you could have fired on our families."

The corporal returned, still at double time, with another Tassini in tow. The second Tassini slowed, then took a knee alongside me as he set a beaded hide bag in the sand. Most of his wrinkled face was purple.

Enslaved Tassini were literate enough to have served Marin's nobility and planters for centuries. And they could learn to maintain and use machines as complex as main battle tanks only too well. But they remained grounded in a nomadic medieval theocracy that preferred a tribal shaman to a medic.

The shaman rummaged in his bag until he found a two-pronged carved bone pipe, which he tried to slip into my nostrils.

I twisted my head away. He whispered something, pressed the side of my neck, and I couldn't twist away any more. Once he got the pipe up my nose, he tapped powder from a smaller bag into his palm, then blew the janga into the pipe. It prickled the insides of my nostrils.

I wheezed. Whoa! Somewhere, my leg still hurt. But I absolutely, positively did not care any more. I smiled at the old man, at Zhondro, even at the corporal. "No wonder you people talk in your sleep."

This was all very nice, but it didn't change the fact that Tassini thought they were doing prisoners a favor by burning them alive. "The condemned man smoked a hearty breakfast?" I giggled.

Zhondro knelt beside me. "Lieutenant, did your commanding officer order you to hold your fire?"

What the hell. I wasn't going to die a liar. I shook my head. "Nope. I disobeyed a direct order to drill 'em all. Ka-boom! The Legion is so gonna burn my ass." I cocked my head. "Not that it matters. When do we get to the part where you burn my ass first?"

Zhondro shook his head at me, as he tugged an aid pouch from the bandolier across his chest. Tearing the pouch open with his teeth, he spit the top into the sand. Then he cut the ropes that bound my hands, and applied the aid dressing to a wound on my forearm that I hadn't even seen. He said, "Burn you? Never. You saved the lives of my family. Now I owe you mine until we meet in Paradise."

"Cool."

In the distance, one Tassini hollered. A Tassini long rifle snapped off a round.

An instant later, more shouts and a crackle of small arms fire followed the rifle shot. Tankers ran in all directions at once.

Zhondro sprang to his feet, shouted to the corporal, and remounted his tank. As he dropped through the commander's hatch, I saw a Kodiak's main gun tube poke over the dune line five hundred yards behind Zhondro's tank.

Maybe the Tassini had grown careless in their anxiety to learn their families' fates. Maybe they just had too few tanks and scouts left to set proper pickets. Maybe somebody had been blowing janga when he should have been on watch.

Whatever had gone wrong for the great Zhondro's outfit, our dead-slow remaining platoons had not just caught up with them, they had caught the Tassini taking a figurative dump in the sand.

Zhondro's tank rotated its turret toward the threat, and its main gun elevated. Too slow, and too little gun.

Along the dune crest, more Kodiak gun tubes appeared, while the lead Kodiak's tube steadied as it acquired a firing solution on Zhondro's tank, which remained four feet away from me.

I smiled at the shaman. "You know, this is the first time I've been blown up twice in one day."

The old man cocked his head, then swung both arms, palms out, in an arc, chanting. It was the gesture that adults made to embrace everything around them, but also the gesture that a child made when it yelled, "ka-boom."

Foom! The Kodiak's muzzle flash outshone the fires all around us, and blinded me.

In the chaos, it occurred to me that Zhondro and I would be meeting in Paradise sooner than he expected.

After the noise, there was only silence so loud that it startled me.

The forest turned silent when I shouted. I knelt just inside the tree line that bordered the clearing where Cutler had run out on us the afternoon before. The echoes of my voice died, then the forest's background buzz resumed.

I shouted again, "Kit? Zhondro?"

It had taken me an hour to retrace the zig-zag path of broken twigs and trampled brush that I had made when I ran from the clearing.

I paused, straining to hear a voice that never came. I knelt in the brush for five more minutes, scanning the opposite tree line for anything waiting to pounce on me.

I knew that Zhondro could be too badly hurt to answer me. In fact, I knew that he was probably dead by now. But Kit shouldn't have either followed me along the path I had just retraced, or stayed close to this spot waiting for me. Not because she liked an ex-baby killer. Because two guns were better than one. Besides, there was the lesson she had taught me about gorts. If we were together, she didn't have to outrun the predator, she just had to outrun the baby-killer.

If I wasn't getting an answer, it was because I was the only one left alive. Still, I couldn't shake the feeling that someone was listening to me.

Finally, I stood, stepped into the open, and ran toward the Sleeper.

Thirty-four

Forty seconds after I ran out of the tree line I reached the Sleeper, flattened my back against its armored outer wall, then panted, holding the Barrett across my chest. I craned my neck and examined as much of the armor as I could see. If there were dents or scuffs more than what the woogs had already put there, I couldn't tell.

They could be alive inside, and hadn't heard me. I banged the wall with the Barrett's stock. "Kit? Zhondro?"

Nothing.

I looked up at the clouds. It seemed to me that the wheeling gorts were thicker above the clearing than normal.

I inched down the Sleeper's side to the door, then tried the latch. It opened. I hissed, "Anybody home?"

Nothing.

I pushed the door back with the Barrett's muzzle, paused, then stepped inside.

Empty. My heart sank, but it was better than finding bodies.

I latched the door shut behind me, pulled a ration pak out of the cryo, and squeezed it to warm. I also popped a plasti of Coke, and drained it in three gulps, while I sat at the table and stared across at the empty bunk stack. Zhondro's prayer scarf lay neatly folded on his bunk, like it always did. A lump swelled in my throat. If he was dead, and it seemed certain that he was, that was the last place that scarf should be. At least, that was how he had explained it to me once.

Zhondro sat propped up in his hospital bed in the detention wing of the infirmary of Human Union Mutual Defense Base Marinus. We were a thousand miles and two months removed from the carnage we had left in the Tassin desert.

My own bed faced his, so both of us could look in one direction out a barred window at the transports that came and went across the base's tarmac. For variety, we could look in the other direction at the locked door with an armed guard outside it round the clock. We shared an infirmary room on our jailers' theory that it was best to put all the rotten eggs in one basket, then watch that basket.

Actually, Zhondro's rank made it a nice basket to be in. The physicians that were putting us back together were Trueborn, as was the medical technology. The food was better than in any Legion mess, and our jailers amused us with endless holos of a Trueborn game called football that they assumed GIs liked.

Zhondro grimaced as he held one corner of his tattered prayer scarf in his teeth, while he folded the other corner over it with his uninjured, remaining, left arm. The organic prosthetic that was growing to be his new right arm still stuck out in front of him in its cast, at a right angle to his torso, so that he appeared to be perpetually signaling first down and ten.

I pulled the burn mask back from my lips and said, "Why don't you throw that rag away?"

He finished folding, laid the scarf in his lap, then sniffed at me. "This *rag* saved our lives."

"Yesterday you said it was the shaman's spell that saved our lives."

"It was that, also. God manifests himself in multiple ways to the virtuous."

I credited our survival less to virtue than to Second Platoon's abysmal gunnery. They had near-missed a five hundred yard shot at Zhondro's tank, an incompetence worse than shanking a two-yard field goal. I sighed. "So how long does a Tassini keep the same prayer scarf?"

"Forever. It must cover him on his funeral pyre before he may ascend to Paradise."

"Oh."

The guard unlocked the door, let in an uncharacteristically squatty Trueborn in a well-cut business one-piece, then pulled the door shut and left the three of us alone.

The Trueborn had lips that protruded like a duck's bill, and gray hair. I recognized him. When the Brigade downshipped through this base at the beginning of our tour, he explained to us from a podium on the runway that the Union tolerated the Legion's assistance to the Seceded Territories, rather than welcomed it.

What he hadn't told us, because we already knew, was that Earth was playing both ends against the middle on Bren. Bren's mines supplied the Union's starship fuel. Earth couldn't allow a disruptive civil war between Bassin of Marin, who had freed his nation's slaves, and his Seceded Territories, whose nobles were exterminating slaves who, if liberated, might become rivals. So Earth engineered a limited war by proxy. Tassini nomads, allied with their escaped-slave kin and armed under the table by Bassin, were the good guys. That left us to be the genocidal slavers' hired guns.

I sighed. Politics makes rotten bedfellows. Politicians don't care, because it's GI blood that stains the sheets.

I cocked my head at our visitor. "Ambassador Muscovy?"

He nodded to us. "Colonel Zhondro, Lieutenant Parker. You both look well."

Even after two months of reconstruction, we looked like crap on a stick. Diplomats! What a cream tour to tell obvious lies, go to work in real clothes instead of battle dress uniform, and get overpaid for it.

The ambassador cleared his throat. "At any rate, your doctors tell me you're both well enough for a substantive discussion of your situation. I—"

Zhondro raised his palm. "What do you know of my family?"

Muscovy cocked his head, but Zhondro's question hardly surprised me. Zhondro asked it of the guards, every day. They didn't answer it, every day. I think both Zhondro and I assumed that meant his family was dead.

Muscovy sighed, then sat on the edge of our therapy table with his legs dangling. "Officially, Colonel, you're a terrorist in our temporary custody for urgent medical treatment. You're awaiting repatriation to the Seceded Territories for execution. I'd be hung if I brought a terrorist's wife and children in here to visit him. So would they."

Zhondro's eyes glistened, and he blinked. "They're alive?"

"No one told you?" Muscovy shook his head as he stared at the locked door. "Idiots. Jesus H. Christ."

Zhondro's mouth hung open while he shook his head. "I didn't know." Then he frowned, "What's to become of them?"

Muscovy stared at his hands. "We extracted them from the war zone on the same premise that we extracted you. They're detained noncombatants awaiting repatriation."

"Repatriation." Zhondro frowned. "Meaning they will be sent back, and shot later rather than sooner."

"Officially? Yes."

Zhondro squeezed the holo remote in his good hand so hard that it snapped.

Muscovy raised his palm. "*Unofficially*, your family appears to have escaped from our custody through no fault of ours."

Zhondro leaned forward, eyes flashing. "What?"

"Relax. We can't repatriate your wife if we don't know where she is, can we? I got your wife an interview for a vacancy in community relations here on the post. But I had to use an identity card with a new name."

Zhondro frowned again.

Muscovy made a patting motion with downturned palms. "It's a citizen position, not an indenture. Remember, Bassin's in charge here. The Emancipation is law. She got an offer. She accepted. She can quit tomorrow and chase butterflies if she wants to. But the job pays well enough that she's house shopping. Her supervisor told me the only thing he doesn't like about her is that she'll get promoted past him in six months and he'll have to find a replacement."

Zhondro leaned back against his pillow.

Muscovy flipped a chip on top of the hologen. "There's an hour of your kids on this chip. I took it myself. They're enrolled under her new name in the same school that King Bassin's nephew and my daughter attend. Your son's performance in the play's terrific, by the way." He paused. "There's ten minutes at the end of the chip that your wife recorded on her own, just for you. I haven't watched that part. Not my business." He paused. "I'd appreciate it if you'd both keep all this to yourselves. They might not hang me if they found out, but I'd finish my career shoveling snow in Antarctica."

Zhondro turned his face away, and his eyes glistened again. "Thank you."

Maybe Muscovy wasn't overpaid, after all. I cleared the lump in my throat.

Muscovy heard me, then turned to me. "Don't worry, Lieutenant. I haven't forgotten you. It's a package deal."

I narrowed my eyes. "Deal?"

He nodded at both of us. "The Legion's employers consider Colonel Zhondro a terrorist who should be summarily hung. Therefore, so does the Legion, common sense notwithstanding. Lieutenant, the Legion's less conflicted about you. You disobeyed a direct order. They're quick to take credit for the licking that you gave Colonel Zhondro's numerically superior force. But they blame your unit's casualties on you. And your disobedience occurred in the face of the enemy. So you're not even entitled to a court martial. Your commanders in the field have administrative jurisdiction to summarily hang you, too."

My heart sank. The guards had informally told both Zhondro and me all that over the last couple of months. But now it was official.

Muscovy said, "However, last month a prominent citizen on Earth asked a favor of my bosses that they dropped in my lap. He needs to quietly hire a couple guys short-term who know their way around old crawler tanks."

I snorted. "That's what you do all day? Hire shady mechanics for rich Trueborns?"

Muscovy shrugged. "You'd be surprised how much of diplomacy is doing big money small favors, Lieutenant. Suffice to say that my employer and yours are willing to let me piss off the Seceded Territories if it helps this gentleman out."

I narrowed my eyes. "There must be a thousand veterans right here in Marinus that know crawlers. Why us?"

"None of those thousand are embarrassing political footballs. If I can do the favor and at the same time get you two out of sight and out of mind here for a while, everybody wins. Besides, King Bassin thinks you're a hero, Parker. And he thinks that the Colonel, here, is George Washington."

First there had been this Christ that aggravated both Cutler and Muscovy. Then football and Antarctica. Now this George person. We were presumed to recognize all of them. Trueborns really did think Earth was the cultural center of the universe.

Muscovy continued, "Actually, I think you're heroes, too. But the Human Union doesn't care what I think. It does care what King Bassin thinks."

I asked, "What would we get for helping you do this favor?"

Muscovy smiled. "For starters, Lieutenant, you'll be awarded the Star of Marin, with Leaves no less, by order of his Majesty Bassin the First. Technically, he still rules the Seceded Territories that you serve. Your brevet rank will be made permanent. You'll be given a medically accelerated honorable discharge, and your ongoing benefits will be those of a commissioned officer."

Muscovy turned to Zhondro. "Colonel, the purpose of getting you off Bren for a while is to remove an irritant. In the couple of months that this job will take, the heat will die down. The King will invite you to return here to Marinus, to your family. He'll appoint you governor in exile of the Seceded Territories. Again, he's still their King, technically. You and your family will live free, while you continue to work to free your people." Muscovy slapped his palms on his thighs. "And what do you two have to do to earn these generous outcomes? Spend a couple months restoring some tycoon's vintage tank, then chauffeur him around in it."

Zhondro said, "That's extraordinary."

"I told you everybody wins. Except the slavers. I think this is worth all the chips I cashed to arrange this for you. For both of you."

Zhondro and I looked at one another, but we said nothing. Orion had told me once that if something seemed too good to be true, it probably was.

Muscovy raised his wrist, tapped his 'puter with a finger, and frowned. "Gentlemen, I interrupted your day because I must have a yes from you both. And I must have it now. Or at least before nine thirty-six tonight."

Just when I was starting to like this Trueborn, he started dictating to us. I wrinkled my nose. "Nine thirty-six? Why?"

Muscovy said, "Because that's moonrise."

"Oh." Then I whispered, "Crap."

Zhondro cocked his head at me. "Why does that matter?"

I said, "Moonrise is when the Legion hangs prisoners."

Muscovy shrugged, his eyes dull as tombstones while he looked first into Zhondro's face, then mine. "I'm sorry. I stalled them as long as I could."

I glanced at Zhondro. He nodded. I said to Muscovy, "Ambassador, tell your Trueborn tycoon he's just hired two crackerjack mechanics."

Thump.

Inside the Sleeper, I straightened as something struck the outer wall, on the side opposite the hatch. I slid the Barrett off the table in front of me while my heart pounded.

Thirty-five

I held my breath while I listened as footfalls stopped, started, and moved irregularly toward the Sleeper's hatch. Too small and few for a six legged grezzen, woog, or striper. Unfortunately, also too irregular to be human.

I exhaled. The dumb ostriches could harass me if and when I left the Sleeper, at least until I shot a couple. Meantime, I was safe in here.

I smiled. Unless they had learned to operate a hatch latch.

There was a bump-and-bang racket right outside the hatch. Maybe one that had followed my scent trail was scrabbling outside, trying to force its way in.

Creak.

My eyes widened. The inner handle of the hatch latch twitched.

I raised the Barrett to my shoulder, and sighted on the hatch center.

Pop.

The latch retracted fully, and the hatch swung inward, admitting a sliver of light. I closed one eye, but at this range aim was optional.

The door swung wide.

"Christ!" Kit threw her hands up and staggered back and out of my line of fire. "Parker! It's me!"

Gasping, I pointed the gun vertical, while it quivered in my hands. I had nearly shot the closest thing to a friend I had left in this world.

She peeked one eye around the hatch edge. "You're alive!"

"You're alive!"

She pointed at my gun. "Almost!"

I nodded. "Close."

"Grezzen?"

"Gone. Parker . . . I've been with Zhondro all night. He couldn't be moved, even if I could've carried him. Spinal cord. And worse."

"But you're here. Is he—?"

She dropped her eyes. "Soon." She pointed at the prayer scarf on Zhondro's bunk. "He asked me to bring that. It's important to him."

"Then he knows he doesn't have long."

She nodded. "He'll be glad to see you first."

She led me back through the forest to the place where Zhondro had finally collapsed. He was tough, and had made it so far away that I understood why Kit hadn't heard me call, earlier.

He lay on his back, eyes closed, but opened them when he heard us. She was right about his condition. If I hadn't seen so much like it before, I would've said he only had a broken leg, which Kit had splinted. But his pallor and drawn features betrayed the extent of his internal injuries.

When he saw me, he smiled. "I knew you must have made it. Kit tells me you tried to beat that animal with a stick." He coughed blood. "You always had more courage than sense. Jazen, my family—"

I touched his shoulder. "Take it easy. I'll be sure they know." If I lived.

He nodded, let his eyes close again.

He opened them when Kit pressed his prayer scarf into his hand. "Thank you. I can go now." He closed his eyes for the last time.

It took us an hour to gather enough dry wood for Zhondro's pyre, a waist-high pyramid of sticks and brush, then lift Zhondro's body onto it. I spread his prayer scarf across his chest, then knelt and lased the kindling at the pyramid's base. It lit with a chuff, and I stepped back alongside Kit.

We stood still and silent and watched oily black smoke that was Zhondro and his prayer scarf twist into the sky. Gliding dragons slid through the smoke, wolfing down glowing ash scraps that never reached the clouds.

To me, Zhondro's Paradise was a security-blanket myth, his cause quixotic, and his family unmet strangers. But I wept for him because he had become my friend.

I caught Kit staring at me, and wiped my eyes. "Smoke."

She reached up and touched my cheek with her fingers. "Soot. You missed a spot. Parker, I'm so sorry."

"Thanks. But Zhondro and I didn't know each other that long."

"Not just because you lost him. Because I made very wrong assumptions about you. Parker, Zhondro knew how badly he was injured when I found him. I did everything I could for him, but we both knew it wasn't enough. So I sat up with him all night and he told me about you. About what you could have done to innocent people, but didn't. And about what it cost you."

"Oh." I stared up into the deluge and sighed. "And all it's come to now is the two of us stranded here in a zoo that's run by the animals."

We stood there until the flames ebbed, then walked back to the Sleeper together in the rain.

She stepped inside the Sleeper, I closed the hatch behind us and we slumped on the dining table bench. She asked, "Tired?"

I nodded while I pulled out two fresh plastis, opened them, and set one on the table in front of her. "You?"

She nodded back as she drained it, then said, "Thanks. Why do you think Cutler did that?"

I shrugged. "I've seen better men than him panic in the face of less danger. But that's charitable. I think the son of a bitch left us to die. I'm gonna walk out of here. Then I'm gonna find Cutler and beat the shit out of him."

"Not if I get to him first." She patted my shoulder and yawned. "But we worry about that tomorrow, huh? Best not to walk any farther in the rain out here. You can't see or hear what's catching up to you. We both need to sleep."

The magic word. It had been a bad couple days. For the first time in what seemed like years, nothing was about to eat me. I wilted like a switch had been thrown, and my eyelids drooped.

Kit dimmed the illumination, stepped out of her fatigues, and climbed into her bunk. It measured my exhaustion that I didn't even notice what she had on underneath.

My top bunk suddenly looked accessible only if somebody winched me up, so I flopped into the coveted lower, just below

Kit's, that had been Cutler's inviolable domain. When I rolled over, the corner of something poked my back, and I dug out Cutler's Reader, leather-bound, monogrammed, and slimmer than a Trueborn supermodel. My first impulse was to punch it as though it was Cutler's square-jawed face. But when you grow up with nothing you don't break stuff for the hell of it.

Reflexively, I moved my thumb to the off button. When I read in bed, I always forgot to encrypt and turn off. Apparently, so did Cutler.

Before I switched it off, I glanced at the screen, and read:

Prepublication Copy
Observations of Cognitive and Communication
Capacities in *Xenoursus grezzenensis*, a Sextapodal Top
Carnivore, Native to Designated Earthlike 476

I rolled my eyes. Now, there was a sleeping pill.

But the next line read, "By Aaron Bauer, Ph.D."

I sat up so fast that my head nearly thumped the bottom of the bunk above, where Kit already breathed deeply and regularly. Bauer. Kit's predecessor. Who said that dead men tell no tales?

Forty minutes later, I dimmed Cutler's Reader display and lay staring up at the bottom of the bunk above me while my heart raced and alien rain drummed the roof.

"Kit?" I reached up and jostled the bunk above me. "Kit! Wake up."

She moaned. "Parker?"

"We need to talk."

She moaned again. Then she said, "Parker, a half inch of hammock foam doesn't alter the fact that you're groping my left breast. If that doesn't change in five seconds, I'll break your fingers."

I withdrew my hand like her bunk was on fire. "Sorry."

"Forgiven. G'nite."

"Wait! I have something down here that you'll want to see."

"I'm sure. Most men offer dinner and a show first, Parker."

"No. It's Cutler's Reader. The dead guide, Bauer? Cutler's got a copy on here of a paper Bauer was going to publish."

Her face, framed in tousled hair, poked over the bunk edge above me, then her arm dangled down while she flapped her hand. "Give it here."

I handed her the Reader. "Bauer's paper says that the grezzen—"

"I know what Bauer's paper says. We probably tumbled to it the same time Cutler's people did. What I want are any notes or studies they may have added." She swung her bare legs over the side of the bunk, hopped down, then sat at the table in her underwear and read.

For the next five minutes, I watched while she scrolled through Cutler's reader, the screen's glow painting the curves of her face and bare shoulders.

Once she nodded and muttered, "Aha. So that's what they're after."

Another time she frowned and whispered, "That rat bastard!" Then she looked up and saw me watching her. Her eyebrows rose. "Parker. You're awake. You okay?"

I ached all over. I had spent the previous night in a bug-infested log. A rat-bastard tycoon had hijacked my tank and left me for dead among monsters who wanted to pick my brain, figuratively and literally. In four months I would have a price on my head, and a mysterious interplanetary spy had just threatened to break my fingers. On the other hand, I was alone with a smart, beautiful, half-naked woman who had allowed me to touch her for five seconds longer than she had to.

I said, "Never better."

Thirty-six

The grezzen, reclining in the evening rain, split the striper's thigh bone, by levering it under his right tusk with his left forepaw, then savored the bone's marrow. His right forepaw remained numb, and he was convinced and annoyed that his overall lethargy was a product of the tiny wound that the dead human had inflicted. The two surviving humans had confined themselves in their immobile shell a brief run away, and were at rest. The grezzen ignored them and reached out. "Mother?"

The pause until she answered was too long. "I am here."

The grezzen sensed weakness in her. And he saw what she saw, which was that humans and their moving shells scurried all around her. He sprang to his feet, and spoiled the marrow when he dropped the bone. The humans' proximity to her disturbed him, but her location disturbed him more. Before the ghosts had come, the treeless rock knob had been a spot for lying out to catch the breeze on a fair day. Now the knob lay beyond the barrier formed by the ghosts. "Mother, you were going to kill him! What happened this time?"

"Listen."

She lay bound by vines the humans had woven from unknown material, while a male human stood in front of her. They all looked alike, but for sexual dimorphism and head tufting. This one's head was bare skin, and black markings decorated its bare forelimbs. It held a stinger between its forelimbs and thought, "You look like *a tired, six-legged panda. Why would Cutler go through all this over you?"*

Then the grezzen sensed the presence of the dominant male called Cutler. Within moments Cutler, who was fractionally larger head to feet than the skin-headed individual, appeared alongside him, and slapped his forelimb on the smaller one's shoulder. "Some CEOs delegate the dirty jobs. But here she is, tied up with a bow, Mr. Liu."

Liu, the skin-headed male, thought, "God, what an ego! Those bastards who died out there probably had more to do with catching this thing than he did." But he audibilized, "It looks sick."

Cutler audibilized, "Mr. Liu, I pay your gang to keep this animal in and the locals out until the xenobiologists get this lab up and running. I pay them to look after the animal." But Cutler thought as he stared at the grezzen, "It does look sick. Christ, I really don't want to go through this again. Maybe it's just because it's doped up, disoriented."

The grezzen, through its mother, felt Liu think, "Gang? Every one of us is a decorated vet. Any one of us could kick your ass." The grezzen saw in Liu's mind the image of Liu striking Cutler with the blunt end of Liu's stinger. But Liu did not reduce this image to action. This perplexed the grezzen, and his mother felt his question.

She said, "The world rarely presents us a circumstance upon which we cannot simply act."

Indeed, the only new circumstance that the world had presented to the grezzen species and its collective consciousness during the last thirty million years was man.

To his mother, humans were annoying competitors who did not fascinate her. But they fascinated him. It was extraordinary. One human could simply withhold its feelings and intentions from another human by failing to audibilize. Or it could audibilize things that were not real. The other human would be aware only of what it heard, and would change its behavior in response to a nonexistent stimulus. They called it lying.

Particularly vivid were the humans' lies about places beyond the clouds. In some cases those places were incompletely realized visions of destinations that the human would ascend to upon death. In other cases those places seemed fully realized visualizations, as though the humans actually, physically, came and went there during their lifetimes. Either was patent fantasy. There was one world, and grezzenkind intended to remain in control of it.

The grezzen's mother said. "It would not have been enough to kill only Cutler. The xenobiologists are not here yet, but they also suspect. There may yet be a way that I can destroy them all, and keep the secret from all the rest."

"Mother, the risk if you fail is too great. The burden cannot rest on you alone."

"You believe I am too weak, now, because I am old."

"You are. That is the way of things. I also believe that two are stronger than one."

"Of course. But I was only able to evade the ghosts by allowing Cutler to transport me. You have no such advantage."

The grezzen paused. His race was perfectly adapted to dominate its world. Grezzen had no need for the mental deceits that humans used to survive their weaknesses. But that didn't mean that his race couldn't learn from humans, and quickly. Deception was unfamiliar to the grezzen, but the humans were excellent teachers by example.

He said to his mother, "Yes, I lack advantage. But I have a plan."

Thirty-seven

I don't know whether Kit stayed up all night burglarizing the contents of Cutler's Reader. She woke me with fingers on my shoulder, while she wafted toward me the aroma of a cup of coffee brewed from Cutler's private stock.

She said, "We need to start early, so we can stop before it rains this afternoon."

I sat up and smiled. "Thanks. Does that taste as good as it smells?"

She smiled back as she set the cup on the table. "Nothing in the universe beats Truebean Colombian. Cutler notwithstanding, there's a lot about Earth that you'd like, Parker."

I sat at the table, massaged circulation into my right leg, and sipped.

Dressed already, in walking weight body armor, she held up a large-bore gunpowder revolver and squinted, counting cartridges. Then she pinwheeled the pistol around her trigger finger and plopped it into a belt holster, like a Trueborn-holo Earth cowgirl. Lifting Cutler's Reader off the table, she wrapped it in plastek, then tucked it down behind her armor's breastplate.

I smiled at her "You know a lot about Earth for a frontier gunslinger. Do you work for Cutler's competition?"

She paused and stared at a ceiling corner. "You could say that." Then she pointed at two overstuffed route-march packs alongside me. "There's a pistol and holster next to your pack. We can't carry those loads and unslung long guns too."

I eyed the packs, each taller and thicker than I was from genitals to nose. "What are the odds against us walking out alive?"

Kit shrugged. "I don't know. Nobody's ever done it. At least nobody who survived to brag about it."

It took us forty-five minutes to suit up. I tugged my pack onto my shoulders, and clucked as I adjusted its straps. "We carrying rocks?"

As she laid her Barrett on the table and field stripped it, she shook her head. "The packs are heavier than you would have carried in Legion basic, because we're packing extra water. When we run out, we'll have to drink local, but the purifying tabs make it taste like vomit."

"I thought the local bacteria couldn't infect humans."

She shrugged into her pack, slung her Barrett, and clumped toward the hatch. I staggered out behind her into the morning heat and the humidity slapped me like a wet rag.

Kit said over her shoulder, "The local bacteria can't hurt us. But when the rain runs over leaves, it picks up mite-sized insectlikes. They physically irritate the human bowel. Twenty-four hours after ingestion, the body starts expelling them. I drank rainwater off leaves when I first got here. Stupid. I lost eight pounds in two days. Be glad you weren't that dumb, Parker."

"Yeah." My belly squealed as my pyloric valve suddenly decided it was a storm drain.

Thirty-eight

The grezzen limped just beyond the sight and hearing of the two humans as they inched back toward the ghosts that would protect them from him. Without their shell the two humans propelled themselves on two twiglike legs, slower than grazing woogs.

The journey they were attempting would take days to complete. More accurately, it would take forever to complete, because they were too slow and soft to survive the vast suite of predators that lay between them and their goal.

Unless, of course, they were protected. Already he felt a scavenger pack that had caught the two humans' scent. The pack was closing on the pair from forward and left.

The grezzen, trotting on five legs with his numb forepaw elevated, gave the humans a wide berth and passed them. Then he interposed himself, unnoticed by the humans, between them and the pack. He displayed himself noiselessly to the scavengers, felt their astonishment and terror, then watched them scamper away to seek a less complicated meal.

He returned to his station behind the humans. Their trail was only too easy to follow. They moved with the male behind the female, in a proximity one to another that grezzen tolerated only in order to mate. The male seemed to have assumed the trailing position to fulfill the responsibility of marking their territory, and its tiny droppings were as disproportionately pungent as they were repulsive. Whether the assignment of this task was a function of gender the grezzen did not know.

In fact, he knew almost nothing of humans. Once grezzen had decided to sequester and coexist with humans, his race had been deliberately incurious about a species they found dangerous and prone to disgusting habits.

By midmorning, the grezzen gazed up at the lazy circling gorts, poked at the too-familiar ground. Already, this exercise bored him, and it was destined to continue for days, particularly given the male's frequent marking stops. Driven more by ennui than curiosity, the grezzen brought the two humans forward out of the vast background hum of intellects available to him.

"Again, Parker?"

The female continued to walk while the male paused and marked territory. She displayed only a hunter's concentration on her surroundings, and anxiety at their lack of progress.

The male crouched in the brush and audibilized after her, "Can you slow down? I'm dyin' back here."

The grezzen cocked its head. He felt in the male embarrassment, coupled, certainly, with anxiety about increasing dehydration. But no life-threatening symptoms.

The female responded audibly to his cry. "Parker, it's only the runs! You're a soldier. Just suck it up!"

The grezzen stopped and drew back on his haunches. He was aware that certain small species could re-ingest their excreta to survive extreme drought. But the suggested behavior in an intelligent species disgusted and shocked him.

The grezzen gritted its great teeth at what it was about to be forced to witness.

The male, however, simply increased its pace. As it hurried to rejoin the female, the male audibilized criticisms of her, but in muted tones so that the female was not instructed at all. That seemed pointless. Males were apparently less intelligent, because this one seemed misinformed about sexual dimorphism in his own species. It was physiologically obvious that the female was not heartless.

The grezzen resumed his meandering trot, but soon felt the tweak of a minuscule consciousness. He paused and flipped over a stone slab with his uninjured forepaw. The flat, green animal that he found beneath he swallowed whole. The individual had displayed barely enough awareness of its surroundings for him to detect it. It was that very insensate quality that made the species a rarely-found treat.

Grezzen rarely tasted humans anymore, either, but they reportedly went down bland. These two wouldn't taste like much. But in the meantime they were proving to be full of surprises.

Thirty-nine

Three days after we left the Sleeper, shortly after the daily rain ended, we encountered again the formidable obstacle of Broad Falls. The river rumbled feet deep over the rock bench, though Kit said the flow was at much lower levels than in some years. At the present decline of flow, the bench would be dry enough to cross on foot by the following morning.

Kit said that the river valley's rock, water-smoothed, pocked and criss-crossed with six-inch wide joint cracks, was avoided by the worst of the land predators, because it was hard on their claws. Safe havens for humans were few and far between on Dead End, but the riverbank figured to be our safe haven for awhile. We gathered wood for an evening fire. Then we stripped off and washed our armor and ourselves in clear pools that the receding river left behind in bowls it had hollowed out from the rock.

About the three days march to the falls, the less said the better. For the first two days, I crapped my brains out. I had struggled to hold Kit's pace, but by the time we got to the river I had recovered to the level of mere soreness and exhaustion.

On our journey out from the Line by tank, we had crossed paths with stampeding woogs, grumpy stripers, and a half dozen smaller species you wouldn't want to meet in a dark alley without your 120-mm cannon. But, walking back in, we were assaulted by nothing bigger than lemon bugs, and one altitudinally challenged gort who drifted close enough to earn a bullet. Kit attributed that pleasant surprise to us being less noticeable on foot. I chalked it up to dumb luck.

Kit and I lay side by side on our backs on the rocks, heads pillowed on our packs, bootless feet up on boulders.

She tugged two Coke plastis from her pack, tossed me one, then tucked Cutler's Reader, which had been inside her armor, into her pack.

I pointed my Coke at the Reader. "Straighten me out here. Bauer was an obscure naturalist. He took a dangerous job in an obscure place because he heard that Rover 'bots were able to sneak up on these fierce animals, even though other animals couldn't even get close to a grezzen. He thought the reason was that grezzen could read a living thing's mind, but they couldn't read non-living chips that performed like minds. A couple months before Zhondro and I got blown up on Bren, you, or somebody you work for, got wind of Bauer's work."

She nodded.

I said, "If there really were intelligent telepaths out here at the ass end of the universe, it was a huge event. But it was very unlikely. So your employer just sent you out to investigate on the cheap. By the time you got here, Bauer had gotten terminally close to his work. You took over his job to see whether he was right. How am I doing so far?"

Kit sipped from her plasti. "On the money. When we heard Cutler was cashing favors to come out here and hunt grezzen, we suspected that he knew at least as much as we knew. But he could have been just one more Trueborn with too much money and a taste for overkill."

"You weren't sure. So when we got here, you climbed into the Cutler party's back pocket." Like Zhondro had said, keep friends close and enemies closer.

She nodded again.

"That's why you had us close our eyes. If the grezzen was reading our minds, it could find us by knowing what we saw. When we saw nothing, it saw nothing that gave away our position. So now we're the living proof that Bauer was right."

She shook her head. "That was a hunch I played out of necessity. To a scientific skeptic, our survival proves squat. The grezz could have been confused, or not hungry, rather than telepathically blinded. People usually live or die of dumb luck. Not because something mystical cares."

I smiled. "Zhondro always thought God cared. I wonder whether Cutler thinks God is on his side, or just on his payroll."

She sighed. "If I had truly understood what a menace Cutler was, I wouldn't have let it get this far."

I turned my palms up. "What's Cutler after? Train grezzen to steal somebody else's trade secrets? Hire them out to armies to spy on the enemy?"

She nodded. "That's what we thought. But based on what I saw in Cutler's Reader, it's bigger. And it's worse. Parker, what's the fastest you could send a message back home to Yavet from here?"

"Why?"

"Just answer."

I cocked my head. "I dunno. If I pay extra so the information gets burst between jumps at lightspeed, it's still ten jumps inbound back to Mousetrap, then another six jumps out to Yavet. Couple months?"

"Try four. Six if you just send a hard-chip Cutlergram that gets mailbagged between jumps on a near-light-speed cruiser. What do you think it would mean if you could whisper a question into a grezzen's ear here on Dead End and have a grezzen on Yavet repeat it over there in the time it just took for me to ask and you to hear what I said?"

I laughed. "It'd mean I'd never buy another Cutlergram."

"No, but you'd buy the new, improved version. And be delighted to pay more for it."

"But it's irrelevant. Even if Grezzen can phone each other jungle-to-jungle here as fast as I could phone city-to-city back home, nothing can travel faster than light in this universe."

She nodded. "In *this* universe. The War taught us a lot of things, Parker. Not least, it confirmed what the theoretical physicists have been saying since the twentieth century. This universe coexists with others. Some of the other ones may be nearly infinite, some are probably infinitesimal. Our guys weren't sure but Cutler's people are very sure, that if grezzen telecommunicate, they telecommunicate transuniversally."

I stared at her. "You do know I was only homeschooled."

"I'm not patronizing you. I don't understand it either. The geeks dumbed it down for me this way. You and I are on opposite sides of a room full of jello, which represents our universe. I can't throw a ball across the room to you faster than it can move through jello, right?"

I nodded.

"But suppose the room has a dropped ceiling. If you and I climb up into the open space above the ceiling tiles, we can exchange fastballs all day. Cutler's people think grezzen telecommunicate above the ceiling tiles. Their information moves out of this universe, through an adjacent universe, then back. The conduit universe may be so small that the thoughts travel no farther than the distance from one side of an atom to the other. Real-time communication among five hundred planets, Parker. It's the jackpot of this century."

I raised my eyebrows and pointed in the direction of the clearing where we had seen the grezzen. "Cutler thinks he can hire five hundred of those monsters to work as telegraph operators?"

She smiled. "The employee of the month would be the one that didn't try to eat you?"

I laughed. "So what *does* he plan to do?"

Kit held up her Coke plasti. "Bottle it. Figure out what makes the grezz tick, then replicate telepathic communication mechanically or organically."

I shrugged. "That's less evil than I expected."

She raised one finger. "Don't underestimate the man. Tycoons don't like competition any better than top predators do. Cutler doesn't plan to share."

I shrugged. "Neither would I."

"But the way he's going to keep competitors from duplicating his work is to exterminate the grezzen once he's got a monopoly on the process."

I snorted. "Tycoons don't exterminate races. Countries do."

"Parker, have you seen Cutler do anything that wasn't overkill? And who do you think's gonna stop him? Earth is the Union's sole superpower and it barely has the stroke to slow down *human* genocide on Bren. Grezzen are long-lived, slow reproducers at the tip-top of a food pyramid that can't support very many of them. This whole planet has fewer grezzen than downtown Eden has parking meters. Grezzen may be hard to kill with antique tanks, but there's plenty of up-to-date technology for sale that can wipe them out. If we just let the Rover 'bots range free, we'd overkill the species down to endangered status in two years."

"Look, he doesn't own the place. The locals—"

"When I told you that the locals here would rename the planet after him if he carpet bombed the grezzen to extinction? I meant it. A bad neighborhood always welcomes a tough sheriff. According to his Reader, Cutler Communications' front entities have already optioned seventy-two percent of the fee simple patented real estate on Dead End. So he will own the place, unless something changes."

I laid back and folded my arms. "So that's what this is about? Your employer wants to exploit the grezzen before Cutler can?"

She shook her head. "There are two kinds of Trueborns, Parker. I—yes, guilty—represent the pole opposite Cutler. The war left us as the only intelligent species in this universe. We want a do-over for mankind, if there is another intelligent race out there."

"If I stick with you, I get to be the good guy for a change?"

She sat up, touched my cheek, and whispered, "That's not a change for you, Parker."

She smiled down at me as the day ebbed behind her. Her cheeks were scrubbed pink, her fine blonde hair was pulled back, and she smelled of soap and water.

I'm not one to impress a date by making her dinner, but I can squeeze a Meal Utility Dessicated until its internal heat triggers, as well as the next GI. I could mix a tube of buttery alfredo sauce with a couple tubes of marini fila, which would showcase my creative, romantic side.

I said, "You busy tonight?"

Forty

Hidden in brush, on a bluff above the river that obstructed the two humans' passage, the grezzen sprawled. The rocky river bank made for poor hunting, which the female had realized in selecting the place to rest. So the grezzen nibbled a yearling amphibian that had strayed farther from the water than normal. The season had been dry, the water low, and the river's residents had altered their habits accordingly. As the grezzen reclined, he physically eyed the humans below while he felt them.

In the dusk, a yellow spark flickered between the two humans. It blossomed into a flickering orange and yellow pyramid from which smoke spiraled cloudward.

The grezzen widened all three eyes and surprise caused him to grunt amphibian blood into his chin hair.

Fire didn't surprise him. He knew fire was a product of lightning, of which Dead End had plenty. He knew that lightning fires thinned and rejuvenated forests, and turned rain to steam that replenished the clouds. Fire was part of the natural balance of the world.

The world needed fire, but grezzenkind otherwise did not. Grezzen moved easily during darkness, were never cold, and preferred their food at just-killed temperature.

Fire frightened him. Unlike most adversaries, fire could not be defeated head on. It could sear his flesh, and easily kill him.

151

So what had surprised him was, first, that the humans had harnessed something that his race avoided.

Second, until now, night in his world had been dark. He didn't know that perpetual cloud had blocked starlight and moonlight for thirty million years. He didn't know stars and moons existed. He simply knew that tonight was not dark, and that was as different for every other living thing in this world as it was for him.

"What's in this?" The male exuded caution about something that the female had presented him to eat. Not surprising. It turned out that the male's trail marking had actually been a product of digestive disruption.

"Chocolate. Aerated sugar. Melted between two graham crackers. Boy Scouts like you love 'em, Parker."

"Hmm. S'good."

"Hold still. You've got a marshmallow moustache. There."

The grezzen turned his great face away, then tried to probe for prey, for danger, for anything but what he was witnessing. He felt in both the male and the female urges that he usually felt only in prey animals as rut and heat.

The grezzen knew that once in his lifetime he would someday come into rut. Then he would couple with a female, who would produce and raise an offspring, as his mother had raised him. His mother had taught him that during rut he would enjoy not only proximity to, but physical contact with, the female who chose him. He shuddered. The prospect was improbable and disgusting. In the meantime, he had as little desire to witness another sentient species do it as he had to participate in it.

Prey animals endured rut and heat only seasonally. But humans apparently came into and out of rut and heat randomly and often. Indeed, after the male had recovered from its illness, a simple word or glance from the female, or even her posture, aroused in the male visualizations of physical contact so strong that the male lost concentration on its surroundings.

The grezzen would, at this stage of his maturity, have found physical contact noxious even with a mate of well-curved fang. Female humans must have been the ones who had harnessed fire. Males couldn't have concentrated long enough.

Now the female had moved closer to the male, and had just initiated physical contact, touching a foreclaw to the male's lips. The male's already elevated heart rate had increased.

"Thanks. I think there's some on your lip, too."

"Parker, I didn't eat anything."

The male escalated the physical contact.

The female audibilized, "What are you—?" But she thought, "Finally! For a minute I thought I was gonna have to draw you a picture."

It was a picture the grezzen didn't care to see. The prospect of spindly human limbs entangled like those of mating woogs was bad enough, but already there was rapid breathing and murmurs that could only get worse.

He brought forward the surrounding animate threads to drown the humans out, then sat bolt upright in the brush. In addition to himself and the two humans, he felt a third presence. It was one that jolted his own heart rate to a level even faster than that of the human male.

It was even possible that a flicker of the grezzen's alarm had leaked back along the human threads that the grezzen had been monitoring.

Forty-one

I raised my head, pressed my fingers against Kit's lips, and peered into the darkness beyond the campfire.

She muttered, "What's—?"

"I just felt something."

"I should hope so."

There was no sound but the fire's crackle and the constant rumble of water over the falls. Not even a hint of breeze. I said, "I must've imagined something."

She stroked my back with both hands. "I'm still imagining something, Parker. It'll go better if you participate."

Forty-two

Nothing in the world could give a grezzen a fair fight on solid ground. The only thing that could give a grezzen a fair fight on any terms was a river snake, and then only if it caught a grezzen in the snake's element.

The grezzen hadn't been alert to the snake's possible presence because in a normally wet season they would have been mating, days swim upstream from the falls. But, as the falls' meager flow reminded the grezzen too late, this was not a normally wet season.

There was no mistaking what species the grezzen felt. A river snake's mental signature mimicked its body and temperament. Outsized, stupid, and perpetually hungry, a snake displayed barely sufficient curiosity and visual acuity to investigate firelight. But it displayed enough.

The grezzen peered physically down toward the river's surface, and saw a wake bulge the water as the river snake approached the two humans, the low whisper of its approach masked by the falls' rumble.

The grezzen stood and paced five-legged, back and forth along the bluff while it peered down. The humans, now horizontal, were intent on one another and in such rude proximity that they appeared to be a single writhing animal.

The river snake was an aquatic organism, no more capable of breathing above water than the grezzen was capable of breathing under it. But the humans were close enough to the river's edge

155

that the snake could easily thrust itself across the smooth exposed rock of the river bed, snatch them up, and then slide back into the river.

The outcome of a battle between a grezzen, even on six good legs, and a river snake was not free from doubt. And that assumed that the grezzen could make his way down the bluff in time to interpose himself between the humans and the snake, which on five legs was also far from certain.

But it wasn't fear of combat that kept him pacing the bluff. The plan on which he was staking revenge for his mother and the preservation of his race depended on these humans remaining alive for now, but only if they also remained unaware of his presence. So he paced.

Below, the snake had advanced so far into the shallows that its great, black back glistened wet above the river's surface. But the humans remained focused on one another.

The grezzen leapt, twisted, and stomped three legs on the ground in frustration.

The snake was now only three of its enormous body lengths away from the river's edge.

Only one option remained to the grezzen, and he might have left it until too late.

Forty-three

Kit whispered, "The snap's on the side, Parker."

"I'm out of practice. Sorry." It wasn't a lie, precisely. You can't practice what you've never tried.

She purred in my ear. "It wasn't a complaint."

I sat bolt upright. "Why?"

"Where?" She sat up too, holding her coverall across herself.

I asked her, "Why should we run?"

She shook her head. "I didn't say anything." She poked my chest. "You said something was coming."

It was my turn to shake my head. "I didn't—"

Behind her, out on the river, I saw something move. I whispered, "Oboy."

I stood and dragged her up by her wrist while she turned and looked where I was looking.

We were one hundred feet from the water's edge, and one hundred feet out in the water, an attack submarine was surfacing, prow-on to us. At least, it was the size and bullet shape of an HK sub, without a conning tower, just a ring of knobby bulges that could have been eyes, where the torpedo tube doors should have been. Water rained off its flanks and boiled into the river as it moved toward us, twenty feet high and lit glistening black by the fire's flicker.

We retreated, walking backwards side by side and staring up at the thing.

I whispered, "No predators, you said."

"No *land* preds! These are all upstream, mating."

"What's this one? Gay?"

"Bite me, Parker." Kit whispered, "Walk slow. It's big. We're little. It's in the water. We're on shore. Maybe it won't—"

The submarine's blubbery prow spread open like the bell of a tuba, until it looked like we were staring into a highway tunnel. Thousands of fist-sized triangular teeth, all pointing in and backward down the snake's gullet, glistened in the firelight, pus yellow against wet pink flesh. The monster reached the water's edge, then lunged and roared.

Ugly as it was, its breath was worse. Its roar flapped Kit's coverall and blew her hair straight out behind her head.

The beast splashed down onto the rock fifty feet from us, then gathered itself for another pulse.

I turned to run, took a first step then realized that Kit was no longer alongside me. She was on one knee, teeth gritted, as she tugged to free her bare foot from one of the six-inch wide joints in the rock.

The monster quivered forward again, now thirty feet away, just six feet short of our fire.

I laid a hand on her shoulder while I tried to work her foot free with the other. No dice.

Her hands trembled as she tugged at her leg.

I said, "Don't worry. We'll be fine. I think the fire's stopped it." In fact, I was pretty sure that the fire had attracted it in the first place.

The snake flopped like, well, a snake out of water, and its lower maw snuffed the fire and scattered burning logs and our dinner in all directions. So much for fire as snake repellent.

Kit pushed me away. "Run! It can't come much farther out of the water." Her foot bled at the ankle, chafed but still stuck fast. I fingered the trench knife at my belt. No. I would die here with her before I carried her out of here in pieces, to bleed to death like Suarez had.

The river snake lunged again, and its lip came to rest a yard from Kit. I hacked the lining of the animal's mouth with my trench knife, and it bled, but seemed undiscouraged. I suppose it had endured its share of woog hoof scrapes to get a snack.

A rehydrated foil packet, the "buttery alfredo sauce," had skittered alongside Kit when the monster scattered our fire and our dinner. I snatched it up, tore it open with my teeth, squeezed the slime down along her ankle, and twisted one more time.

Pop.

If I sprained her ankle, she'd thank me later. Her foot came out clean, and I snatched her beneath one arm and dragged her away just as the monster lunged forward again.

I thought we were moving away fast, but it wasn't fast enough. The monster scooped up both of us, the alfredo sauce, smoldering branches and kindling, and assorted debris like it was a sapper brigade's bucket loader clearing a shell crater.

The sides and roof of the beast's razor-toothed mouth contracted like a giant had pulled a laundry bag's drawstring. The lips closed completely and the night got even darker for us.

Forty-four

The grezzen reached the bottom of the bluff at full gallop, though slowed by his still-numb forepaw. He skidded to a stop as the river snake's mouth closed around the two humans. With the stimulus of the firelight and of food removed from its consciousness, the snake undulated and backed its immense bulk toward the water. Perhaps he could still attack the snake, but the battle would not be won soon enough to salvage the humans.

The grezzen shared the death throes of the two humans as they struggled inside the beast, kicking and screaming while needle teeth jabbed into their flesh. The only evidence that the two humans and their fire had ever existed was the residue of feeling that still washed over him, of their ebbing panic and pain as they struggled, and faint wisps of fire smoke that curled out of the river snake's closed mouth.

He hung his great head. He had realized that Cutler had somehow warded off the ghosts' attacks when Cutler encountered them. It seemed likely that the two humans would be able to do the same. The grezzen had planned to sneak past the ghosts by staying close to the two humans, though unknown to them. The grezzen didn't know the human story of the Trojan horse, or even what a horse was. But he was learning guile from humans quickly. Now his plan had failed.

The great snake paused and twisted. It raised its head, then dropped it, then repeated the motion. The river snake was accustomed to digesting living, struggling prey. It was not accustomed to the irritation of fire smoke in any quantity attacking the lining of its mouth and throat. It thrashed one more time.

Then it sneezed.

Forty-five

Ka-boom!

One moment I felt consciousness sliding away forever as I suffocated in the dark, while a thousand knives pricked me.

The next moment I was rolling and bouncing over uneven rock, my vision an alternating flicker of dark sky and darker stone. Finally, I came to rest in a heap, alongside a water pool in a hollow.

I turned my head and saw the river snake slide back into the water tail first, like a remastered holo of a steamship being launched.

Kit's body lay limp and face down on the pool's opposite side. The red dots of tooth marks measled her torso, arms, and legs, which were covered in thick yellow slime and gobbets of the snake's less fortunate meals. So was her hair. I crawled toward her on hands and knees. "Kit?"

Nothing.

I scrambled faster, reached her, and touched her cheek.

She moaned, then opened one eye. "Parker, I've never been so glad to see a man who looked like vomit."

I bent, kissed her cheek, slime and all, and said, "You too. Me too."

She got to her knees, then stood. Breathing through her mouth, she extended her arms and watched while the snake's digestive juices and gut contents oozed down her arms, then dripped off her fingers. "This slime won't digest us and the bacteria in this

162

rotten gut meat won't infect these cuts. But if I have to stink this bad for ten more minutes I'll kill myself." She slid into the pool, drew a breath, then submerged and popped up squeezing water from her hair. I joined her.

A half hour later, we had gathered our scattered gear and huddled together in the dark, seated with our backs against a rock and my sleeping bag wrapped around our shoulders. She laid her head on my chest and sighed.

Then she started shaking all over. "I thought I was dead. Really dead."

I pulled her closer, but she kept shaking.

She said, "Thank you, Parker. I owe you my life."

I held her tighter, until her shakes subsided. "No. You owe a snake with an itchy nose your life."

She sighed, I sighed, then we sat, leaning on each other half asleep, until false dawn lit the clouds.

I said, "Y'know, all things considered, this was the best date I ever had."

She sat up, then stared at me. "When we were, you know, why *did* you tell me to run?"

I shook my head. "I didn't. Like I said, *you* told *me* something was coming."

We stared at each other. Then we each turned around and peered out into the gathering morning ground fog.

Forty-six

The grezzen sat again on the bluff, peering down. Below, the two humans, stings cradled in their forelimbs, skittered across the dripping bench of the falls. Low morning fog swirled around their tiny feet, and they teetered beneath bundles nearly as large as they were.

Grezzen needed to buy nothing, and had less to sell. So the grezzen had no concept of business. But business was what he was back in this morning. With him as unseen escort, the humans continued toward their home base.

Regrettably, the humans' suspicions about the capabilities of his kind were now heightened. But his warning had been subtle enough that they remained uncertain of his presence, much less of his capacity to feel them.

Meanwhile, the humans, their foot placements on the slippery rock ledge obscured by fog, extended their forelimbs like gort wings for balance. The female stumbled, and the male enveloped her with both forelimbs to prevent her from plunging into the water, six of her body lengths below.

"Thanks, Parker."

They lingered, ventral side against ventral side, longer than necessary for her to regain her balance, and the grezzen felt from each of them mutual affection, and pleasure at the physical contact.

The grezzen shook his head, surprised in three ways.

164

First, he was surprised that a species which balanced on just two limbs of its meager four had survived the engine of evolution at all.

Second, Parker had last night endured pain, indeed risked his continued existence, to protect another human who was not his mother. Kit—a corollary, lesser surprise was that he now thought of them by their human identifiers—seemed to have developed a reciprocal attachment to Parker, who was not her son.

The grezzen's brief, anonymous warning to them the previous night was the first grezzen-to-human communication made since the first humans tried to sting the first grezzen decades ago. That first encounter had ended badly for the humans. So would this one.

The third surprise was that the prospect of dismembering Kit and Parker, inevitable though it remained, no longer pleased him.

While he waited for Kit and Parker to make their way out of sight of the river, so that he could replicate their crossing, he reached out. "Mother?"

No reply. His contacts with her during Kit and Parker's labored passage to the river had been spotty. He had attributed it to her advancing dotage. But it became apparent that Cutler and his subservients were able to induce lethargy in her, similar to what he experienced from his recent sting.

He was bounding down from the bluff, testing his forepaw and finding it fully recovered, when his mother's reply came back to him, at last.

"I am here." Her thread was so weak that it flickered.

He felt, and saw through her, that she was now enclosed in a human nest far beyond the ghosts, and therefore inaccessible to him. Just beyond this enclosure he felt humans as numerous as a woog herd. So her prison was one chamber within a vaster human nest. The vision of humans scurrying and tumbling, often touching, reminded him of splitting a log and finding larvae swarming within.

He watched as Cutler approached the round-headed Liu. "I should fire you! All of you!"

Liu's anger welled as he responded. "He was off duty. He had a drink."

Cutler responded, "Duty? A discharged legionnaire's duty is to do what he contracted to do. And that was keep his mouth shut."

Liu waved his forelimb at the grezzen's mother. "The locals got nothing to worry about from this thing. It's half-dead. Invite 'em in to see for themselves."

"That's beside the point! The natives are restless, thanks to him. I paid for discretion."

The prospect of pay withheld swelled anxiety in Liu. "Mr. Cutler, the main thing you pay us for is security. My men can handle anything a bunch of civilians got." Indeed, Liu thought. "And we'd like to."

Cutler expelled his breath. "This Libertarian republic's nothing but a mob armed to the teeth. If they come after the monster, it won't be with torches and pitchforks."

Liu's anxiety turned to anger, and he touched a small stinger attached to his waist. "Tell 'em to bring it on!"

"My scientists won't be able to work if your goons are out there cracking skulls. I've brought a lot of resources across a lot of space for this."

The grezzen thought, "Mother, what if there really is more space than the world? What if the humans are from another place?"

"Nonsense. There is nowhere else. The others are within this nest. I will simply wait for them to show themselves."

"At least wait for me."

"That's not an outcome I can force." Her thread weakened again. "I will rest, now."

The grezzen's ability to see and feel the humans faded as her awareness lapsed again. He picked up his pace and wished his humans here would do the same.

Forty-seven

The night following the night by the river, when we stopped, Kit and I traded off sleep and turns on watch. It was less fun than getting acquainted, though more fun than getting eaten. But except for the river snake, nothing much bothered us on our walk back.

On the fourth day, our packs were lighter by what we had eaten and drunk along the way. They weren't lightened by expended ammunition, because we hadn't had to shoot much. All in all, we covered ground faster than either of us had expected to.

We had been forcing our pace for three hours when Kit pointed up at a tree, higher than a woog's shoulder would rub, and pumped her fist. "The TAP Line, Parker!"

A day-glo lime marker tacked into the tree bark winked down at us. The visual marker designating the Transponder Array Perimeter was meaningless to the local fauna, but a welcome sight to a couple of scared, tired humans. In neither of our minds had we expected to cross it today, much less this morning.

A homing-limpet mine field, which was basically all the Rover 'bot line amounted to, was bordered by transponders augured into the ground at intervals, and by durable visual markers, like an invisible fence for livestock. The TAP line prevented the Rovers from wandering out while it also warned friendlies not to wander in.

I glanced up at the marker. We were now five hundred yards from safety, at least safety from grezzen. "Almost home."

167

Ahead of me, Kit nodded. "Almost. Once we make another five hundred yards, if a grezzen comes after us, it's committing suicide."

"You think rat bastard Cutler made it back to Eden with the female?"

Kit shrugged. "Probably. The Rovers are adjusted to respond to the mass and motion of a grezzen. As far as they're concerned, she's just part of a cargo trailer. Cutler had enough fuel to make it back here and top off his supply. We made it back *without* a tank. I don't know why Cutler would have had trouble making it back *with* one."

In fact, except for the river snake, we had walked without incident for four days through a forest so deadly that I had barely survived it one night.

I shifted my pack against my sweat soaked shirt back. "You ever wonder why it was so easy? On Yavet we say that if something seems too good to be true, it probably is."

She sighed. "On Earth, we say don't look a gift horse in the mouth, Parker."

I rolled my eyes. There was a polite word the 'zines used to smooth over these Trueborn references that the rest of us were assumed to understand. Terracentric.

I shook my head, as if a bug had crawled under my hat, and shuddered. Somehow, I couldn't shake the feeling that I wasn't the only party to this conversation who had never seen a horse.

Forty-eight

The grezzen planted all six legs in the moss of the forest floor and stopped still and stunned as his two humans' thoughts struck him. He had trailed them, undetected, at a distance that he had come to understand represented a half mile to them. He had been prepared to creep stealthily even closer, and thereby secure safe passage through the ghosts. Now, without warning, his plan was shattered.

Grezzen didn't tell jokes, much less good news-bad news jokes. But the good news for a telepath was that he knew exactly what the other guy was thinking. That was also the bad news. The grezzen's two humans had been surprised when they so suddenly were about to walk beneath the Rovers' protective umbrella. And so he had also been surprised.

Also, Kit and Jazen had never until now had occasion to think about precisely how Cutler had provided the grezzen's mother safe passage through the ghosts. So he had not known. The grezzen had simply extrapolated from what he observed in his world. He knew that small runners moved closely among the woogs, and thereby avoided mid-sized predators. He assumed he would be able to avoid the ghosts in the same way, by staying close to his humans. But now he saw that his two humans—he didn't know when, precisely, he had begun to think of Jazen and Kit as his—would not have kept the ghosts away in any event. What now? His mother would know. She always knew.

"Mother?" No reply.

He waited. "Mother?" Again, nothing. Her inattention was becoming intolerable.

Finally, he exhaled so vigorously that brush stirred. His two humans suspected, and so remained a threat to his race. His mother's last instructions to him had been to kill the two humans. Kit and Jazen weren't protected yet. But if he delayed even an instant longer, killing them would become impossible for him.

He sprang forward, and accelerated across the few yards that separated him from Kit and Jazen. He wasn't pleased at what he was about to do. But he was resolute.

Forty-nine

Crash.

Kit and I took off running for the Line at the sound, unslinging our Barretts as we went.

I looked over my shoulder, hoping to see a blundering woog, maybe a striper that both barrels from a Barrett could discourage.

Instead I saw three red eyes, tusks, fangs, and claws bearing down on us so fast they were blurred. Stopping to fire the Barrett at a charging grezzen merely wasted time. I saw Kit drop her pack, and shrugged out of mine, too.

Maybe the grezzen would stop to investigate.

It roared as it trampled right over them.

We were still three hundred yards from the Line, and the grezzen would be on us in thirty yards. Hopeless. After all I had been through, after all Kit and I had been through, this was the way it would end for me. I thought of my mother who I would never find, now. I thought of Orion, who had sacrificed so much just to bring me to this.

Kit stopped running. She turned, and faced the grezzen.

It was fifty yards from us, now, looming larger than a house, glaring down at us. Its growl and footfalls shook the ground beneath my boots.

I spun, ran back, and grabbed her arm. "Come on!"

She shrugged off my hand and stood facing the grezzen.

The grezzen, twenty yards away, raised its clawed forepaws to swat us dead with a single blow.

I raised my gun.

Fifty

The grezzen raised a forepaw to strike as Kit stood tiny in the grezzen's path on two hindlimbs, forelimbs folded, Jazen at her side.

Jazen raised his stinger, though the grezzen felt in Jazen that the male knew the gesture was futile. Jazen's last thoughts were, as the grezzen supposed his own would be, for his mother.

Kit pushed down the tip of Jazen's stinger, and the grezzen felt her, as strong a female presence as his mother had ever been. "If you kill us, you know that your mother will be lost. But alive we can help you save her."

Kit's thought so stunned the grezzen that he froze, barely a forepaw's length in front of the two tiny humans. He peered down at them and cocked his head.

No, Kit couldn't know. Not after all the efforts of all the grezzen over all the years to conceal their race's ability and intelligence. She wasn't sure. She was just casting out a thought. She, like all humans, understood him and his race to be inarticulate brutes. At least, she couldn't be sure that grezzen were otherwise.

But even as he thought this, he realized his blunder. His pause had just confirmed for her his awareness and his intelligence. But he could still kill them and the secret would die with them, as it had died with the male called Bauer. He rumbled at the two of them, raised his paw again.

Fifty-one

I tugged at my Barrett, but Kit kept her hand wrapped around the muzzle, while the grezzen loomed, staring, above us, ten feet away. Its breath rumbled like a diesel and echoed through the forest that surrounded the three of us.

As she stared back at the beast, she said to me, "No, Parker! First, your gun can't hurt him. Second, if he were going to kill us, he would have by now."

I swung the Barrett back and forth from Kit to the grezzen. "You two are talking?"

She kept staring at the grezzen and it kept looking down at her with three giant eyes. It sat back on its four rear legs without taking its eyes off of us.

Kit shook her head as she stared up. "He's not talking back. Not now, probably not for a while. But he's been eavesdropping. Haven't you?"

My jaw dropped. "Goddammit! You've been talking to him the whole time we've been out here?"

Kit shook her head again. "Not 'til right now. There was no point trying unless the grezzen perceived a benefit in listening. Which they obviously haven't for decades. But when this one reached out and warned us about the river snake, I realized that he wanted us alive. Jazen, our chances of walking out after Cutler abandoned us were less than one in ten. The reason we made it this far has to be that we've had a bodyguard."

I squinted up at the monster. It didn't look friendly or intelligent. Its mouth dripped greasy, gray saliva. What it looked was hungry. But it hadn't killed us. And there was no doubt that it would have made a very effective bodyguard. And there had been the constant feeling that someone was listening to me.

I asked Kit, "Why would it protect us? Because of the grezzen that Cutler took?"

She nodded. "Unless I've misread this, she's his mother. The bond between a grezzen and her offspring's closer, and more enduring, than between a human mother and child." Kit talked to the beast, like he was a big Labrador retriever. "She raised you, taught you everything, didn't she? You're inside her head, and she's inside yours, even now. You want her free again."

I flexed my hand on the Barrett's stock. This imaginary conversation was all very well. But this monster might just be momentarily curious. I often admired a cheeseburger for a second before I dug in.

I said, "Kit, I don't see a lot of ice breaking between you two, here. Could he tap his foot for yes?"

"He won't respond, Jazen." Kit actually smiled at the giant hairball. "You're keeping your options open, aren't you? For now, you're pretending that you're just another animal?"

The grezzen stood up on all six legs, lifted the right rear, and peed a rumbling, steaming stream into the mossy forest floor, enough gallonage to sink a dinghy. That was the action of just another animal. Or the action of an intelligent mind reader who wanted someone to think that he was just another animal.

Kit slung her Barrett over her shoulder, and walked back around the grezzen to retrieve her pack. Finally, I followed, but I didn't turn my back on the beast. It turned slowly, keeping us both in its sight, and a paw swipe away from becoming raw meat.

As I shrugged my pack back on, I said, "Should I pet it?"

"No!" Kit shook her head. "Grezzen only touch other animals to kill them or eat them. They live alone. This one probably hasn't been within five hundred yards of another grezzen, not even his mother, since he was weaned. He hasn't needed to be. He's got a built in cellular 'puter with unlimited networking to every other grezzen on this planet. He's got plenty to eat, no natural enemies he can't whip or avoid. He never has to compromise on the thermostat setting because it never gets too hot or too cold for him here. Accommodation and cooperation are as foreign to him as, well, we are."

Kit walked toward the Line, saying to the air, "So listen to me, my big friend. Yes, I can get you past those things up ahead that can kill you. I know that's part of what you want from me. Now I'm going to tell you what I want from you in return. We call it compromise."

The grezzen stood motionless, breathing like thunder in the distance, while it watched her walk away.

I held my breath and followed her.

If the grezzen was a beast, it would pounce on us. If it was intelligent, and was reading our minds, it would pounce on us, because it knew that it had to kill us now. Otherwise we would slip through its claws and regain the protection of the 'Rover 'bots.

She turned back and faced the eleven-ton monster, hands on hips. "I'm trusting you. Now you have to trust me."

The grezzen crouched like it was about to pounce.

Fifty-two

The grezzen growled as he watched the two humans walk away. He should kill them. And he could, with a single paw swipe. But Kit was right. His mother's fate, his ability to snuff out Cutler and his suspicious ilk, depended on cooperating with these two for the time being.

But what if they were—what did they call it?—lying? He couldn't be sure he understood all of what they felt. Humans were devious in a way that stripers and woogs lacked the intelligence to be. The humans seemed to be leading him safely to his mother. But they could be leading him into a trap, where the ghosts would kill him. The prospect of death frightened him. He felt the same fright in the two of them as they walked ahead of him.

Yet they now walked with their backs to him, stingers lowered. Trust. Compromise. That was what Kit had called it.

Grezzen would never trust humans as a species. Grezzen would never compromise with humans as a species.

But Kit and Jazen were no longer a species to him. They felt fear, like he did. They felt affection, like he did. It was easy to dislike a species, hard to dislike an individual who was like you. And it was much easier to trust, and to compromise with, someone you knew.

He trotted toward the ghosts, alert, but following carefully in the tiny footsteps of his new allies.

He could always kill them later.

Fifty-three

We arrived at Kit's Line camp at noon. The predators gave us a wide berth, or more accurately gave a wide berth to our bodyguard.

The grezzen acted neither intelligent nor dumb. It just followed us like an eleven-ton puppy. A puppy that had swatted dead a green toad the size of a two-passenger Urban that had been unfortunate enough to be in our way. The grezzen had then gathered the carcass in the crook of a forepaw and carried it along for a snack, the way a human hiker might pick an apple to eat when he stopped for lunch.

When we entered the cleared area, the grezzen curled up on the knob's warm granite. It plopped the two-ton toad carcass down, wrenched off a seven-hundred-pound drumstick, and stuffed it into his mouth bones and all.

I winced, but what the grezzen was doing was no different than converting a cow into cheeseburgers, with the middleman eliminated. Feeding eleven active tons is a full-time job, I suppose.

Still, I was glad when Kit waved me to follow her across the clearing and into the camp's cavern. When we swung the armored doors closed behind us, putting six inches of supposedly grezzen-proof armor between us and our new puppy, I exhaled. I knew that I hadn't held my breath since the grezzen had appeared, but I couldn't remember taking one, either.

I let my pack plop to the cave floor and the thud echoed. I asked Kit, "Now what?"

She stepped to the land line phone. "First, we figure out what Cutler's been up to."

Before she rang back to Eden Outfitters, I stepped alongside her. "How about first I find out what you and I have been up to?"

"What do you mean?"

I pointed at the armored doors, toward the beast cracking bones just outside. "I mean what do you expect to do with our new friend? You can't book him a room at the Eden Hotel. And if you could I don't think the Dead Grezzen Lounge would serve him."

"He hasn't killed us. That should prove something to the locals."

"It doesn't even prove anything to you! He still may be planning to kill us both. If he doesn't, the locals will shoot him on sight. Then hang you for letting him inside the Line."

"I'm not going to march beside him down Main Street. I just need to persuade him to acknowledge that he, and his species, are intelligent."

"Isn't Cutler doing that?"

"For my purposes, I need proof. For Cutler's purposes, he needs to extend the absence of proof, at least until his R&D people synthesize telepathy."

"Why does Cutler need to extend anything? Dead End has the social order of a plane crash. He's already gotten away with murder by grezzen."

She sat on a stool alongside the mike, then tugged me down onto the stool across from her. "You're half-right. Trueborns suck at rooting out evil on the frontier. But we've got centuries of guilt stored up when it comes to exploiting indigenous races. Cutler's an Earthman. His corporate assets are Earth-centered. I can trip him up back home, even if I can't here. The Intelligent Species Protection Act was passed after the War."

"Never heard of it."

"Why would you? After a half century and five hundred planets, we haven't found any intelligent species for ISPA to protect. But if Cutler violates ISPA, he kicks over a big barrel. Felony prosecution for him and his officers and directors, delisting of stock, loss of government contracts. A tycoon's worst nightmare."

"Hasn't he already kicked over the barrel?"

Kit shook her head. "ISPA only applies after a finding that a new species is intelligent. That sounded easy when the act was written. We'd land on a planet. We would find bipeds that would smile and wave, then cure cancer for us. People who write endangered species legislation expect an intelligent species to be cute and helpful, not eleven tons and grumpy. They especially don't expect that species to be so intelligent that it would play dumb."

"ISPA's why Cutler's keeping this quiet? To the point of letting us die?"

"You know the man. You put it past him?"

I pointed at the doors again. "But if you get that thing to stand out there and recite Shakespeare, Cutler can't exterminate the species?"

"By the time the bureaucrats even fund a study on a planet ten jumps out, Cutler will have his alternative telepathy in place. The grezzen will be exterminated before the first ISPA inspection team packs its bags to leave Earth." Kit shook her head. "It doesn't matter what that grezzen does on Dead End. We need him to recite his Shakespeare on Earth."

"Earth? You can't even transport an alien banana on a starship."

"Dead End organic exports have been off quarantine for years."

"Organic export? A grezzen's not a banana! No starship Captain would ever let you bring an eleven-ton killing machine—"

She raised her palm. "I can take care of that."

I snorted. "Right. Assuming, which I don't, that you could, how is kidnaping an intelligent being better than what Cutler's doing?"

"Who's kidnaping? I'll talk the grezz into making the trip."

"And then I'll stuff a horse down my pants." I rolled my eyes. "Trueborns!"

She raised her eyebrows. "You got a better idea?"

I shrugged.

Kit fired up the land line back to Eden Outfitters, but got no answer, which was odd. She rang her boss' Handtalk, then put the call on speaker when he answered.

"Oliver?"

"Kit?" Crackles and pops broke behind the old man's voice. At first I thought it was just old equipment and Dead End atmospherics, then I recognized a sound I'd heard before. Oliver was in the middle of a gunfight.

Kit said, "Oliver, what's going on there?"

"Cutler said you were dead."

"Long story. Parker and I are fine. Is that gunfire?"

"Cutler's an idiot! He's got a grezzen caged in that warehouse he rented. But I suppose you know that. There's a disagreement in progress between Cutler's thugs and a few of the neighbors who found out that they have a grezzen next door. Cutler asked me to stop by and visit with him about it."

Boom.

"What was that?"

"Fragmentation grenade."

Kit and I turned our heads and stared at one another, mouths open.

I said, "Welcome to the neighborhood."

Kit asked Oliver, "What did Cutler want from you?"

"An escort out of town. He went to the Port, to catch the evening Upshuttle. He left his goon squad to hold the fort."

"He's abandoning his project?"

"Don't think so. Just leaving the kitchen 'til the steam blows off the kettle."

I shook my head at Kit. "That's our boy."

She leaned toward the mike. "Anybody hurt?"

"I've seen worse after a Saturday night fight. Unless you count the grezzen."

"What?"

"The goons say they're gonna kill it."

Kit looked at me, eyes wide.

We both stood and raced to the armored doors.

Fifty-four

The grezzen lay outside the covered hole down which Kit and Jazen had vanished.

While he waited, he reached out to his mother. No response.

He sifted until he found Cutler's thread.

Cutler, like Kit and Jazen, was in a hole. Light filtered down through a roof above the hole, but it was a hole. Cutler spoke to a subservient human, "No luggage to check."

"Have a nice flight, sir."

Flight. The reference was to flight like a gort flew, not flight to escape. He was learning slowly to distinguish between what humans imagined and what they actually experienced. The flight reference was clearly only something that was imagined.

Humans could no more fly than he could. However, the better he came to know them, the more convinced he became that humans were clever enough to construct flying shells for themselves. One of the first grezzen who had encountered humans claimed to have seen such shells. But that seemed illogical. Where in the world would they fly to?

Which made him wonder what Cutler and the other human were talking about, now.

"I am here." His mother's weakness was now too severe too ignore. And he felt anxiety surrounding her, in the way that smaller animals caught up in a woog stampede displayed anxiety.

She could see little, and therefore he could see little. He felt the smoke that hung in the air she breathed.

Grezzen were not prone to quotable clichés. Nonetheless, the grezzen thought that where there was smoke there was fire.

He clamped his jaw, fearful for her.

"Mother, what is happening?"

"The humans are fighting among themselves. Cutler has escaped."

"What will you do?"

"There is little left that I can do. I misjudged this situation."

Through his mother's eyes, the grezzen saw Liu approach her, along with two others. One held a large stinger, the other a three-legged root. The second set the root on the ground, then both busied themselves attaching the stinger to it.

Liu said, "I didn't sign up to get killed over some hunting trophy. Cutler's run out on us. If these hicks want this thing dead, then we'll give 'em dead."

"Mother?"

"We'll see whether this one can do what it visualizes." She struck at the bars of her cage, and two of the humans retreated.

Liu turned and shouted at them, waving a forelimb. "Get your asses back here!" Then he crouched behind the stinger that the two had left behind.

The images faded. The grezzen couldn't tell whether that was a product of his mother's weakness, of his own anxiety over her predicament, or something that the humans had done to her.

He sprang to his feet, and ran to her.

Fifty-five

Kit ran out through the open armored doors, spun and looked in all directions. Then she threw her hat to the ground and kicked it. "Goddammit!"

I said, "Maybe it—"

"You know where he went as well as I do, Parker! He's headed for Eden. When he gets there, he's going to kill somebody. Everybody, if he can. Unless they kill him first." She tweezed her closed eyes while she shook her head. "What was I thinking?"

I turned and ran, pointing at the doors. "You've got a Sixer in there. Maybe we can get there in time to do something."

She returned to the mike and warned Oliver that trouble was on the way while I backed the Sixer out. Then she jumped in beside me and I drove us, bouncing, down the road back to Eden like the place was on fire and we had the only water bucket on the planet.

Fifty-six

*The grezzen had been running toward his mother for two hours,
and night had fallen, when he felt the first humans, directly ahead.*

*He had run directly down the path the humans had cleared
between the hole where he had left Kit and Jazen and the nest that
the humans called Eden. He chose the route, though he had never
traveled it before, for the same reason that he followed trails worn
by prey animals. Because that was where he would find them.*

*He felt humans and paused. There were two, side by side, con-
cealed along the trail, a human mile ahead of him.*

*"You don't really expect it to come walking down the road, do
you?"*

"Path of least resistance. It gives us a clear shot with the RPG."

"I don't even know if an RPG will kill one."

*"You rather just hide out in the woods and wait for it to sneak
up on us in the dark?"*

"We got snoopers."

*"They had snoopers thirty years ago and look where it got them.
Radio back that we're in position."*

*The grezzen understood that an RPG was a large stinger. He
also understood that he could easily kill these two, regardless. But
that might alert the others ahead, and his objective was first to
learn his mother's fate.*

"How long do they want us to stay here?"

"All night."

"*Grezz aren't the only things that can kill you at night.*"

Indeed not. But if these two were killed, it wouldn't be by him. He circled wide around these first humans, then continued.

A tree snake as thick as his thigh dropped down onto his back, sadly misinformed about what it was attacking. The grezzen tore the snake off his back. Then he bit off and spit out the snake's head, which was all gristle, fangs, and venom. The fleshy body he wrapped around his neck, to eat later. His run had sapped him of energy he would need when he reached the Eden nest.

As he came closer to the human nest, a red glow became visible, reflected off the clouds. Human stingers crackled, and he felt a vast jumble of human confusion, as well as fight and flight reactions.

He reached again for his mother. Her lack of response this time was unlike the hesitations that had become increasingly frequent.

He was forced to contemplate the probability that she would never respond again.

A human hour later, he reached high ground from which he could not merely feel the humans, but could look down upon their nest. Flames snaked skyward from one spot, around which humans had concealed themselves, some hidden behind movable shells, others behind stationary objects.

Sporadically, stingers in the hands of the concealed humans spit fire and rattled. Equally sporadically, fire spit and rattled back from the place that blazed.

He felt Liu shout, "Cease fire! Cease fucking fire, you yokels!"

The flashing and rattling crescendoed. "Go to hell, you mercenary bastards."

"You got what you wanted!"

"Not because we listened to you! And now there's another one inside the Line."

"The second one's not our doing, or our problem."

"It's gonna be everybody's problem! You don't know what you're dealin' with."

"I do. I been trying to tell you. We killed this one, no problem. So back off."

The grezzen stiffened. He had feared this result. And he had known that this moment would come, as it came to all sons. His mother had prepared him to live without her. Indeed, she would disapprove if he didn't handle his sudden independence responsibly. His first responsibility, he decided, was revenge.

Fifty-seven

By the time we got within Handtalk range of Eden, we saw the red glow of fire, lighting the bellies of the clouds above the town. The drive had been uneventful, except for a couple of idiot look-outs who almost ambushed us with an RPG. If they represented the dull point of the human spear, the grezzen had probably gotten into Eden easily.

Kit raised Oliver and asked, "Oliver, what's going on?"

"Nothing good, Kit. Cutler's thugs killed the first grezzen with an antitank missile. Then the second grezzen showed up."

"Casualties?"

"The thing just roared into town like a runaway mag rail. Ignored everybody else, went straight for that warehouse where Cutler's thugs were holed up with the other one. Peeled back the roof plating like it was cardboard, then jumped down in there and tore them all apart. You would have thought it knew."

Kit said, "It did."

Oliver continued, "Since then, it's just been sitting down in that hole, next to the dead one. We can hear it howl. Frankly, though, I hardly weep for those bastards it killed."

"Maybe you shouldn't. Their boss kidnaped his mother, then those bastards killed her." I looked over at Kit. Her eyes reflected moist in the fire's glow.

While Kit and Oliver talked, and we bounced closer to town, I peered up through the Sixer's windscreen. A triangle of red, winking navigation lights appeared in the darkness as the evening Downshuttle broke through the cloud ceiling. It glided over Eden, then disappeared over the hills that separated the town from the port.

Kit asked Oliver, "What's everybody planning to do now?"

"Kill it, of course. The plan is to flood the warehouse with kerosene while it's down in there, then burn it to death. The grezz never seemed to like fire. We're bringing up a tanker truck now."

Kit rubbed her fingers across her forehead. "Can you wait 'til I can talk to the vigilantes?"

"People are done talking. Kit, I'd keep my distance if I were you. This new grezzen got in through your section of the Line. That makes you about as popular as Cutler right now. I imagine half of town was glad to look up and see that Downshuttle."

Kit and I looked at one another. The evening Upshuttle took off only after the Downshuttle landed safely. The appearance of the Downshuttle in the night sky probably *had* caused half the population of Eden to think that Cutler was out at the port and about to escape from this planet. If that many people had thought it simultaneously, the grezzen had probably noticed.

"Sonuvabitch!" Oliver's shout rang from Kit's hand talk as I swung the Sixer onto Main Street and headed for the flames that marked the warehouse compound.

"The goddamn thing just jumped out of that hole like it got shot from a cannon! Like it knew what we were planning. Now we don't know where it's headed!"

Kit switched off the Handtalk, turned to me, and said, "I do."

I pointed out the windscreen. "Me too. Hang on."

I hit the brakes and swerved. The Sixer flipped and rolled onto its roof.

Fifty-eight

As the grezzen ran, he leapt up and over the human shell that hurtled on a collision course toward him. Beneath him, the shell toppled and rolled like a tripped woog.

As he passed above the tumbling object, he fleetingly felt Kit and Jazen, or so it seemed. Then the immediacy of the moment seized control of his thoughts again.

He took no satisfaction from killing Liu and the others, and his mother's death left him hollow. But he had seen with his own eyes the flying object that had burst through the clouds. His mother, his race were wrong. Humans did not merely imagine that the world was bigger than grezzen thought it could possibly be. Humans knew that it was bigger. He was uncertain what to make of his new knowledge.

But one thing the grezzen did know. Cutler, who the grezzen counted among those responsible for hastening his mother's death, now waited beyond the hills that bounded the Eden nest. But shortly Cutler would escape, unless the grezzen reached him first.

The grezzen sought and found Cutler's thread.

"Now boarding First Class Upshuttle passengers holding reserved accommodation vouchers aboard HUS Yorktown." Cutler walked forward, toward a human-sized opening in the largest shell the grezzen had yet seen.

The grezzen searched among his peers for knowledge of the terrain through which he ran. He had never been here, within this

189

small area of the world that had been ceded to the human race. But his ancestors knew the territory, and so he knew it. A narrow canyon led through the hills. If he cut through it, he would reach the place where Cutler now was sooner. The canyon was a place where his ancestors had ambushed and slain many humans. Surely such terrain would still favor him.

The grezzen altered his course toward the pass, and lifted his pace.

Fifty-nine

I hung upside down, suspended by my seatbelt against the Sixer's driver's seat.

I twisted and saw Kit, also suspended, limp, in the same posture. "Kit? You okay?"

No answer.

I pulled myself up until I could release the seatbelt, dropped onto the Sixer's roof, then crawled to Kit. Her eyes were closed, and blood trickled from her nose down toward her hairline. But she was breathing.

My heart pounded. Should I move her?

She moaned, then her eyes opened.

I said, "You okay?"

She nodded. "Get me down."

Two minutes later, we stood and examined the Sixer. The right front wheel had snapped off at the axle, and two left side wheels folded beneath the chassis like bent jar lids. Even if we could have righted the vehicle, its close encounter with the grezzen had left it undriveable.

We limped, arm in arm, toward the dying flames that marked the warehouse complex.

I said, "You think it's after Cutler?"

"What else? But I don't think it understands that it can't reach him. There's no reason to think grezzen even understand the concept of space beyond this world. Much less travel through it."

191

"If Cutler gets away after all this, you think he'll abandon his project?"

She shook her head as we walked. "No chance. He'll have to pay the locals more, maybe move his operations outside town. But the costs are peanuts compared to the profits."

Headlights, tall and accompanied by a big displacement diesel's bellow, winked on at the opposite end of main street.

I shielded my eyes. "I imagine that's Oliver's kerosene bomb tanker."

The diesel, towing a two-hundred-barrel tank wagon, rumbled toward us down the mud street, lit by fading firelight. The truck's brakes squealed as it stopped and idled alongside us. A dozen armed men and women, faces smoke-blackened, clung to the tanker's sides.

Oliver leaned out the cab window. "You two all right?"

Kit looked up at him. "Nothing serious. Where you all going?"

"They spotted the thing. It's making for the Cageway."

Kit said, "The Cageway's blocked at the other end."

"Exactly. Once it gets inside, we'll close the doors on this end. Once it's trapped inside, we can set up hoses and pump kerosene in through the roof bars. We'll roast it just like we planned. Just in a different spot."

I said, "That thing nearly wrecked a main battle tank. You might want to just leave it alone."

"I saw what happened to the tank. It's still parked down by the warehouse. But tanks weren't built to keep grezzen on the outside. The Cageway was. It was built of one hundred percent newsteel. The Cageway'll keep a grezzen from getting out just as well as it'll keep one from getting in."

A bearded man in a black stetson, straddling the tanker's top hatch, waved a rifle. "Let's go, Oliver!"

The old man looked back at the posse, nodded, and the tank truck lurched away in the direction of the Cageway.

Kit said, "We can't let them kill the grezzen."

"In their shoes, I would."

"You're not in their shoes! Parker, you refused to kill children. The grezzen are as innocent as children."

"Children don't commit mass murder. That grezzen just did."

As the tanker's rumble faded, distant thunder replaced it.

The Upshuttle rose above the hills, through the darkness, navigation lights flashing.

"Parker, you know the two situations aren't equivalent. And we'd be dead now if the grezzen hadn't bodyguarded us back to the Line."

"It didn't do that to for us. It did that to get inside the Line! That's pretty obvious, isn't it?"

"You blame it? For reasons it doesn't understand, its only family was taken away from it. It's been sentenced to be shot on sight, just for being born. Do you think that's right?"

Kit had just described my own life. I didn't think that was right for me. I couldn't very well think it was right for the grezzen.

I stood in the street for a moment, thinking. Then I pointed at the sky, where the engine flare of the Upshuttle had just disappeared into the low clouds. "Can you really fly one of those?"

"Why?"

"Come on!" I took her arm and dragged her behind me down Main Street, toward the smoldering ruins of the warehouse.

Sixty

The grezzen raced through the narrow canyon that led to the place where he had felt Cutler. He was slowed by the canyon's open, barred roof, against which his back would crash if he ran with his normal, bounding stride. The bars admitted the dim light of night that reflected off the clouds, but the bars had obscured his view of the object that had roared overhead moments before.

He sifted threads until he found Cutler, and was horrified to realize that the man was gone, already above the clouds—yes, there really was more of the world above the clouds—and already planning to return and do to other grezzen what had been done to the grezzen's mother.

The grezzen skidded all six legs to a stop in the confined space, then slammed a forepaw against the bars above his head, as though he might strike down the shell in which Cutler had escaped him. His effort served only to release his frustration, as well as his sorrow at his mother's passing.

Now what? He felt and heard humans behind him, but none close ahead, so he continued to trot forward, out of curiosity. Soon he arrived at a pair of great doors, like the ones that protected the hole into which Kit and Jazen had retreated. These were barred, like the canyon roof, and against them, on the side away from him, lay a massive but wrecked human shell.

He advanced to the doors, then slapped at the bars. Most things that humans made he could slice with his claws, less easily than flesh, but more easily than a grezzen's bone. These bars were made of sterner stuff. He scratched them at other spots, but with the same failed result.

Finally, he simply put his shoulder to the obstacle and shoved. The doors and the heap of human debris groaned, but did not give way.

He turned and trotted back the way he had come. He had covered half the distance to the canyon mouth when he heard a great thud that echoed toward him. Simultaneously he felt humans exult.

"Got him!"

"Yeah, well, maybe he's got us. Keep your distance and keep your weapons sighted on those doors."

"For how long?" The speaking human displayed a feeling of weariness.

"It'll take most of the night to get the piping and hoses up the hill." This the grezzen did not understand.

"You sure it's in there? What if it breaks out the other end, then doubles back on us?" The weary human was also anxious.

"The gates on the other end are strong as these. And they got a bus lying against them. Every bar in the Cageway's newsteel. We'll be fine." The dominant human spoke with a confidence that the grezzen felt was false.

"Those dead mercs in town were supposed to be fine."

The grezzen slowed as he approached the end of the canyon through which he had entered. As he feared, the humans had now blocked it with doors similar to those at the canyon's opposite end. They had trapped him.

No. He had trapped himself. In his rage, and his disdain for human capability, he had underestimated them again. And they had surprised him again.

He now found himself confined. Restrained. Humiliated in the way that Cutler had humiliated his mother.

He peered ahead toward the closed gates. Unlike the gates at the opposite end, which he had been unable to budge, no heavy debris buttressed this obstacle.

He paused in the darkness. Each breath rumbled and echoed as he filled his lungs. He allowed his rage, at his mother's death, at Cutler's escape, at his own miscalculations and hubris, to swell, knowing it would strengthen him.

Crouching back on his haunches, he gathered himself, then sprang forward. He accelerated over the distance that separated him from the gates, speed multiplying his mass. His shoulder struck the gates at the hinge point where one gate connected to the rock wall. At that hinge point, the gates should be most vulnerable, just like a striper's knee was vulnerable.

The gates held fast, and he rebounded and staggered backward.

A crackling storm of human stinger pellets struck the gate bars, exploding bits of fire in all directions. The pellets couldn't penetrate his integument, but if one struck an eye, he could be injured.

He retreated as the humans beyond the gates yelped.

One shouted, "Shut up! And hold your fire!"

"Sonuvabitch! Did you see that thing? It's as big as that Trueborn's crawler tank back at the warehouse."

"Bigger. Reload. The little one back there nearly wrecked that tank. This one could still wreck those gates."

The humans need not have worried. The gates at both ends of the canyon had proven robust. Given time to study them for weaknesses and nuance, it might be possible to solve them, but not while harassed by humans with stingers.

For thirty million years, grezzen had taken any and all competition head on, because that had been the easiest way to win. That didn't mean that they weren't clever enough to take on competition obliquely, if need be.

He twisted his head, and looked up at the dark and light stripe pattern made by the roof bars and clouds far above them.

The grezzen stretched tall, teetered on his hind legs, and extended his mid legs for balance. Then he reached up with his forepaws and sawed at the thick roof bars with his claws. Historically, the materials the humans used to make their shells were harder than bone, harder than most rock, but when grezzen had tried, they had been able to cut through them.

He worked until the lack of circulation to his uplifted limbs weakened them, then dropped down on all sixes. When he examined the bars, he saw that his efforts had barely scratched them.

His ancestors' good hunting in this canyon had taught the humans yet another lesson. He examined the points at which the bars that imprisoned him were attached to the rock walls. The humans had extended the bars into the rock walls in the way that a tree extended its roots into soil, probably deeply. Trees were deceptively difficult to uproot, rock was harder than soil, and the humans apparently planned some further action against him by the time daylight returned.

He paced the narrow canyon that imprisoned him.

Now what?

Sixty-one

The Abrams, scarred by its earlier encounter with the grezzen that Cutler's goons had killed, squatted in the fenced yard of the warehouse amid smoldering rubble. I ran to it, and mounted over the intact fender. Dropping inside, I wriggled into the driver's seat, and pressed the starter. My heart thumped, then it whined to life like an old friend.

With my head poked up through the open driver's hatch, I pumped my fist. "Alright!"

Kit had followed me, and crouched on the fender. "Parker, what are you thinking?"

"I'm thinking that you're right. If somebody kidnaped my mother then killed her, I'd be mad, too." I jerked my thumb at the turret. "Crawl in there, and check the ammo and fuel."

She pointed in the direction that the fuel tanker had gone. "Ammunition? Parker, you can't make war on those people! Idiocy's not a crime. And if it was, nobody elected you sheriff."

"I thought you were on the grezzen's side."

"I am! But I don't kill people just because they act in reasonable fear for their lives."

"Just tell me two things. Will that thing do what you tell it to?"

"The grezzen? The only orders it's ever taken were from its mother."

"I'm not talking about orders. Is it smart enough to act in its own self interest?"

198

Kit cocked her head. "I think so. Probably more rationally than you do, because this sounds—"

I held up my palm. "Second question. Do you know how to fly? Seriously?"

She rolled her eyes. "I'm certified on everything from sailplanes to multi-engine shallow orbitals. If there was a lesson my parents could buy me, they did."

I jerked my thumb at the turret again. "You're hired. Climb in."

She crossed her arms and stared at me. "What are you thinking?"

I levered the driver's seat up so that, with passive night goggles, I could see ahead and drive without Kit directing me from the commander's cupola. "I'll tell you on the way. You expected the grezzen to trust you. How 'bout you trust me, for once?"

Ten minutes later, we were out of town and winding uphill along the narrow gravel road that detoured around the Cageway.

I finished explaining my plan to Kit, then drove on in silence.

After five minutes, she said over the intercom. "Parker, that's insane. But I like it."

Sixty-two

The grezzen paced its prison while it sifted among the threads of the humans beyond the gates.

"We're gonna need more piping. And a portable welder."

"I just talked to Tucker. That's on the way."

"And an inline pump. Kerosene doesn't flow uphill."

"And fast."

"Look, that thing's not going anywhere."

"Don't underestimate a grezz. I'll believe it's done when I see it burn."

Burn? Humans controlled fire. The grezzen was beginning to suspect that they controlled a great many things beyond what his race had understood. But at the moment, fire was his immediate concern.

He probed deeper into the humans' consciousness. He saw humans moving thin logs, dragging them up the hill alongside the canyon. That was actually happening. He also found a vision of water poured down onto him. But it wasn't water, it was fire.

Was that a vision of something the humans could do, or merely something they wished they could do?

He searched his prison until he located a narrow overhang beneath which he could shelter a part of his bulk. Water extinguished fire. He found a rain-filled depression on the canyon floor as long and wide as he was, but no deeper than his ankles. Perhaps he could roll in the water.

200

But the more he thought the more he understood that he had no satisfactory options.

High above him, beyond the barred ceiling of his prison, he heard clicks of metal against metal as the first humans arrived. He heard them whisper, but only when he felt them could he understand the meaning of their words.

"Can you see it?"

"I think so. Hell, I dunno. It could be a boulder."

"Use the light."

"I don't want to spook it."

Then the first whisperer spoke to others, distant. "How long 'til we're ready?"

"It's slow work in the dark."

"Be light soon."

"Not soon enough for me."

The grezzen turned onto his side, then scraped the canyon wall beneath the overhang with all six paws, to enlarge his shelter.

He paused and regarded the tiny pile of scrapings his efforts made, and the even tinier dent in the rock.

It was hopeless, but he kept digging because he had no better idea.

Sixty-three

"Parker! We're sliding over the edge!"

I corrected our course, and the Abrams' upslope fender squealed as it scraped rock, and sixty-nine tons teetered back onto the narrow trail that ran parallel to the Cageway.

I stopped the tank and flexed my fingers, stiff from clutching the steering yoke's grips. The view through passive night snoopers was narrow, like seeing the world using a pair of toilet tissue roll spools as binoculars. Slow going.

The good news was the sky was lightening. The bad news was that we had been driving all night and our detour still hadn't brought us to the Cageway's port-end gates.

Kit was monitoring the vigilantes' progress by eavesdropping on their Handtalk conversations. I asked her, "How close are they to finished?"

"Too close. But that doesn't mean drive faster!"

I sighed, twisted the throttle, and we inched forward again, downslope.

Sixty-four

"Can you see it yet?"

Slowly, the grezzen pressed himself back beneath the overhanging ledge then froze. Every hunter knows that movement attracts attention. Now, for the first time, he was the hunted and not the hunter.

In the distance he now heard an ongoing metallic, human buzz that echoed off the hillsides that formed the canyon's walls.

"No. Can't see a thing."

"Goddammit, it's daylight!"

"Still dark down in the canyon, 'til the sun gets higher. Spotlights won't reach. I think maybe it's hiding under a ledge."

He felt conversation from a new voice. "Soak this and toss it down."

A moment later something clanged the bars above his head, then fell through to the canyon floor, four of his body lengths distant.

Fire! He shrank back. The tree branch just lay there, wrapped in something, burning with an alien, smoky pungency. The odor resembled the scent humans' shells left on the wind when they moved.

"I dunno. I maybe see something."

"Try more torches!"

Four more flaming branches tumbled into his prison. Soon, black smoke filled the narrow space.

"Well, that was fucking brilliant. If it is down there, now we can't see it for the smoke."

The grezzen remained still and, in time, the small fires died.

"Still can't see anything."

"Pump down the kerosene and see what happens."

The buzzing sound grew louder, then rain spattered the bars above, and trickled down onto the canyon floor.

It was not, he knew, rain, but the same pungent, greasy liquid that had coated the burning branches. The rain grew to a torrent, so drenching that puddles formed on the rock floor.

The liquid dripped down from the overhanging ledge, soaking the fur on his left rear thigh, which, no matter how small he compressed himself, was exposed.

Another burning branch tumbled down through the bars, landed in a puddle of the liquid, and set it aflame.

The grezzen shrank back even further as the flames spread across the dampened rock toward him. The flames sprang at his hind leg, and set his fur afire.

As he felt the heat, he howled, more from surprise and fear than pain.

"You hear that?"

He sprang from his hiding place, as though he could run from the flames, beating at them with his left middle leg.

"There! You see it?"

Bam. Bam. Bam.

The humans' pellets struck around him, one glancing harmlessly off his flank.

"It's on fire! We got it!"

Bam. Bam. Bam.

"Damn, that thing's fast!"

The grezzen sprang through the smoke and flame, found the water pool, and rolled through the muddy liquid. The flames on him died, and he darted through the smoke, away from the spot where he had hidden.

"Where'd it go?"

"Maybe it's dead."

"Smell that? We burned it, alright."

Twenty body lengths down the canyon, away from the area where the flaming kerosene lakes crackled, the grezzen paused. Hidden from those above by roiling smoke, he twisted around and examined himself. His fur was singed, but the skin and muscle beneath undamaged. The odor of his own burned hair caused him to snatch his head back. He realized as he did so that he had eaten his meager ration of stored snake hours before, and there was no prey in this cage to restore his strength. Soon his weakness would slow his reflexes.

"Now what?"

"Let the fire burn out. Breeze down the canyon'll clear the smoke. Meantime, have somebody walk a box of grenades up here."

".44 magnum rounds didn't faze it. Grenade fragments are smaller and slower."

"Nothin' to lose trying. Ask 'em how long to get another kerosene tanker connected to the line."

The grezzen felt a dull flicker of life, saw, then snatched, a fifty-legger as big as a tree branch out of a wall crevasse. He wolfed it down without even peeling its exoskeleton.

He sighed as he realized that the energy he had expended to catch the thing almost equaled the energy its digestion would provide him.

"They say an hour to get the next load. What if that doesn't kill it?"

"That thing's gonna run out of places to hide before we run out of kerosene."

He sat back and tried to comb out his singed fur with a foreclaw. The human was right. Unfortunately, the grezzen was learning that when the subject was killing, they usually were.

Cutler had escaped. The grezzen's plan was a ruin. Grezzen-kind's secret would be out soon enough. And he was going to die here, restrained and then drowned in liquid fire. He rumbled softly as he raised his forepaws to his face and held it between them.

"Can you hear me?"

At first the grezzen thought it was his executioners above, talking amongst themselves. Then he thought that he had become delirious from exhaustion, fear and smoke, and imagined his mother was speaking to him, the way humans imagined things that were not. The contact he felt was, after all, female.

"It's Kit. We can help you."

He felt back along the thread until he found her, just beyond the blockage at the canyon's far end.

"I'm sorry about your mother. But it wasn't anything we did."

He sat up. Wrong! She and Jazen were human, and humans had killed her. Trust? Cooperation? What had it gotten him?

Kit reached to him again. "Goddammit! Talk to me! It's bad enough for you to decide you're going to die. But you have no right to take the rest of your race down with you!"

He sat in his human prison, hidden for the moment from the humans above by smoke, hidden from Kit's nagging by his silence.

"Bombs away!" The humans above whooped.

Clang.

Through the smoke he saw an egg-shaped black rock, the size of a lemon bug, bounce through the bars and drop to the rock floor. There it spun. He felt glee, and a flinch, from the humans above. He turned his face away from the little rock, and closed his eyes.

Boom.

Shrapnel buzzed and swarmed around the grezzen, but didn't penetrate his fur, which was more protective than steel cable. The instant's warning, that he gained from the human flinch that he felt, saved his eyes. But the grenade's concussion, confined between the canyon walls, rocked him.

He felt Kit. "What was that? Get out of there!"

Dazed, he blinked.

Clang. Clang. Clang.

He stared at the three new eggs, then leapt across them.

Boom. Boom. Boom.

He dashed through the thick smoke, sprang through the flames that leapt up at him from the kerosene pools, and ran toward Kit and Jazen.

Sixty-five

I maneuvered the Abrams alongside the wrecked bus that leaned against the Cageway's gate. Kit stood in the road in front of the tank and directed me with hand signals.

The sounds of grenade detonations and the roar of flames echoed beyond the gates.

I shouted to her, "You think it's still alive?"

Whump.

Before she could answer, something struck the gates like eleven tons of wet leather. The gates groaned, but didn't budge.

We both spun and stared through the bars, where the grezzen peered back at us through three red eyes. Its ochre fur was singed black in places, and its breath rumbled in ragged gasps.

Kit shouted to be heard over the tank engine's idle, which seemed superfluous if it was reading her mind. "You know that even you're not strong enough to break out of there. We can break you out. If we do, you can probably kill us. Then maybe you can hide from all those angry humans who are trying to burn you. But you can't kill them all, you can't get back out through the robot mines, and they'll get you eventually."

The grezzen just stared at us, but if it was reading her mind and was as smart as we thought, it knew she was right.

She shouted again, "When you get free, we're going to ask you to do things that you won't like. I'm asking you to trust us again."

He just kept staring.

Kit turned to me and nodded.

I shrugged, which she couldn't see because my shoulders were buried behind sixty-nine tons of steel.

An Abrams can pivot on its tracks in no more space than its own length, so I spun it, dug its prow into the back end of the wrecked bus, and gunned the turbine. I've never seen a horse, but an Abrams engine pushes with the power of one thousand, five hundred of them.

The bus creaked, then sheet metal crumpled.

I backed off a couple feet, then butted the wreck again. A fifteen-hundred horsepower truck might spin its wheels trying to push a bus, but a tank's tracks, held down by gravity tugging on sixty-nine tons, just dig in and push.

Chassis members groaned, then snapped. Then the wreckage moved. Slowly and messily, but it moved. I cleared a space in front of the gates as wide as the tank, then backed away.

Kit shouted to the grezzen again while she made shooing motions with her hands. "Back off!"

The beast tiptoed back from the gates. As a GI, I understood divulging nothing but name, rank, and service number. But I, at least, no longer bought the grezzen's mute act.

My original idea had been to blow the gates with a main gun round. But we might have hurt our big friend, and the noise might have alerted the posse. Based on the grenade explosions, small arms fire, and smoke plume still coming from over the hill, they still thought our friend was trapped below them. Also, they had no idea that Kit and I were in the mix. If we got as far as part two of the plan, we wanted to keep things that way.

Kit scrambled aboard and I backed the tank off while she rotated the turret to opposite lock, with the main gun tube pointing backward, to avoid damaging it.

I dropped back into the driver's seat, dropped it down, then pulled the driver's hatch shut over my head, to avoid damaging myself. Then I released the brake and rumbled the tank straight at the gates.

My emotions were mixed. As a tanker, I hated to abuse the old girl. But she was Cutler's, and the thought of running up his insurance premiums made me smile.

Ten seconds later sixty-nine tons of Abrams rammed the grezzen-proof Cageway gates at forty miles per hour.

From where I was sitting, I've hit speed bumps that were worse. The gates collapsed onto the turret as they were carried along, then they slid off on both sides, and crashed to the canyon floor.

I reversed the tank out onto the road that led to the port, then peered out through my periscopic windows. The grezzen trotted out of his prison, stopped, and stared.

My heart pounded. He could run away. Based on the damage that his elderly mother had already done to this tank, he could probably rip our armor like a MUD tube filled with buttery alfredo, then gobble us both alive.

Sixty-six

The grezzen blinked as he emerged uninjured from the shadowy prison in which he had expected to be burned alive. He cocked his head at the shell that held Kit and Jazen, which sat, rumbling, two body lengths from him.

He felt Kit, hidden inside the shell. "I told you we would free you. We did what I told you we would do. Now I am asking you to trust me again. I am inviting you to accompany us on a journey. It will be difficult for you. You will be confined for a long period."

The grezzen snorted. He had just experienced what confinement by humans meant for him, and for his mother. Never! He turned away. He would regain his strength, then he would hunt and kill humans until either they were all dead or he was.

"The worst of the confinement will only last a short time. Aboard a small ship like the one you saw. The one that Cutler just left on."

Cutler! The grezzen paused.

Kit continued, "Most of the journey you'll spend on a much larger ship. Cutler's on one like it now. If you come with us, you can stop conflict between our species. What happened to you won't be allowed to happen again. You need to decide now. Those people aren't going to keep dropping grenades into smoke forever."

The shell spun round, and clattered off, away from the prison from which Kit and Jazen had rescued him.

The grezzen watched the shell crawl away. He felt in Kit her confidence that the future would unfold as she predicted. But he also knew now that all humans were not of a single mind, in the way that all grezzen were. Her proposal was physically repugnant to a grezzen, dangerous, and unlikely to yield the results she promised.

But wherever Cutler had gone was where Kit now proposed to take him. It was his only chance to get to Cutler and then to kill him. And that was all that mattered.

The grezzen trotted off after his two humans.

Sixty-seven

The port would have been an hour away, but after an hour it remained miles distant. That was mostly because we made an unscheduled stop while the grezzen picked up lunch, in the form of an unlucky woog that crossed our path.

Between Cutler's wild ride and all the maintenance we had skipped, the tank's tranny was grinding, and she was running hot and grumpy. If the Abrams quit on us out here, the posse would catch us. Aiding and abetting a grezzen may not be a crime, but Kit and I would probably be lynched for it anyway.

I begged and pleaded with the tank like it was a living thing for the remaining miles.

The Abrams delivered us to the port's drop-off entrance, squealing like she was wounded. Which she was.

The bald guy who had cleared me through customs appeared at the top of the stairs that led down into the dugout terminal building to investigate the noise. One hand was visored above his eyes, and after a heartbeat, he ran back inside and clanged the door shut behind him.

A visit from a main battle crawler tank will do that. More so when the tank is accompanied by an eleven-ton monster with a bloody water buffalo carcass dangling from its jaws.

Two minutes later, a Sixer shot up and out from the warehouse's ramp and roared away from us in the opposite direction. I saw a driver and one passenger inside. The night shift, as I recalled, consisted of two employees, one in the terminal and one in the warehouse, so we now had the place to ourselves for awhile.

I drove the Abrams to the hangar, and pulled it between the two shuttles parked there. The tank's engine died before I killed it.

All frontier outworlds follow the same routine. One shuttle's always either in parking orbit, or coming or going. One, usually the most recent Downshuttle, is being unloaded, cleaned, and repaired. Because an outworld's only links to the rest of mankind are its shuttles, a third, "hot" shuttle always sits fueled and ready in case of emergency.

This, it seemed to me, was an emergency. It was also a crime, but I was already a convicted felon.

Kit climbed down from the Abrams' turret while I lifted myself out of the driver's hatch.

I paused a moment and laid my hand on the Abrams' rock-solid forward armor. The old girl's armor was scarred and muddy. One fender was pretzeled, and soot coated all of her paint that wasn't blistered. Her chassis had rolled off an assembly line on Earth, which was now an invisible light point in the sky, during a year when the first two digits on the calendar read 19. There was no telling where she had been and what she had seen over the course of the next century and change, but if steel was capable of expectations, I think she had exceeded hers. I gave the tank a pat. "Good girl."

Kit turned to me. "What?"

"I was talking to the tank. When you think about it, she's actually a Trueborn. But I don't suppose she realizes it."

Kit looked up at the clouds. "Yeah."

Then we stood staring up at the enormous old wedge that was the hot shuttle.

I said, "You really can fly this?"

She nodded. "Flies itself, really. A space plane's more automated than a single-engine atmospheric. The hard part's landing, and we aren't doing that."

"What's the penalty for grand theft space plane?"

She smiled, arms crossed. "Let me worry about that."

I jerked my thumb at the grezzen, who was enjoying a snack behind us. A woog thigh bone is as thick as a roof beam, and makes the same sound when pulverized. "You can worry about him, too."

We walked up the shuttle's cargo ramp into its hold.

The grezzen trotted up behind us, but stood at the base of the ramp on all six legs. It plopped the bloody woog carcass in front of it, then peered up with three blinking eyes.

Our footsteps echoed in the hold, which had been big enough to transport the Abrams, crated, with room to spare. I said to Kit, "Cozy stateroom for our friend. For how long, you think?"

Kit called up a schedule on the bay's bulkhead flatscreen, read it, then said, "The *Yorktown* broke orbit seventy minutes ago. The *Midway*'s due to match orbit day after tomorrow."

In the distance, I heard vehicle buzz. I ran down the ramp and peered out through the hangar bars. A half dozen vehicles crawled toward us like black ants.

I called back up the ramp to Kit. "The posse's onto us. How long will it take to get out of here?"

Kit jogged down the ramp looked up at the grezzen, and said, "You need to get in there."

The grezzen growled, and didn't budge.

In the distance, rifle shots crackled.

Kit ran back up the ramp and shouted over her shoulder, "Parker, I've got work to do! You talk to him!" Then she disappeared through the hold's forward hatch, toward the crew compartment.

I never had a pet, and I've never been much for small talk. I felt foolish talking to a hairy, six-legged monster, much less trying to persuade him to board a spaceship.

I pointed up the ramp. "You don't want to do this, I know."

Visions of tanks afire and friends and family lost welled up in me. "But I know what you just went through. I've been through it, too. This is the best thing you can do right now. Believe me."

The fuel pump hydraulics whined as Kit began the shuttle's start up sequence.

The grezzen cocked his head at the sound.

I backed up the ramp until I stood in the hold, alongside the lever that would lift the ramp, closing Kit and me in and the grezzen out.

Kit's voice sounded from the intercom speaker. "Don't make me come back there, you two!"

I pleaded at the grezzen, palms up. "Were you this much trouble to your mother?"

The grezzen dropped its head, bit into the woog, then side-stepped six-legged up the ramp, dragging the carcass and leaving a smear of blood on the ramp as wide as a Sixer's wheelbase.

I yanked the up ramp lever, it whined up, and Kit lit the engines.

I swear that as we taxied, bumping and rumbling, out onto the runway, a voice said in my head, "More trouble, actually."

There is no seat belt for a six-legged monster, so the grezzen spread-eagled all six legs against the hold's bulkheads.

A shuttle's hold is separately pressurized from the crew and passenger spaces. Therefore, you pick your side of the hatch before takeoff and stay there for the duration. The grezzen looked scared. Actually, I had no idea how he looked. But I knew I would have been scared if I were in his shoes, all six of them.

Rather than leave our infrequent flyer guest alone on his first flight, I strapped into the loadmaster's acceleration couch for the Upshuttle trip.

The grezzen made it through boost phase intact, the dead woog less so. This became apparent only when the shuttle made parking orbit, to drift through space awaiting the arrival of the *Midway*.

Kit's voice crackled through the hold's intercom speaker. "Everything okay back there, Parker?"

The grezzen drifted weightless, six limbs outstretched and all three eyes wide, as though it were a parade balloon. Its weightless fur fluffed out like it had been blow-dried. But that wasn't the worst of it.

I said, "It's a shit storm back here!"

"Grow up, Parker."

"No. It's a shit storm. The boost phase squashed the dead woog's intestines like toothpaste tubes. Crap's floating everywhere."

"Oh."

"It's not funny!"

"Look on the bright side. It's only thirty-nine hours until the *Midway*'s due. And at least the grezzen's not airsick."

I somersaulted so I could see the grezzen. "I dunno. He looks a little green around the tusks. He might—"

You have no idea how much floating vomit an eleven-ton animal can spew in thirty-nine hours.

So I was too busy to notice the details of the secret handshake Kit used to get a mile-long *Bastogne*-class star cruiser to take a hijacked shuttle and a monster aboard.

I suspect the good citizens of Dead End were perturbed that we got away, but glad to see us gone. The last feeling was mutual.

Unfortunately, our reputation had preceded us with the good people aboard the *Midway*.

As soon as the *Midway*'s docking bay was pressured up, I cracked the shuttle's rear ramp and let it whine down. The grezzen, subject again to gravity, courtesy of the big cruiser's rotation, slid down onto the bay's deck plates with all six legs splayed, as weak and dopey as a dehydrated puppy.

The bay inner doors opened, and a combat engineer sergeant motioned an engineer team, wearing full eternad armor and dragging welding gear and plasteel girders, forward into the bay.

A wide-eyed embarked Marine security platoon, also full-armored, weapons locked and loaded, scurried in behind the engineers and surrounded the grezz, while the engineers welded a custom plasteel wheeled cage around him.

I admired their caution, but not their grasp on the reality I knew. If the grezz chose to pick a fight, even weak as it was, those Marines and engineers would be smeared on the bulkheads like strawberry compote in a half minute.

The cage finished up just smaller than an assault transport. Therefore, it just fit into the docking bay's radial elevator, one of thirty-six elevators that ran up and down shafts that led like bicycle spokes from the docking bays ringed around the cruiser's beltline down to the centerline cargo bay.

Kit and I rode down the dark, echoing shaft with the grezzen and his jailers.

Once we offloaded the cage in the bay, one marine popped his helmet faceplate and drew a breath.

He saluted Kit, who had changed into pilot's coveralls during our flight. No such amenities for the grezzen and me.

She returned his salute, then he scrunched up his nose while he jerked a thumb at the grezzen. "Colonel, is that thing as strong as it smells?"

Actually, he was probably smelling me as much as the grezzen. After thirty-nine hours I could no longer smell myself, for which I was grateful. But I did smell something unfamiliar.

I looked around the cargo bay. Another of the thirty-six elevators from the docking bays clanged down. It was full of export kerosene bladders. I glanced at the grezzen. I have no idea how a *Xenoursus grezzenensis* looks when it's terrified, but I was pretty sure the way he shrank back against the far wall of his new cage was it.

I thought, "Don't worry. That smell doesn't mean these guys are going to burn you."

If my assurance relaxed him, it didn't cause him to move away from the cage wall.

Then I realized what the jarhead had just called Kit. I stared at her with my mouth open. Colonel? My five thousand soldier brigade was commanded by a colonel.

She smiled at him. "You don't want to find out, corporal. Sling the rifles. The grezzen won't bother you, and the rifles wouldn't do you any good if it did."

"As you say, ma'am. Uh. Captain Halder sends his compliments. He'd like to see you and this gentleman," he nodded to me, "on the bridge immediately."

It took ten minutes for the jarhead to escort us to the bridge, clumping along in armor with his rifle at port arms. There Kit was piped aboard like, well, the full bird colonel that she apparently was.

The *Midway*'s "captain" was actually of equivalent rank to Kit, but he was gray enough to have been her father, and had bushy eyebrows. He wore a Colonial shoulder patch that marked him as non-Trueborn, which I counted as a strike in his favor, though it probably meant he had hit the promotion ceiling, and would never make admiral no matter how well he did his job.

Kit saluted him first, he returned it, then frowned. "Colonel Born, we had to dig pretty deep into the recognition files to verify the codes you transmitted. But you check out. May I ask why I have turned my ship into a spook circus train?"

She dipped her head and smiled at him. "I appreciate your cooperation. And your concern."

I raised my eyebrows. Kit had been very polite. She also hadn't uttered one substantive word that answered his question.

"Concern? Do you know how much it costs to hold a *Bastogne*-Class cruiser in orbit, like I've just done for you?"

She nodded. "I do. And I'm sure you know that the spook budget's big enough to cover it." It was Kit's turn to frown. "I'm afraid us spooks are going to have to impose on you further, Captain Halder." She drew a pad and stylo from a pocket in her coverall's sleeve, scribbled a note, and passed it to him. "Grocery list for our big guest below. Could you arrange to have these items acquired, and upshipped on the next shuttle?"

"This is a big ship. We have plenty aboard to feed it."

"He's picky."

"You've already put us behind schedule. I'm afraid we won't be able to wait on the next shuttle."

"I'd appreciate it if you would."

Halder's eyes bugged like she had asked him to swim through grezzen puke. Trust me, I know the look.

Kit smiled again. "So would my boss."

The captain pressed his lips together, but he didn't speak. Then he waved the officer of the deck over, handed him Kit's note, and said, "Russ, please have Logistics and Procurement attend to the colonel's requirements. And please re-plot an extended parking orbit."

Wow. Most armed forces called their intel people spooks. And most regulars didn't like their spooks. But Kit was apparently a very important spook.

Halder also said, "Please find the colonel a suitable billet." He nodded my way while he made a face. "And something for this gentleman. Preferably with an immediately available shower."

Kit smiled at Halder. "Why, thank you, Captain."

Kit might be the spook from hell, but her smile could charm even an old squid like Halder. He smiled back.

Kit said, "On the subject of accommodation, could you separate the animal and the kerosene bladders? He doesn't like the smell."

Halder's smile vanished and he stiffened. "Ma'am, the bay's the only space aboard big enough to hold our legitimate cargo and yours."

Kit nodded, and Halder smiled again. I think she served up the last demand so he could smack it back and feel good. I knew she was tough, I knew she was smart, I knew she could be funny. Now I knew she could be diplomatic. Each new side of Kit Born that I saw I liked. The beauty of a multi-jump cruiser trip was that I'd get to see even more of her, especially if we shared a cabin.

Ten minutes later, a steward led us to our quarters, Kit first, then me.

Unlike most of the great and aging cruisers that linked the worlds of the Human Union, the *Midway* didn't see action in the War. On the ways when hostilities ceased, she wasn't even commissioned until two years later, the last ship built before the vast shipyards of Mousetrap closed down.

Combat configured, a *Bastogne*-class cruiser like *Midway* could bunk a ten-thousand-soldier embarked infantry division, in addition to its own crew.

But on peacetime runs to the far outworlds, passengers were scarce. On the outbound legs, cruisers carried manufactured goods to build up the outworlds. On the inbound legs, the cruisers carried to Earth stuff like Weichselan diamonds, which made sense to me, and kerosene, which didn't. Apparently Trueborns found kerosene too environmentally noxious to refine at home, but so valuable for charming mood lighting that they would overpay for it. The 'zines called the system commercial symbiosis. I called it neocolonial exploitation.

So the troop spaces of warships like *Midway* were reconfigured. She was like a wet bottom tramp steamer, with space for her crew, which was military, like Kit, and separate space for a handful of civilian passengers, into which I would have to fit. There was just one billet available for Kit, sharing a cabin in female officer country with the *Midway*'s chief engineer.

Accommodations for the colonel's anonymous gentleman friend were less deluxe. I was installed in the only vacant passenger space, a second-class cabin. But in a cruiser's embarked division space lots of relics got left in place because somebody was too lazy to remove them. Therefore, my "cabin" was a junior non-commissioned officer's sleeping drawer that shared a sanex with another "cabin."

As a Yavi and a tanker, I didn't mind the close and spartan quarters. But Kit and I would be able to visit only in the ship's public spaces. So much for having her all to myself.

That afternoon, she invited me to lunch with her in the officer's mess. We carried buffet trays to a corner table and sat facing each other.

I raised my linen napkin. "Officers travel well. Colonel? Really? You could have told me." I wasn't really angry about her lack of candor. After all, I was a fugitive from justice and I still hadn't told her that.

She swayed in her chair. "I'm not a real colonel."

"Halder seems to think you are."

"I mean I've never commanded a brigade, or anything like that. My outfit was organized during the Blitz, before I was born. The Army drafted every civilian extra-terrestrial intelligence geek who it could find and told them to win the War. Now there's no War. My rank's more like a parallel civil service designation."

"You don't shoot like a civil servant. I just watched you fly a low orbit hypersonic like a pro. You've probably got a Ph.D. in xenobiology."

She smiled. "Master's. From Dartmouth. I'm one of your favorites, a Trueborn rich kid."

"I was a soldier because I couldn't be anything else. Why the hell are you a soldier when you could be a surgeon, or a diplomat, or a yacht racer? Or at least study planets that won't kill you."

She looked down at her tray and smiled. "My parents ask me the same thing. The Borns have never suffered the embarrassment of a common soldier before."

"I don't think you're common."

I think I made the full bird colonel blush.

I said, "So? Why do you do it?"

She shook her head. "It's a story you don't have time for."

"It's nine jumps just to Mousetrap. Time I have."

She smiled, laid her palms on the tablecloth. "Okay. There are three kinds of planets, right?" She ticked them off on her fingers. "First, Earth. Second, the Seeded Worlds—the triple handful of planets where abducted Earthlings got planted or left behind thirty thousand years ago. Third, the Outworlds."

"If I was Trueborn I'd study Earth. I hear it's nice."

She paused, smiled, then shook her head. "Too nice for me. Familiarity breeds boredom. The Seeded Worlds can teach us more, as a race. Take Yavet."

I smiled. "Thanks. I've already taken plenty of it."

"Yavet shows Earth the future it escaped. Human industrialization melted Yavet's ice caps. Oceanic encroachment reduced crop land and packed Yavet's population in so tight that being born became a capital crime."

My heart skipped. As a perpetrator of said capital crime, I wanted this topic dropped immediately. "Maybe you will bore me."

She held up a finger. "Yavet shows us what the Motherworld might have been if the War hadn't changed things. But it's hard to study because Yavet's the most self-isolated, repressive society in the Union. No offense."

"No argument."

She said, "The Seeded Worlds add to what we know. A person could spend a lifetime studying them . . . "

"But?"

She smiled. "But they're still too familiar for me. Now, the Outworlds! Parker, the Outworlds don't just add to what we know! They're everything we *don't* know! They cover more territory than the imagination can see. The Outworlds are where the action is."

"The action can kill you, though. It almost killed both of us. Now it might kill that big thing we brought with us." I twisted in my chair and stared aft and up at the ceiling. In a starship, the floors face toward space, the ceilings toward the centerline axis around which the ship rotates as it travels forward. Back in the centerline cargo bay the grezzen lay.

Kit left her homeworld for adventure. Why had the grezzen left his? I didn't believe, and surely neither did she, that he had followed us home like a lonely puppy. If he really was people-smart, was he simply intellectually curious? Was he an adventure seeker, like Kit?

He was risking a lot more and enduring a lot more than I would chasing curiosities or adventures. It seemed to me that if he was really as smart as I was, something more had to be driving him.

Sixty-eight

The grezzen lay, alone and restrained within the shell the humans had woven around him. Imprisoned deep within the vast human nest called the Midway, he scratched at a cage bar. His foreclaw easily chiseled away flakes of plasteel that trickled into a small heap on the deckplates. He brushed the flakes with his forepaw, dispersing them. If he wished to, he could scratch through the bar in seconds. Seconds, he had learned, were a way humans subdivided time.

That wasn't all he had learned. He had passed his time in this shell regaining his strength after the ordeal he had shared with Jazen in the smaller ship. Now he also sifted through the minds of the thousands of humans in this new and vast nest they called Midway. In this way he learned about plasteel and deckplates. Also about starships jumping through temporal fabric insertion points, vacuum, and Cavorite impellers. Even about jelly doughnuts, about why Machinist's Mate Yakoubian was a jerk, and about football.

In football, males hunted an animal skin, head-butting each other like bull woogs. Frequent committee meetings were punctuated by violent episodes. But a foot seldom contacted a ball. Time ran backwards. Afterward, all participants fled, and no one ate the skin.

Football, like most of what he learned about humans, mystified him. And he had no more intention of revealing that he was capable of learning it than he had of escaping.

222

Escape he rejected for several reasons.

In the first place, dissecting this cage would simply free him within the larger restraint of what the humans called the cargo bay. It was an enormous space, tubular in the way of a log hollowed by rot. It stank of kerosene, the terrifying liquid that had nearly killed him.

The remainder of the ship Midway *in which the humans nested wrapped the hollow of the cargo bay like a log's bark, and extended forward, a warren of tubes and open spaces only large enough for humans. His bulk prevented him from moving beyond the cargo bay and into those areas except by clawing through the ship. That he could do, of course, as easily as he could disembowel a woog. But if he did he would stop the ship as certainly as disembowelment would stop a woog. The area behind him was made up of larger, but sparsely populated spaces that housed the mechanisms that made the ship* Midway *move. If he escaped into the cargo bay he would simply endanger himself. If he tried to perfect his escape either forward or backward, he risked stopping the ship's progress.*

The last thing he wanted was to stop the ship. Cutler, the human who he held responsible for his mother's death, remained beyond his reach, in a separate ship. But this ship and Cutler's would ultimately reach the same destination.

There, and only there, would the grezzen escape. Then he would hunt and kill Cutler. He would also kill the humans who suspected that his race were more than simple brutes. Even Kit and Jazen, though them without relish.

For all the grezzen had learned, he remained imprisoned by the simpler paradigm of the world that he and his species knew. He couldn't understand the impossibility of his quest, or the vastness of the race he was challenging, any more than he could understand football.

This plan, and everything he had learned, his cousins knew as well as he did. Despite increasing distance, the grezzen and his cousins remained linked as immediately as they did at home.

But though his cousins knew what he intended to do, knew what he saw and heard and felt and even smelled, none questioned him or disagreed with him. How he acted was his decision alone.

None of them questioned his decision to be here, nor counseled him on future action. He was as behaviorally free from them as he was, and had always been, physically isolated from them. The grezzen did not realize that his was a truly libertarian society, albeit one facilitated by biologic accident. He didn't appreciate the irony that the human-on-human violence he had just survived was justified as libertarian.

He did realize and appreciate that he already longed to be home and free again. And he realized that the price of preserving freedom for his home and for his race might be his own life. And the lives of Kit and Jazen, and of anonymous humans from whom he had learned about jelly doughnuts.

For the next forty-two days he lay still, husbanded his strength, and allowed the ship to carry him farther from home and closer to Cutler.

Sixty-nine

Kit and I floated weightless in the rotating fifty-foot fish bowl that was *Midway*'s forward centerline observation blister while the cruiser drifted toward Mousetrap. Kit, myself, and a couple of other passengers were turning knees-tucked somersaults at the prospect of the imminent layover. A cruiser offers plenty of room and diversion to its passengers, even when freight-configured. But after forty-two days and nine jumps, leaving *Midway* behind for a few hours, even to visit the drilled-out gut of a nickel iron meteor, had people bouncing off the ceiling.

I'd shipped through Mousetrap twice as a legionnaire, but was always quartered on the windowless troop decks aft of bulkhead ninety. So on this visit my mouth hung open.

For anyone who's been under arms, it's the history, sure. First Battle of Mousetrap. Second Mousetrap. The shipyards that birthed the armada of cruisers, like the *Midway*, that had finally won the war.

But to see the twenty-mile football of a moonlet spinning slowly in empty space, silhouetted black and tiny as a peppercorn against the orange disc of the gas giant planet Leonidas, overwhelmed a Yavi who had grown up inside a layer cake.

Kit swam to me and tapped my elbow. "I thought I'd visit the museum. Maybe dinner and a holo. You in?"

I shook my head. "Seen it. Headache. Good time for a nap."

The cruiser matched rotation and lined up with Broadway, the central tunnel through Mousetrap from which radiated its ship-yards, mines and docking platforms. Then *Midway* drifted in through the end lock, and on down the fifteen miles to the south end berths where cruisers docked.

A double chime preceded the purser's voice, which echoed in the observation blister and throughout the great ship. "Ladies and gentlemen, let me be the first to welcome you to Mousetrap, cross-roads of the Human Union. If you're transshipping, follow the signs to the appropriate shuttle or hotel. If you're continuing on with us to Earth, the ship will be reconfigured here to accommo-date additional passengers, so we'll be berthed here for ten stan-dard hours. If you disembark, the Pseudocephalopod War Museum and Memorials are accessed by *southbound* transport. The captain has asked me to remind you that he is unable to assume responsibility for your safety if you elect to visit Shipyard, or the other abandoned quadrants accessed by northbound trans-port. Passengers returning from Shipyard are subject to medical screening and contraband search as a precondition of reboarding."

While *Midway* kissed its mile-long bulk up to the berth fifteen miles south along Broadway, Kit and I returned to our cabins. I lay on my bunk with the hatch open.

It would take Kit ten minutes to disembark, make her way to the transport platform, and catch a southbound to the museum.

I lay still for fifteen minutes, to be safe, disembarked, and arrived on the transport platform two minutes before a graffitti-smeared tuber whispered up. The green-lit sign on its prow glowed behind grime:

NORTHBOUND LOCAL—SHIPYARD.

The arrival chime rang, the doors squealed open, and I stepped aboard.

Seventy

The grezzen sat up in his cage when the human entered the larger cargo bay.

She pushed a rolling device on which rested two objects, in the aggregate as large as she was, as she walked toward him.

Molly the human slid a woog haunch between his cage bars, as she had each day of the past forty-two. "Extra popsicle today, ogre!" She slid a side of ribs in behind the haunch. Humans, he had found, audibilized even to inanimate objects or dumb animals, which Molly assumed he was. Of course, he allowed her to assume.

She said aloud, "Won't see you tonight."

Why not? The grezzen almost cocked his head, then caught himself. Molly was incurious for a human, but he didn't want her to wonder whether he understood her.

His anxiety rose. He reached out and felt other humans, then relaxed. No, the ship had not reached the end of the journey sooner than he expected. But it had stopped, now enveloped within an even larger hive.

"I got liberty on Mousetrap. Paar-tay!"

Molly left him alone with his meal, as she always did. He bit into the lifeless meat and rumbled a sigh. He preferred fresh kill, but could survive on rotted carrion. Actually, it wasn't rotted, though it was not fresh kill. The humans retarded the growth of unappetizing parasites by lowering the temperature of the meat. The unfamiliar coolness added a tang to the bland meals.

While he ate, he reached out to locate Kit and Jazen's threads. What he found so startled him that a rib dropped from his mouth to the deck. He had become accustomed to the thousands of human threads of consciousness in the ship, but now there were more. Many more.

Now the ship rested within a larger nest. A great sea of threads washed over him, dwarfing the thousands to which he had accustomed himself. This new nest, Mousetrap, was far larger than the Midway. Indeed, it was far larger than the nest back home that the humans called Eden.

And, from all that he sensed along the individual threads that he had studied during his journey, uncountably larger nests—entire worlds!—of humans made up the vast buzz that underlay everything that every grezzen felt every moment of every day.

His mother had been wrong. His race had been wrong. There was no containing this species. There was no competing with this species. There was certainly no destroying it. Even the idea of deceiving this species by the notion that grezzen were simpleminded seemed to grow more hopeless hour by hour.

He cast about in the vast sea of consciousness that now engulfed him. Gradually, he pieced together understanding along individual threads, by feeling and seeing through them.

The Mousetrap nest, like the Midway, was a place of human-sized burrows punctuated by grezzen-sized spaces.

Much of the verbalization he encountered in his explorations proved to be nonsense. Bills of lading led him to counterfeit bills led him to duck bills, then Buffalo Bills. He growled and pounded a paw against the deck plates.

He longed to sense the familiar, to feel Jazen and Kit. He tried to bring their threads forward out of the newly enlarged mass. But in the vast tangle of real and false human threads, he often followed false trails.

He brought forward one female's thread because the forest that played in her head closely resembled his home. Then the female, who he assumed was Kit, ingested a contaminated fruit and fell unconscious. He roared in anguish. She recovered, then sang and danced, delighting seven undersized males with whom she cohabited. He discarded the false thread.

At last the grezzen found Jazen's thread. Jazen was in motion within the larger nest, tingling with the hunting reflex, but at the same time uncharacteristically melancholy.

Seventy-one

I stepped off the tuber at Lockheed Station, in Shipyard. The basic look and smell of Lockheed Station hadn't changed in the two years since my first visit, when I was a laid-over Legion basic skinhead bound for his first duty station.

Lockheed Station was a fifty-foot ceilinged neon and steel cave hollowed out of the nickel-iron captive meteor that was Mousetrap. Music and voices echoed out of a half dozen bars, and four establishments with active picture windows offered other distractions for hire if you didn't need a drink. The crowd that boiled in all directions across the deck plates was as unruly, uncaring, and unsober as ever.

Directly across from the platform, Lockheeds' pink-and-green sign still blinked. The bar, which had once been the tank plant's cafeteria, used to be a friendly place that offered two-for-one whiskey with a Legion tanker ID. But Lockheed's had been face-lifted to attract Trueborn tourists who sought a homogenized taste of North Mousetrap. The urine on the deckplates in front of Lockheed's still smelled the same, but the customers who staggered out and deposited it were now much better dressed.

I passed Lockheed's without a glance, and turned down the first side passage. The light got dimmer and harsher and the ceiling dropped to a Yavi-friendly seven feet.

During the last years of the War, the shipyards and armaments plants of Mousetrap's north quadrants were the best places in the universe to go if you needed hardware to lay waste to worlds.

After the War ended the last ships were commissioned. The yards shut down. The generation of 'Trap Rats born in, raised in, and then left unemployed in, Mousetrap holed up in the abandoned mines, factories, and passages that laced the moonlet's north quadrants. Eventually the squatters declared Shipyard a "free city." That actually meant that in Shipyard nothing was free. But everything was available, if you paid in cash. The new anarchy didn't disrupt the flow of commerce through Mousetrap's south end, so Shipyard was left to fester. Or bloom, depending on one's world view.

Shipyard soon attracted, or had dumped on it by overstuffed penal systems all across the Union, the best and brightest. Their fields of expertise ranged from prostitution to drug peddling, and bounty hunting to forgery. The hollowed-out cone that was Mousetrap's north end became the cornucopia into which a universe funneled its miscreants. Shipyard could still help you lay waste to a world, as long as it was yours.

I peered into a familiar double wide hatch. Fatso's had been named for its bouncer, but the half-empty bar no longer needed one.

Inside, the fog of second-hand janga was the worst—or best, I suppose—that I'd experienced since Second Platoon had mistakenly incinerated a Tassini drying shed with parachute flares.

I stepped to the bar, behind which a woman with middle-aged skin and teen-aged artificials raked empty bottles into a brown carton.

I cleared my throat. "Ms. Suarez?"

She held up one hand to shush me while she glared at a het couple squirming in the corner. She hefted an empty glass bottle labeled Imported True Tennessee Sour Mash that I was certain had never been within nine jumps of Earth. She flung it at them and it shattered on the rough iron wall behind them. "Do him in the john, honey!"

Fatso's prided itself on offering a higher class experience than most Shipyard bars.

She turned back to me and frowned. "Nobody's called me Suarez in a while." She smiled. "But I can be anybody you want."

I took a breath. "You probably don't remember me—"

She raised her palm, shook her head. "Repeaters same price."

"I was a friend of Hector's."

Her face fell.

I swallowed. "I was there. He died a hero."

Suarez' mother stared down into the box and slammed another empty into it while her eyes glistened. "Heroes don' die fighting other people's wars."

She stared up at the crusty ceiling. "He was a good boy. You know?"

I blinked back tears, myself. "I know."

We stood there listening to music thump down from the ceiling. Somewhere in back of the bar, a toilet flushed.

She wiped her eyes with the heel of her hand, squinted at me, then nodded. "I remember, now. Jazen, is it?"

I nodded back.

"The Yavi Illegal?"

Crap. I had been drunker than I thought when Hector had introduced me to his mom.

She nodded. "Ah. So when's your drop-dead date?"

The only thing more routine in Shipyard than a fugitive from sobriety was a fugitive from justice.

I whispered, "April twenty-ninth." When I said it out loud, it seemed closer. I shuddered.

"And you came in here looking for a hub scrub?"

I looked around the bar. Nobody was paying attention. "I thought you might know somebody."

"Honey, I know everybody. You got cash?"

"I will have. I'll be back through here well before the twenty-ninth."

She scribbled on a cocktail napkin and slid it across the bar. "This guy can hook you up."

A drunk staggered up from a table and tapped his empty glass on the bar. As she turned to take his order, she said to me, "Jazen? Don't be late. And thanks for coming in. I miss him."

"Me, too." I turned, walked out the hatch and back to Shipyard Platform.

Mothers and sons shared the same something everywhere in the universe.

I glanced at a bar down the platform, then at my 'puter. Still eight hours until *Midway* closed her hatches. I'd go have one whiskey. For Orion. I had all the time in the world.

Seventy-two

The grezzen felt Jazen as the human sat in a dark and noisy space drinking tiny containers of a bittersweet liquid that dulled his consciousness and made his vision blur. The human stared at a tiny image that glowed from a box he set on the table in front of him. The image was a female whose tufting bore the grayness that marked human aging. Orion. Jazen identified it as his mother. Orion was not the female who bore him, but she had raised and taught him.

The situation was not unheard of among grezzen. A female might perish, or suffer injury or illness.

The grezzen had never reflected on human upbringing. They existed in roiling hives, like the nest within a nest within which he presently found himself. So he had assumed they were raised communally, like larvae in a log.

The grezzen had felt emotion well up during Jazen's visit to the birth mother of the dead human, Suarez. Jazen's emotion had momentarily replicated what Jazen now felt for Orion. The grezzen retrieved the ongoing thread of the female, Suarez, curious.

She remained in the dark place where Jazen had sought her out, but spoke audibly to another, who had not been present during Jazen's visit.

"Petey, I got a job for you. Tube over to the Nasty Nurse. This time of day you should find a guy at the third table from the corner on the left side." She extended a forelimb. "Give him this note. Tell

232

him the guy's an illegal whose drop dead date's comin' up fast. And tell him this tip squares us. I don' owe him no more."

The prepubescent male called Petey wagged its head up and down. Then it audibilized. "How will I know it's him?"

"They don' call him One-eyed Jack for nothin'."

The grezzen leaned back and scratched its jaw with a forepaw. The female called Orion had clearly accepted a transferred bond from Jazen's birth mother. The female, Suarez, had also seemed to feel a tender bond toward Jazen.

But as she contemplated the task she had set to the prepubescent male, Petey, Suarez didn't project tenderness. She projected guilt.

Seventy-three

Three lines had swollen up in front of the *Midway*'s boarding hatch by the time I got back. The longest line was for transfers from other ships and for Mousetrap locals boarding for the first time, who had to go through ID vetting and carry-on bag inspection.

Reboards from the clean, touristy south destinations just got their passes scanned and walked aboard.

There weren't many of us reboarding from the north. But our line moved slow, because we got scanned for sexually transmitted diseases, and searched for weapons and dope. I shuffled forward, my head pounding. It had developed into more than one whiskey.

Something poked my back, and I stiffened.

"You don't look like the headache got better."

I turned and saw Kit beside me, a duty-free bag dangling from one hand. I said, "I stepped out for a drink."

She leaned close and sniffed. "Several."

Good. She didn't suspect that I'd done more than I had just said. I hated withholding the truth about my status from her. But if Orion had taught me anything, it was that Illegals told nobody—nobody. On the other hand, I had apparently outed myself to Suarez and his mother a couple of years ago, in a drunken stupor, and that indiscretion hadn't come back to haunt me.

Kit said, "Well, if you're feeling better later, we could have dinner. Captain's mess. My treat." She stepped across to the line waiting at the reboards portal.

I fingered the cocktail napkin with the ID doctor's name on it that honesty, rather than deceit, had just bought me.

I was almost home free. One of the things that made Mousetrap the crossroads of the Union was that Earth was only one jump and a medium-short sublight run away. Motherworld-to-Mousetrap was the most traveled route in the Union, with cruisers outbound daily. As soon as we delivered the grezzen to Kit's senior spooks, and I got my bonus out of escrow, I'd grab the first ship back here, get scrubbed, and then—what?

I stared at Kit, pert and lovely in her civvies. She was a Trueborn, a field-grade officer, and had enough mysterious stroke to order cruisers around. If—if—I got scrubbed, I would be nobody. But that was a step up from being something so subhuman that it was never supposed to have been born.

They say that relationships forged during extraordinary trauma collapse when the participants wake up back in the real world, with bills to pay and toilets to scrub. But she was the best thing that ever happened to me.

She went through the pass reader, then turned and gave me a wink and a wave before she disappeared inside the ship.

I set my jaw, and my headache seemed to throb less. I *would* meet her in the Captain's mess tonight. I would tell her that I thought she was special. No, I would reach across the linen cloth between us, take her hands in mine, and tell her that I was in love with her. I would tell her the truth about me, and I would ask her to wait until I could start fresh. It would be like stepping out that jump door at four thousand feet in Airborne Basic, except that this time I wouldn't have a chute on. But maybe . . .

The throbbing that had been in my head shifted to my chest. I shifted from foot to foot, willing the line to move faster. Didn't these people know I had an appointment to finally take control of my life?

I turned and glanced at the even slower transfer and local boarding line, thirty feet away across the platform. A guy with his back to me was checking a couple gun cases at the steward's table. The guy, who had black hair that hung in strings over the back of his collar, unbuckled a pistol belt from which dangled a flap-holstered gunpowder automatic. He got back a claim chip from the steward.

He coughed. It was a squealing wheeze. And one I could never forget. My heart skipped.

Then he turned around and faced me. A salt-and-pepper moustache curled around his lip, then dangled below his chin like grezzen fangs. He nodded while he stared right at me, then winked one eye. The other was covered by a black patch.

The two lines converged as they passed through the ship's hatch. We were fifteen feet apart, then ten, then five. My heart hammered.

He eyed me like a wolf eyes hamburger.

This was no time to level with Kit about my past. It had just caught up with me.

Seventy-four

Parker's flight reaction swelled within him as he approached another male among the mass waiting to pour into the ship. The other male was unremarkable, except for a damaged eye.

The other showed his teeth, and audibilized, "Well, well. Some days the fish jump right into the boat." The other male continued, his voice low and hissing, "I'd know you anywhere, Parker. The bitch only left me one eye to see you with, but that's just enough."

Parker dipped his head and audibled, "Jack." Simultaneously he thought, "This can't be. In a whole universe! He can't have found me. How? Suarez' mom ratted me out! It had to be. Now what? Think, Jazen!"

The two humans moved side-by-side into the movable nest.

The one-eyed male said, "Guess we part ways here, my friend. Third class this way, for poor me. Wouldn't the bitch be proud to see you up in second class?"

"If Lupe Suarez tipped you off, you know I've got Legion immunity, Jack."

The one-eyed male thought, "Not for long." But he laid a foreclaw on Jazen's shoulder. "Of course, my friend. You have a pleasant trip."

Their paths diverged. The one-eyed one moved closer to the grezzen's prison, while Jazen moved in the direction where the grezzen had last located Kit.

The grezzen found her again, and brought her thread forward. Kit was audibilizing melodically while she bathed herself. What-ever so troubled Jazen apparently did not trouble her.

The high-pitched whistles sounded again, then the great nest healed its openings again, as it did when it prepared to move through the vast emptiness.

The grezzen sifted among the human threads until he relocated Captain Halder. He had first encountered Halder when the male clashed with Kit, immediately after she and Jazen had brought the grezzen into the Midway.

Halder had proved fascinating on many levels. Though he was a male, he directed the Midway *in the way that a grezzen matriarch directed her far smaller family. Remarkably, Halder's control extended not only over subservient males, but over females.*

Halder's dominance seemed perverse to the grezzen at first, but Halder seemed to have performed competently. It had, in fact, occurred to the grezzen that there was really no reason that a male, given training and hard work, could not and should not be afforded the same opportunities as females.

"Take her out, Ms. Farini." Halder, at that moment, in fact, had delegated the complex job of moving the Midway *out of the great nest of Mousetrap to a female. Halder simultaneously directed sub-servients of both genders by spoken exchanges, manipulated so that they covered longer distances.*

"Mr. Thompson, how's my girl configured now?"

The first time the grezzen had heard Halder refer to his female, the grezzen had been confused. The grezzen could find no such female's thread. But he had come to realize that Halder was refer-ring to the Midway *as though it were a living thing.*

Humans, the grezzen found, often referred to dead things that they had constructed, and to things that moved, as though they were alive.

In this way the grezzen came to understand why the ghosts back home were deadly to his species. The humans had made the ghosts. Though the ghosts moved like living things, they were not alive. Therefore his species could not feel them. Therefore the ghosts were able to approach and kill grezzen. It wasn't humans' nature, or certainly their strength, that made them so dangerous. It was their capacity to multiply destruction.

The subservient who Halder had questioned answered, "We took on three hundred new steerage passengers at Mousetrap, sir."

"Six dormitory modules in the cargo bays, then?"

"Yes, sir."

"Are the cooks ready to feed three hundred new mouths?"

"Feed, sure. It's only a week, subjective. But the 'Trap's hydroponics were down. You know we're always heavy with Trueborns from Mousetrap to the Motherworld. They'll bitch 'cause there's no fresh fruit."

The grezzen felt irritation swell in Halder. "Trueborns. Speaking of which, we got enough of Colonel Born's cold cuts left to feed that thing that's stinking up my cargo bay?"

"We could throw it a couple Trueborns."

Halder found this entertaining. Then he said, "Seriously, it worries me having that thing aboard my ship."

"The animal or the spook, sir?"

"Stop cheering me up, Russ."

"When do you want to run lifeboat drill, sir? They all hate that."

"Right after the first Trueborn orders strawberries."

The grezzen felt no movement, but he felt a stir of activity among the thousands of humans whose activity Halder coordinated. Then the great nest of the Midway once again leapt across the emptiness. From the threads he had just felt, it was clear that his journey was approaching its end.

Once he reached the human Motherworld, he would find Cutler.

The grezzen curled his body upon itself and willed himself to sleep, to gather strength.

Seventy-five

"This is crap!" I waved a hand at the other passengers, milling and grumbling by the hundreds around the *Midway*'s lifeboat deck.

Kit stood staring at me, arms crossed, head cocked. "It's just lifeboat drill. What is your *problem*, lately, Parker?"

I drew a breath, blew it out. My problem was that I was short.

The problem itself was, I suppose, common among soldiers since Hannibal's first elephant driver approached the end of his hitch. But the expression originated among conscripts serving in a proxy war between one of the seminal Trueborn democracies and some competing totalitarian ideology. The unfortunate neutral site (smart ideologies break other people's furniture, not their own) was called Vietnam.

Short was a state of irrational, pugnacious risk aversity. It was induced by surviving most of one's time in hell and not wanting to have the world screw it up in the last couple weeks. Short soldiers ducked hazardous duty, slept in flak jackets, snarled at anyone who got too close to them, and were huge pains in the ass.

I tugged up my sleeve and read my 'puter. March 21. I had thirty-eight days remaining immunity. Per the purser's office onboard, Cutler's bonus to me had cleared escrow. Too small for him to notice and revoke, but everything in the world to me.

I had been a felon under summary death sentence since the day I was born. Now all I had to do was get to a bank on Earth, with a retinal scanner and a teller that dispensed clean Trueborn dollars.

240

I might even find such a bank in the New Denver Terminal. Then I would book a return trip to Mousetrap. The cash would buy a Shipyard ID scrub, a first-class one, complete down to bone-deep alteration of my Legion tatt.

Thereafter, my corpse wouldn't be worth a Weichselan franc to a bounty hunter. I would be just another broke legal, but for the first time in my life I wouldn't have to sleep in a mental flak jacket.

No bounty's paid on an immune. So even though Jack had me penned up here aboard the *Midway*, killing me now was a businessman's worst nightmare, unprofitable. But knowing that the clock was ticking while he was on my ass didn't make me a smaller pain in Kit's.

Ten feet from us, in front of one lifeboat hatch, six Trueborns linked arms and started singing about how they longed to rest their eyes on the fleecy skies and the cool green hills of Earth. The ship's speakers had begun playing the song before morning announcements. Apparently, it got played daily on the Mousetrap to Motherworld run. I hadn't been so ready to vomit since the grezzen had spewed on me in the shuttle's cargo bay.

I pointed at the singing Trueborns and rolled my eyes. "If they assign us to that lifeboat, I'll just go down with the ship."

Kit gave me a smile so beautiful that I ached. "Lighten up, Parker. They're just glad to be going home. And the sky really is fleecy and the hills are green."

She took my hand in hers, traced the finger of her other hand up my forearm. "I can show you. I know a beach place in the Caribbean."

I pulled my hand away. "Not now."

Her forehead creased and I read hurt and incomprehension in her eyes. "Now more than ever. Now, finally. We hand off the grezzen to my boss in New Denver. I've got accumulated leave. You're discharged with a bonus." Her voice dropped and so did her eyes. "I thought that you . . . "

I did. More than anything in the world. But a Yavi who didn't have the right to be born couldn't tell that to a Trueborn colonel with a master's degree from Dartboard.

"Look, I just have some things I need to take care of."

"Let me help. Just tell me what—"

Tell her I was a capital felon? And that I had concealed my rap sheet from her since the day I met her? Now, there was a way to begin a relationship.

I raised my hand. "Spare me your Trueborn condescension."

Her eyes narrowed. "What in the hell are you—? I thought I knew you."

"Well, you don't! Maybe that's best." I turned away so she couldn't read my eyes.

A purser's mate stepped up to me, chipboard in hand. "Sir, I need you to stay in line."

I stepped out of line, instead. "Better?"

He stared at me the way I would stare at a Trueborn. "You have to have a lifeboat assignment."

I stalked back toward Second Class, pointing over my shoulder at Kit. "Put me in the one that's furthest away from her!"

Second Class has several bars. I spent the next six days hiding in plain sight in them, uncommunicative and alone with my misery. The purser herself tracked me down in one. She patiently explained lifeboat safety. She politely told me how her assistant was just doing his job. I was a complete dick with her, too. She entered a note on her chipboard, which I imagine read, "Complete dick. No lifeboat."

Finally, I decided to spend some time with the only person aboard the *Midway* who was more uncommunicative, alone, and miserable than I was.

And he wasn't even a person.

Seventy-six

The sleeping grezzen opened his center eye when he felt a human enter the cargo bay.

Jazen said, "When we land, you and me will go knock back a few."

Jazen's system was depressed, his reflexes slowed. The grezzen had learned this was symptomatic of knocking back a few.

Jazen had been the first to visit him here in his prison, shortly after the two of them had been so uncomfortably confined in the small shell. Jazen had used a snakelike apparatus to spit liquid through the cage onto the grezzen's body. At first the grezzen had recoiled, horrified, thinking the liquid was kerosene. In fact, it was warm water mixed with a surfactant that cleansed his fur of the filth to which they had both been subjected, and it felt wonderful.

The episode had ended when other humans native to the Midway discovered them. Jazen was restrained, until Kit chased off the other humans.

Now the grezzen sat up as Jazen approached.

The little human sat on a small rack in front of the grezzen's cage and said, "Came down to say goodbye."

The grezzen understood that soon the Midway would descend into an uncountably vast nest of humans. Somewhere among them Cutler lurked, and so did the grezzen's moment of revenge. All that the grezzen had endured he had endured in anticipation of that *moment. Yet he would miss Jazen. Not his thread, which the grezzen could touch from anywhere. He had grown fond of seeing and hearing, almost of smelling, Jazen, as he had of Kit.*

The relationships were, however, what humans called one-way streets. He continued to withhold his consciousness from them. It was no longer just a matter of protecting his race. He had persuaded himself that if he did not reveal himself to Jazen and to Kit, if they merely believed and suspected, he would not be obliged to kill them.

At that moment a double chime echoed throughout the cargo bay, and a human voice said, "Ladies and gentlemen, we'll be landing in New Denver two minutes ahead of schedule, in six hours and twelve minutes. Our approach takes us over the North Pacific Ocean and American end of the Rocky Mountains, and views should be spectacular. Dining and shopping facilities will close in one hour, in preparation for arrival. If you're unfamiliar with C-drive vessels, our descent will be imperceptible, but you will be required to return to your berthing deck at that time to assure proper passenger distribution to lifeboats in the unlikely event of . . . "

At the mention of lifeboats Jazen muttered something and sighed. The grezzen understood the disagreement that had separated his two humans. It made the grezzen's silence more difficult to maintain, because he knew that both were miserable without the other. He could fix things with a few thoughts to each.

The human voice continued, " . . . and we've just passed within the orbit of Luna, so we're now on Earth Standard time. If you would like to reset your 'puter, the local time at New Denver is ten twenty-three A.M., *April 30, 2108."*

Jazen stood, and the grezzen felt alarm and fear spike through the small body.

Jazen thought, "My immunity expires April 29, 2108."

The grezzen watched Jazen snatch at one forelimb with the other, then squint at the little ring around his claw. He said aloud, "March 28, 2108." Jazen exhaled. "I must have misheard her."

At that moment, Molly, the human who brought the grezzen his meals, entered the cargo bay, pushing the cart that held his food.

She showed her teeth at Jazen. "Mr. Parker. Lookin' forward to the fleecy skies and cool green hills?"

"Molly, what's the date?"

She turned her forelimb. "Let's see. I just reset my 'puter. April 30, 2108. We always lose a couple days time dilation Mousetrap to Motherworld."

The grezzen felt Jazen's heart rate increase. "A couple days? My 'puter says it's March 28!"

"Well, yes, sir. Almost nobody makes ten back-to-back jumps like you and Colonel Born just did. You've easily lost a month and a half." Molly showed her teeth again. "Bad news, you maybe missed somebody's birthday. Good news, now you're a month younger than they are!"

Jazen's shoulders sagged, he sat again, and thought. "How stupid can I be? Getting a theoretical month tacked on to the tail end of my life by time dilation always seemed as irrelevant as prescription drug coverage. Now—"

"Mr. Parker? You alright? I—"

Jazen waved a claw at her. "I'm fine, thanks, Molly."

She left the cart alongside the grezzen's cage and stepped back toward the hatch. "You're sure?"

Jazen nodded, and she left Jazen and the grezzen alone in the cargo bay.

Moments later, the grezzen felt another human presence close by.

Seventy-seven

Clack.

I winced without thinking. The sound of an automatic pistol slide chambering a round is a sound no GI who has heard it mis-identifies.

Twenty yards away in the cargo bay, One-eyed Jack sighted along the barrel of a gunpowder automatic pistol he steadied on me, two handed.

Jack lifted one hand off the pistol, and tapped a finger on the 'puter strapped to his opposite wrist. " 'puter running a little slow, Parker? Mine's on the money. So to speak."

He rewrapped his hand around his pistol, slid his finger onto the trigger, and shuffled toward me.

I stood and raised my hands.

Jack flicked his head at the grezzen. "What the hell is that?"

"Friend of mine. Don't piss him off."

Jack smiled. "Bet I would. If he knew what I'm thinking."

"He does. He reads minds."

Jack poked the pistol forward. "Read this, wise ass! It's easier for me if you walk off this ship. You fetch the same price if I turn you over alive as dead. But keep smartin' off and I'll shoot you now, and carry you off. All it is to me is a weapons violation fine."

"Why are you here now, then? Why didn't you just follow me off the ship?"

"Competition. In my business, the early bird catches the Illegal."

To our left, something rumbled.

Then plasteel squealed, as the grezzen pushed apart its cage bars like they were taffy, thrust a paw between them, and slapped at Jack.

Jack leapt back. "Holy shit! Holy shit!" He fired at the grezzen twice.

While Jack was busy, I ran. I had one foot through a man hatch in the cargo bay bulkhead when I looked back. The grezzen was completely out of the cage now, on all sixes, snarling down at Jack, who lay on the deck, squirming.

Jack fired one round at the grezz, point blank. Then Jack scrambled to his feet, chased me out the hatch, and fired another round that spanged off bulkhead steel six inches from my ear.

I ran for my life.

Seventy-eight

The grezzen, alone and free in the cargo bay, retreated as six times six humans, perhaps more, entered the space and rushed at him, stingers crackling. These were the hard-shelled strain of human that had surrounded him when he had entered the Midway.

As he backpedaled, he tried to think. He could simply stand still. These little stingers wouldn't harm him, and the hard shells were disciplined, pragmatic little things. Eventually they would calm down. But the cage that would replace the one he had just destroyed would be as strong as the one in which he had almost burned alive back home. There would be no escape, no pursuit of Cutler.

Despite the damage to his plan, he still felt that his reflexive intervention to prevent Jazen's death had been unavoidable, and not even inconsistent with the role of beast that he was playing. But it had complicated matters without advancing his cause. Slaughtering these humans would make matters even worse.

He continued backing up, through a series of tubular chambers of decreasing diameter, until he could retreat no further.

Now what? These humans were subservient to Captain Halder, who always seemed to know what was going on. He sifted threads, searching for Halder's.

Three of the humans in front of him brought forward a larger stinger, one with attached legs. Why, among all the human apparatus he had seen recently, did it look familiar?

Then he found Halder's thread, and brought it forward. Halder's heart rate was elevated, and he was moving quickly for an elderly human, so he puffed as he spoke aloud. "What's up, Russ?"

"Sorry to wake you, Sir. Firearm discharge alarm aft."

"False, I hope? 'Cause I'm tripping over my pants running for the bridge."

"Keep running, sir. A passenger got hold of a checked weapon prior to disembarkation."

"How the hell did that happen?"

"Convinced a steward that a pistol case was a camera bag. Said he wanted to take a picture of the Moon as we went by. Sir, I had the Marine detachment armor up on the move. They're engaged back there now."

"Good boy. A hard-shell platoon to take down one nutball may be overkill. But there's no such thing as overkill where my ship's concerned."

"Uh. It's not the shooter they've engaged. The animal's loose."

"What? Has it killed anybody?"

"Apparently not yet. The animal's too big to enter the populated spaces forward. The Marines've forced it aft, into the engineering spaces. When it's cornered inside the starboard impeller boom, they'll kill it."

"What's Colonel Born say about that?"

"Dunno. We paged her. No response yet."

"She said that thing eats small arms rounds for breakfast."

"I remembered. When the Marines drew armor, I had 'em draw a rocket launcher, too."

There was a long silence. Then Halder said, "Russ, your first posting was internal security officer aboard the *Iwo Jima*."

"Boo-yah, sir."

"How could a terrorist bring down a cruiser?"

"Sir, a terrorist couldn't. A Bastogne—class can take any punch. And this guy's a goof, not a terrorist."

"Hypothetically, then."

"Hypothetically? Sever a cruiser's impellers and it flies like a brick. Actually, just cut one boom and residual momentum would snap the other one like straw. I suppose a small explosion in a confined—oh, Jesus!"

"Russ, freeze those jarheads! Now!"

The humans in front of the grezzen did, indeed, have jars covering their heads. The grezzen recognized the stinger. It was the kind that had killed his mother. The jarheads intended to use it to kill him, and based upon Halder's extraordinary anxiety, that would be a very bad thing.

The grezzen crouched and watched the three jarheads manipulate their stinger.

One said, "Fire!"

The grezzen leapt over their jar heads, landed beyond them, and ran forward, into the larger chambers through which he had retreated.

Boom.

A flash brighter than a lightning strike bloomed. He turned as he ran, and saw a great black void open behind him. A maelstrom sucked him back toward the void, so violently that he was forced to dig his claws into the deck plates to arrest his slide. The jarheads tumbled like insects on the wind, and vanished into the blackness.

Then a great door behind him contracted the way a prey animal's eye did when exposed suddenly to bright light, and closed out the void.

Calm and silence surrounded him. He found himself once again alone in the cargo bay.

He found Halder's thread again.

The Captain said, "Oh, shit."

Seventy-nine

I ran through the deserted passages that honeycombed the aft engineering spaces until I dead-ended against the outer hull, in the circumferential passage of the aft portside lifeboat deck. I looked both ways. Nothing. There was never a purser's mate around when you needed one. The low lighting reflected from cold rows of hatches that had once led to lifeboats for an infantry division that wasn't here.

Jack staggered into the lifeboat deck, wheezing, his shirt sweated through, but his gun aimed at my chest.

I had counted four shots, and his automatic held nine, even if he hadn't reloaded.

I said, "Smoking'll kill you, Jack."

"You wish, you little prick. You'll pay—"

A deep and distant groaning vibrated the deck beneath our feet. Suddenly, I felt lighter. That meant that the *Midway*'s rotational gravity had decreased, which was bad. Or something had interfered with the main impellers, and the whole gravity cocoon had gone south, which was far worse.

Red lights flashed above all the lifeboat hatches, and the alert klaxon hooted.

The purser, the one to whom I had been a dick extraordinaire about lifeboats, voiced over the klaxons.

"Ladies and gentlemen, we have encountered mechanical difficulties. Captain Halder has requested that you move calmly, but

251

immediately, to the lifeboat station nearest you. Please do not, I repeat, not, try to reach your assigned station but proceed to the nearest available boat, and await assistance from a uniformed crew member."

Crap. It was worse. The purser was blowing off assigned lifeboat stations. That meant that whatever had gone wrong, it was going wronger fast.

Jack coughed, and raised his eyebrows. "Goddamn!" He paused, his only eye wide. Then he waved his pistol at the hatches that stretched to our left and right. "Lucky us, Parker. You and me got lifeboats out the ass. All we need's a uniformed crew member."

Something else groaned, then there seemed to be a great snap, and the *Midway* shuddered. Objects a mile long seldom shudder.

I pointed at the hatches. "Jack, the embarked infantry used to bunk back here. About twenty years ago. You think there are still lifeboats behind those hatches?"

He paled beneath his beard, then he stood and waved his pistol barrel to march me ahead. "Then we go forward. To the front of the ship. We know there's boats there."

I shook my head and stayed put. "Those groans? Hull breaches. There's probably sixteen decks between us and the nearest functional lifeboat station. Every hatch in every bulkhead in every deck on this ship locked down automatically at the first pressure drop. We can't get anywhere that'll do us any good."

His jaw dropped. "Son of a bitch."

The purser's voice came on over the klaxons again. "Ladies and gentlemen, if you haven't boarded a lifeboat at this time, please board any available boat. Family groups may have to separate, but there's plenty of room." She spoke slowly, but her voice was an octave higher.

I stepped to the nearest hatch, scrubbed years of grime off its inspection porthole, and peered out. Where there should have been the ass end of a lifeboat there was only an empty tube that led to black, open space.

As I watched, a red spark flew past the opening. The *Midway* was already skipping across the thin upper wisps of the Earth's atmosphere. It was free falling so much faster than the speed of sound that friction was spalling red-hot steel bits off the hull. As the dead ship dropped into thicker air, it would arc across the fleecy skies as a streak of flame, then strike the cool green hills of Earth in the biggest explosion Trueborns had seen since the War.

I stepped to the next port while I pointed Jack in the opposite direction. "Start checking those other ports. And pray somebody was too lazy to scrap every one of the boats that used to be in these bays."

Eighty

The grezzen felt an upwelling of panic, the sort he felt when woogs were stampeded by his scent. The panic shuddered the thousands of threads of the humans with whom he now rushed through space. He understood that the jarheads had inadvertently wounded the Midway. But he didn't know what that meant for his future. Or for the futures of Jazen and Kit, an ungrezzenlike concern that he now found entirely natural.

He sifted until he found Kit's thread. She was trapped in a mass of humans moving in one direction, while she struggled to move in the other. One of the others wept.

A male thrust his foreclaw against Kit's shoulder.

Kit said, "Let me go!"

"Ma'am, get in the boat."

"There's somebody aft."

"I'm sure they just boarded another boat. There's plenty of capacity. You really need—"

Kit folded a foreclaw and struck the male with it. "I'm not taking your word for it!"

A second male seized Kit's opposite shoulder. "Colonel Born?"

"Tell this clown to let me go aft, Lieutenant!"

"Ma'am, every hatch aft of us is locked down. There's no way to get back to the animal—"

"It's not the animal who I'm—"

"—And they've killed it by now, anyway."

"What? No!"

"Went rogue back there."

"That's ludicrous."

"Certainly, Ma'am. In the boat. Now."

"Get your hands off me, you fucking squids!"

The two males hurled her into a small space, then sealed her in with several other humans.

Kit's irrationality confused him. She usually made sense.

Halder, also, usually made sense. The grezzen sought and found Halder's thread.

"All the boats are loaded, sir. Including this one. But I'd prefer to be on the bridge with you, Captain."

"And I'd prefer you to be right where you are, Russ. As I recall the chain of command, Captain's preference wins."

"Then you should be in a boat, too. Sir, you can't steer a flaming rock. With respect, going down with the ship is old school crap."

"I'm not staying for show, Russ. If one system on a B-class is over-engineered, it's the auxiliary electrics. This thing'll be in pieces on the ground and the lights'll still be on. If I vary the aerodynamics by opening and closing the docking bay doors, I can steer. A little."

"Sir?"

"I may be able to hold her stable 'til all the boats are clear. Then skid her down on the oblique someplace out in the middle of nowhere. That beats auguring in on top of downtown Seattle. Old school can be a pretty good school, Russ. Remember that when you get your own ship."

Halder and the younger male were silent for a time.

Then Halder said, "Hull temperature's rising. All boats. Prepare for release on my mark."

The grezzen's heart beat twice.

Halder said, "Mark!"

The grezzen physically felt hundreds of tiny shudders through the Midway's hull, and felt thousands of anxious threads recede as they fell away from him.

Halder's thread remained serene, and focused on manipulating the Midway's travel through the sky, though it was now apparent that he was soon going to die. Halder could have left the Midway along with the others. For such a self-absorbed species, humans could be so selfless.

Selflessness was so ungrezzenlike. But the grezzen thought that perhaps it could be a good thing.

Now the Midway *began to shudder and buck in the way that the ground could shake if lightning struck close by. Also, the walls that confined him began to radiate heat.*

He reached out and found the threads of a handful of humans, not those who had been within the Midway. *They rode atop a shell that bobbed upon blue water, many human miles below him. Through their eyes he saw the* Midway, *and so, in a way, himself. The ship boiled high above the humans, across a sky without clouds, that was the color of the water. The* Midway *had become a flaming streak, moving so fast that the thunder of its passage arrived only later.*

One of the humans on the water whispered, "Madre de dios!"

The warm walls around the grezzen glowed red, and then white, and the air became hot as he breathed. Heat expanded metal, and he heard bulkheads groan and metal creak and tear. Electrical conduits twisted and sparked.

Something else had changed about the air that surrounded him in the cargo bay. It was filled with smoke.

Kerosene poured from one of the ruptured vessels in the cargo bay. Sparks ignited it, and fire swept toward him. He retreated until he was backed up against the elevator shaft that led back to the docking bay through which he had been brought aboard the Midway *so long ago.*

He turned toward the shaft and began tearing at its steel wall, seeking any escape from the encroaching flames. The roar of the fire, and of the Midway's *passage across the sky, increased to thunder.*

The more he tore at the steel, the weaker he felt. It troubled him that he was about to die not proudly, but in panic like a stampeded woog.

Finally, consciousness slipped away.

Eighty-one

The great ship was still, and the grezzen found himself alive within it. There was no fire.

He didn't know that he had saved his own life. In his panic, he had torn open an elevator shaft that led to a docking bay that Captain Halder had opened to the atmosphere. In this way he had slewed the Midway *onto a new trajectory, toward a landing site where it would do less damage.*

The open path that the grezzen had opened between the cargo bay and the virtual vacuum of Earth's ionosphere had depressurized the cargo bay and starved both him and the fire of oxygen. That, in turn, had rendered him unconscious and snuffed out the fire.

He felt for Halder's thread and felt it faint and near. Then it ebbed and died. The grezzen felt no other living threads within the Midway.

The other factor that had saved the grezzen's life was the sheer strength of his body, a physicality that neither Halder nor any human shared.

The crash taught the grezzen one more lesson about the differences between humans and grezzen.

He was strong of bone and muscle and so he had survived the great crash. Humans were weak, yet nearly all of them had survived, too. They had compensated for their weakness by communal

257

cleverness, and by the sacrifice one of their number chose to make for the rest.

Now, alone in the great ship, he was enveloped in steel and in total darkness, and he knew that the Midway *had fared more poorly than he. The cargo bay's collapsed bulkheads pressed against him, but he peeled back the sheet steel as a yearling would shrug off a moss blanket. Then he clawed and dug through twisted girders and hull plate until he encountered the outer hull panels. When he slashed an opening in the panels, they tumbled away.*

He peered out and saw that he was a body length above the ground. At least, he presumed it was the ground. It was pure white. It stretched away, featureless and as flat as a lake, toward a dim, blue sky horizon.

He leapt the body length to the ground and sank to the first joint of his limbs. The ground had less substance than river sand, than water, than moss. And it, like the air he breathed, imparted a curious feeling, like wading a stream, but more intense. Similar to the sensation of mouthing the meat his jailers had offered.

He swatted at the ground with a forepaw, and it exploded and sparkled in the light.

The grezzen had never known a temperature of less than fifty degrees Fahrenheit, so snow was a mystery.

As he watched the particles adrift in the air, something appeared on the horizon, gliding through the sky toward him. A gort, he thought at first. It had wings, like a gort, but it was larger, much larger. As large, in fact, as himself.

He backed beneath the wreckage, so it could not see him.

It was intelligent. He felt it speak to another.

"Kaktovik Temporary Deputy Three to Kaktovik base, over."

"This is Kaktovik base. What you got, Herbert?"

"I just earned my deputy fee, Lowell. I'm lookin' at the wreck."

"I got you on the scope two mile south of the coast and twenty mile east. I'll call it in to the Fairbanks."

The flyer's voice became a high-pitched sound. Then it said, "You ever seen a cruiser? Holy crap, she make a gray whale look small. Like a seal pup. What's left of this one's flat as a hotcake."

"You see any debris strung back southwest? FAA say when she came down she was breaking up. Dropped a junk heap six hundred mile long, from Nome up to us here."

"There's plenty junk down there."

"They say people got out in lifeboats. They should have come down along the debris field axis. You see anything orange?"

"Nope. Nothin' movin' around the wreck, either. I can set down on the river and take a walk round, if you want."

Walk? Ah! It was a shell with a human inside, like the flying shell that had carried him away from home. But this one was smaller.

"No. FAA says concentrate every available resource around Nome. That's where most of the lifeboats came down. You get on back here, Herbert. Big blow comin' in over the pole."

"Roger. I can see the front out to the north. Hope all those folks did come down around Nome. 'Cause anybody alive up here's gonna get a whuppin' from that storm. Kaktovik Temporary Deputy Three returning to base. Out."

The shell of Herbert turned and buzzed away and out of sight.

Silence returned. The grezzen was hungry. He was terribly thirsty, too. He reached out. Six times sixty humans clustered in the direction toward which the shell of Herbert had disappeared. A nest. Food. But the humans there would have stings. Perhaps kerosene. He wouldn't head in that direction.

In this world he felt a distant human buzz far vaster than he had ever before felt. But the only other consciousness nearby lay in the direction opposite to the debris. He felt two individual intellects. One was dull, the other rather brighter. He crawled out from his hiding place beneath the wreckage, and trotted off in search of a meal.

Eighty-two

I woke with a headache worse than any hangover, shivering. My breath puffed out as fog. I sat on the floor of the leftover lifeboat that we had found and ridden down. I was bent forward at the waist, with my wrists bound to my ankles by breathing mask cords of transparent plastic.

"Well, Parker. The sleeper has awoke." Across from me, Jack leaned against the padded inner hull of the lifeboat while he lit a tobacco cigarette with one hand. In the other he held his automatic.

From the stink and haze in the lifeboat, it wasn't his first cigarette in here. I had been out for awhile.

"Fuck you, Jack. Where are we?"

"Alive. On the ground. Someplace goddamn cold."

I dragged myself upright and peeked out the lifeboat window opposite the one Jack looked out of.

When I touched my nose to the porthole quartz I recoiled. Goddamn cold was right. If this was Earth, where were the cool, green hills? What I saw was snow windblown into shallow drifts, twisted hull plates, girders, and unrecognizable debris. Out at the horizon rested a black lump that was either the wreck of the *Midway* or a wind-scoured mountain. It was logical that we had wound up close to the wreck, because we had probably been the last boat out, and had followed the *Midway*'s trajectory.

260

This boat's momentum had probably burrowed it into the snow, its orange hull as invisible as the fire extinguisher's tank. There could be other boats buried around us, that we couldn't see. But I had seen scatter diagrams of airborne operations gone wrong, which basically described lifeboat deployment from a crippled star cruiser. If any other boats had made it down, they would probably be dispersed over an area of hundreds of square miles.

Jack tapped the boat's control panel. "Heater's gone. We stay here, we freeze and starve. Or we make for the ship. I vote we make for the ship." He waved the pistol. "My vote counts. Yours don't."

Actually, I could hardly disagree with him. A lifeboat's not much more than an upside-down, insulated bucket, with a heat shield like a ceramic dinner plate welded over the open end of the bucket. Retro rockets are strapped to the dinner plate, parachutes to the other end of the bucket. Twenty can ride, if they get friendly. They're barely more than the cans Trueborns used to lob monkeys into low orbit before the War.

And this one seemed about that old.

Jack untied my hands, rummaged in a gear locker, then tossed me an orange jacket that cracked when I unfolded it. After I put it on, he made me pull out another jacket and lay it out, so he could cover me with his gun while he put that one on.

Then he made me load my jacket's pockets and a rucksack with everything in the lifeboat that wasn't screwed down. The lifeboat radio's batteries had probably been dead for decades. But we ripped the radio loose because we might find fresh batteries in the wreck. There were rations, which have a surprisingly long shelf life if you're hungry enough, even old-school chemical flares. I sighed. Jack was keeping me alive as a pack mule. For now.

Once we got over to the ship, my utility might be ended.

By the time we were ready to exit the boat, our breath had fogged both portholes. He motioned to me to crack the hatch. When I did, wind slammed my face like a side of frozen beef. The sky had darkened.

He shouted over the wind, "Just in time. Storm coming."

Storm already here, it seemed to me.

We climbed out into the snow and started for what was left of the *Midway*.

As we trudged off, me leading, Jack following, gun trained on my back, snow cut at us blown horizontal by the gale.

Eighty-three

The grezzen bounded across the flat landscape, tracking the two nearby intelligences. They had begun to move, but slower than a grazing woog.

He knew his body well enough to know that his faculties were impaired. By thirst, most prominently and immediately. Also by hunger, perhaps by the alien absence of warmth. Perhaps even by some undefined injury he might have suffered when the crippled nest Midway had struck the ground.

For whatever reason, he felt the two intelligences that he sought in an uncharacteristically indistinct way. One of the intelligences he was approaching was wary, threatened. The other was aggressive, dominant, and quite prepared to kill. It exhibited a cold guile no simple predator like a striper did.

As he ran, his great paws exploded sparkling clouds of whiteness with each landing. He breathed in the particles suspended in the air, and their form changed. In his mouth, they turned to liquid. Water, in fact. He dropped his head into the stuff, scooped it in, and in this way drank.

The grezzen had seen fire transform rain water into vapor, when lightning struck a tree during a storm. He assembled his previous observation together with this new phenomenon, and deduced that the heat of his body had transformed the stiff water into liquid in the same way that the heat of lightning transformed liquid water into clouds.

Grezzen seldom reasoned about their world. But it wasn't because they lacked the capacity. For thirty million years they had simply lacked the need.

The stiff water yielded little liquid, so frequent pauses to slake his thirst slowed his progress. But the stuff was everywhere. His most life-threatening need, for water, was now satisfied.

Renewed, he bounded ahead, toward the two intelligences that would satisfy his need to eat.

As he ran, the wind strengthened, and bore distant gray clouds toward him from his left. He welcomed the familiar clouds as a reminder of home. But the cold that they brought with them numbed his extremities.

The ground was not entirely flat, after all. He moved up a shallow slope, crested it, then paused to drink while he peered down a shallow decline. Beyond that slope, even flatter terrain stretched to the horizon. In the distance, where the slope changed, something moved awkwardly.

Eighty-four

I stumbled forward, my eyes slitted against blown snow, bent beneath the rucksack Jack had made me hang on my back. At each step my booted leg punched knee deep through the snow, then I had to lift it and punch in the opposite foot. About every fourth step, under the weight Jack had piled on me, I stumbled. Each time, as I levered myself upright, panting frigid air and spitting out snow, Jack bitched.

Finally, he stepped alongside me, held my arm, and shoved the gun's muzzle against my ribs while we walked side by side.

I peered off at the clouds racing toward us. At this rate, the incoming blizzard would envelop us before we made it to the wreck's shelter. An infantryman in self-heating Eternad armor could survive for days in a blizzard. In aged, general-purpose survival gear, we would last hours, not days.

Eighty-five

The thing that lurched in the distance was scarcely more than a speck, black against the white ground. It seemed to have four legs. Though the grezzen still felt two intelligences, he saw only the single animate object.

However confusing that circumstance was, one thing was certain. This flat and empty place was utterly unlike the brushy forests that he had so recently thought constituted the entire world. This barren plain offered no possibility for a hunter to conceal itself while stalking prey. As visible as his prey was to him at this moment, so he would be to it. The wind was in his face, so his scent would not be carried to the prey. But the grezzen would simply have to dash forward and rely on speed and power, rather than surprise.

Normally, the long run to the kill would have been of no consequence. But thirst, hunger, and the debilitating strain of his long voyage had drained the grezzen. He could only hope that the unfamiliar creature could not outrun him once it became aware of his presence.

The grezzen gauged the distance between himself and the prey, painfully aware that he had no sense of scale against which to measure the creature's size. If he could overtake the creature, he had no idea what its speed or capabilities might be. It could be as harmless as a woog, or as venomous as a lemon bug.

He drank one more time, then plunged headlong down the shallow slope toward his prey.

Even in his weakened condition, the grezzen covered the distance between himself and his prey in a few beats of his great heart.

At closer vantage, the creature became more distinct. Its body was covered in fur, closer and sleeker than his, but of a similar shade of brown. In plan the creature's body was far more like his, thick yet elongate behind its head, rather than spindly and bipedal like humans. Like the humans, the creature had just four limbs, but unlike them it had the apparent good sense to walk on all of them. At the moment, the creature was walking rapidly because, as the grezzen had already felt, the creature already feared something even before he approached.

The creature turned its head toward the grezzen, and he felt its flight reaction strengthen. It ran away from him faster.

"Ran" was a poor description. Its limbs were flaccid and spatulate, so weak that the creature simply dragged along on its belly, not so different from the way a river snake moved when it hauled out on land.

When the grezzen came within a few body lengths of the creature, he felt its flight reaction turn to fight. It skidded across the white surface until it stopped, then turned and faced him, bellowing like a cornered bull woog.

The grezzen also skidded to a stop, and simply cocked its head from curiosity.

The creature was as large as some of the smaller shells in which the humans moved, near in size to his mother's memory of his own size as a yearling. Just two eyes stared at the grezzen out of the creature's flat, broad-nosed face. The creature's most striking features were two down-curved tusks, each as long as a human forelimb. The creature's overall appearance was pleasantly grezzenlike. And it bellowed and swayed in a display of defiance that would have made a grezzen yearling proud.

Grezzen as a race had no concept of cute, but to him that's exactly how a hauled out, bellowing, two-ton bull walrus looked.

The grezzen paused as he stared at the calf-sized animal and felt its rage. He also felt the animal's fear, because it had encountered something completely unexpected, and much larger and faster than itself.

The grezzen paused. Had he mistaken this creature's simultaneous, conflicting reactions of rage and fear for two separate creatures? The grezzen looked around. He and this animal, that he intended to make his meal, were the only objects visible for as far as he could see.

Yet the grezzen felt the presence of another hunter, quite near.

As he stood eyeing his prey, he heard a creaking, as though a storm-weakened tree, pushed by the wind, was about to topple. The sound grew louder, and was joined by additional creaks. He glanced down at his forepaws planted on the ground. Angular, black lines radiated from them, and grew in all directions.

Then the ground opened and swallowed him whole.

Eighty-six

I once heard a Trueborn complain about abrupt and violent cyclonic ice storms on Weichsel. But the Earth blizzard that now enveloped and blinded One-eyed Jack and me was no less deadly.

We staggered in the direction where we hoped we would encounter the wreck of the *Midway*. We had more going for us than blind hope, though not much more. In among the survival supplies, I had found a magnetic compass. I was pretty sure Trueborns had invented compasses, which suggested that Earth had a reliable magnetic field. According to the compass, the black hump which we assumed was the wreck lay along a line due northeast. So even though we could no longer see the wreck, we could still see the compass' face.

At least one of us could. Jack assigned me to read the compass and stumble ahead, while he covered me and followed the trail I broke.

We staggered northeast for fifteen minutes. The wind and visibility worsened until we were reduced to crawling through snow in which we sank to our elbows.

Jack, crawling behind me, grabbed my ankle and shouted over the wind. He had to pause after each sentence, short of breath. "We're going back to the boat! Wait this out."

I looked back. The wind had already covered our tracks.

"No! The boat's too small a target. In this stuff if we miss it by ten feet we'll never see it, Jack!"

It was true, but I also didn't want to try to return to the lifeboat because I knew what waited for me there. A bullet, eventually. The wreck was a bigger place. There might be survivors inside, there might be stuff inside, ergo options for me. There I might be able to think of something.

Jack coughed. "Yeah. You're right. Now we find the wreck or we die." He prodded me with the pistol, then pointed it ahead, in the direction we had been moving. "You first, Parker."

Eighty-seven

Dark water surrounded the grezzen and he plummeted downward, flailing all six limbs as he struggled to regain the surface, to breathe. The water tasted of mineral, and seemed even colder than the stiff water that had turned to liquid in the warmth of his mouth.

He had first seen snow scant hours before, yet had divined its basic nature in moments. But the concept that stiff water could coalesce and form a hard substrate eluded him. Snow-covered ground and snow-covered pack ice were indistinguishable to his three inexperienced eyes. Equally alien was the idea that ice thick enough to support a two-ton walrus would crack beneath the grezzen's eleven tons, and plunge him into the near-shore shallows of the Beaufort Sea.

The waters beneath the ice remained liquid even at temperatures below the normal freezing point of water, because dissolved salt lowered sea water's freezing point.

What it all meant was that this frigid, salty surprise was drowning him. But the salts dissolved in the sea water also rendered the solution denser. He was more buoyant than he was in the fresh water in which he often swam at home. Therefore, his struggles lifted him back toward the surface. But his head crashed against the underside of the ice. He butted the translucent ceiling, slashed at it with a forepaw, but without success.

Lungs near bursting, he saw an area of light, and kicked toward it with all six limbs.

His head broke the surface into open air, he breathed, then he looked around while he trod water. He was afloat in a pool of open water perhaps twice the size of his body. Within the pool floated chunks of stiff water. He recognized that this was the place where he had broken through the stiff water, as though he had stepped on a rotted log.

Three body lengths from the pool's edge the legless, tusked brown creature regarded him, now with more curiosity and less dread. The creature's outline had become indistinct, partly obscured by windblown flakes of stiff water.

The grezzen paddled to the edge of the pool, splayed its forepaws on the stiff water to distribute its weight, and kicked its hind legs to propel itself forward.

The tusked creature watched long enough to satisfy itself that the grezzen no longer posed an immediate threat. Then it turned and waddled away, eventually vanishing in the swirling clouds of stiff water.

Hunger pangs overtook the grezzen as his meal escaped. He realized that the creature's spatulate appendages adapted it to live awkwardly on solid ground and stiff water, but gracefully down here, in the sea. If one species lived in this water, others did too. The grezzen was accustomed to diving for meals. Indeed, river amphibians were a favorite.

He paused there, half in and half out of the water, weighing the hazards of hunting in the frigid and roofed over liquid water below, versus pursuing the tusked waddler through the fog of stiff water above.

Beneath the water, something bumped his left rear leg. The ungainly waddler's dull intellect had receded. But now the hunter's presence that the grezzen had felt before had returned.

The grezzen kicked, then felt the unmistakable prick of teeth as jaws clamped his leg, and tugged him backward.

Whatever clamped his leg represented a threat, to be sure. But it also represented food. He had already let one meal get away, and meals appeared to be few and far between in this world.

The grezzen opened his mouth, gulped cubic yards of air into its great lungs, and plunged back into the water.

Among the evolutionary gifts that had sustained the grezzen's species were transparent ocular membranes, similar to the nictitating membranes that protected the eyes of less formidable predators *like sharks and housecats. The grezzen's membranes flicked down and protected his eyes like goggles, and they enabled him to see and hunt underwater. He knew nothing about nictitating membranes. He simply knew what he saw in the dim, murky sea.*

The creature that held his leg in its mouth was of streamlined shape, with spatulate limbs, adapted for swimming. The limbs were in the places analogous to forepaws and hind legs. The form was familiar, the animal's great size and power were not. It was fully as long, nose to tail, as the grezzen, and of similar bulk. Its body was black, with white patches surrounding its eyes, and covering its belly.

It clamped harder on the grezzen's leg, then shook its head with power as great as a striper's. The animal's teeth did not penetrate the grezzen's integument. The grezzen could feel that this annoyed and puzzled the animal.

And that was the most remarkable thing about the animal. A striper, a woog, the peculiar tusked creature that the grezzen had just encountered, all exhibited a low level of awareness. In the grezzen's experience, only humans displayed grezzenlike intelligence. But this animal was more aware than prey and lower predators. In some ways it was like himself.

The grezzen didn't know that in fact he had encountered the animal on Earth most like himself. A killer whale was eleven tons of perfectly adapted top predator, gifted with more intelligence than it needed to dominate its environment. Toothed whales had ranged unchallenged throughout the environment that covered two thirds of their world for a lazy thirty million years. Killer whales organized socially into matriarchal pods, and communicated by high-pitched waterborne sound over distances as vast as those across which grezzen telecommunicated.

At the moment, however, the animal was nothing but an adversary, and one that he had to dispatch quickly, while he held his breath.

The grezzen twisted around beneath the water, then clasped his middle paws around the black and white predator's midsection.

The cetacean clung to the grezzen's leg, its teeth too soft to break through matted fur tougher than carbide steel cable, its jaws too weak to crush the dense bone and tissue beneath. The animal squealed, frustrated and puzzled, as it rolled its body in the water, trying to shake the grezzen loose.

In that moment, the grezzen felt the animal's realization that its adversary was not simply a much larger version of land animals that it hunted and devoured routinely. This was something vastly stronger, vastly stranger.

The animal's blood lust turned to fear. It released its hold on the grezzen's leg, and struggled to withdraw.

The grezzen slashed a forepaw across the animal, just below its jaws, and tore at its belly with a hindclaw.

A cloud of red blood infused the dark sea, even as a cloud of astonishment exploded in the animal's consciousness.

Another slash, lower on the body, and entrails spilled from the mighty predator's gut and drifted in the water.

The beast thrashed, rolled. The grezzen held fast, avoiding the jaws that were the animal's sole weapon.

Finally, the beast weakened. None too soon. The grezzen swam upward, clutching its prize, broke the surface, exhaled explosively, and breathed.

Then the grezzen felt another presence. Three, in fact.

Something blunt pounded his left side, another his right, so powerfully and painfully that he released the dead carcass.

Ducking back below the surface, he saw the rear limbs, joined into a single, horizontal tail, of another animal like the one he had killed, flapping as it disappeared into the murky water.

He felt the approach of his next assailant. It shot at him out of the clouded water and tried to ram his midsection with its head. He twisted in the water, and the beast brushed by him harmlessly.

The grezzen had been wrong when he evaluated the killer whale's available weapons. A killer whale pod's coordinated and multidirectional ramming, six- to eleven-ton bodies hurtling head-first at thirty miles per hour, could defeat even sperm whales, far larger than himself. Nearly as large, in fact, as the river snakes he contended with at home.

He felt a surge of combativeness. He felt his adversaries, hovering beyond his sight, preparing to rush him again. And he felt something else.

The female that had attacked him had separated from her pod. She had ventured beneath the pack ice because smooth-backed prey like seal and walrus sheltered there. They sheltered there because killer whales' tall dorsal fins dangerously reduced their mobility when they squeezed beneath the shallow sea bed and the hard ice ceiling in the shallows. She had accepted the risk because her pod was hungry and she was its matriarch.

And so he felt the outrage of her sons, who sought revenge against him just as he sought revenge against Cutler.

In their anger, they would take disproportionate risks, as he had. If he waited for them, he could slash open the gut of each of them as it passed by him.

He paused beneath the water and reflected. He had made his kill. He was out of his element, in a strange place. He was outnumbered. He was starving. And he felt something unfamiliar to a grezzen. Empathy. Empathy for fellow orphans.

Based on what his mother had taught him, he would cede the field. She had taught him to act pragmatically in all things, because that was the grezzen way.

He decided that he would cede the field. But as he decided, he realized that pragmatism was no longer all that drove him. His recent experiences, first with humans and now with these alien but kindred creatures, had begun to teach him that the grezzen way was not the only way.

While the animals regrouped, he maneuvered himself below the dead female's carcass, swam up beneath it, and pushed it with his forepaws until it slid out of the liquid water and onto the stiff water. The stiff crust cracked beneath the carcass' weight, and it slipped back into the water. He pushed again. The crust gave way again, this time more slowly.

He felt the three sons rush him again, and had to abandon his efforts while he repelled them again.

He repeated his exercise until he had pushed the carcass onto stiff water thick enough to support both his weight and the weight of his prize.

Then he lay sprawled on his belly, gasping. The wind robbed heat from his soaked body. Alongside him the blood of the orphan's mother, who would now preserve his life, ran in a small river down to the open water.

Crash.

One of the sons hurled itself up and out of the water and wriggled forward, much in the way that the river snake had hurled itself after Jazen and Kit, so long ago and so far away. The enraged male's dorsal appendage wobbled side to side above it, and its toothed jaws snapped.

He kicked the animal's black snout, as he crawled farther from the exposed water. The son slid back, its grief and frustration penetrating his own consciousness.

The episode explained why the tusked creature had displayed fear when the grezzen had first felt him. In a land where predators were otherwise unable to conceal themselves, predators could prowl unseen beneath the stiff water. Then, at places where an opening was found, they could rise up and snatch prey.

The realization that he was now in a world that he neither understood nor dominated made the grezzen feel as no grezzen had felt in thirty million years. Humble. And afraid.

He huddled alone in the darkness of the storm, cold, wet, hungry, and, most of all, far and forever away from home, and alone.

Jazen sometimes seemed to have felt that way. The grezzen reached out, searched halfheartedly among the uncountable numbers of human threads in this enormous world, and hoped to find the little human. But he did not.

There was little that the grezzen could do to improve his misery, but there was something.

He crawled through the storm to the dead animal that had so recently been a son's mother. With one great claw he peeled off a massive strip of integumentary fat, and began to eat.

She tasted awful.

Eighty-eight

We stumbled on through the howling storm, blind and weakening. I hobbled on two numb knees and one numb arm, while I held out the compass in the other. I've never been much of a land navigator. If we had drifted left or right, we might already have missed the wreck altogether. In that case, we would just wander until we died. It seemed we should have reached the *Midway* hours ago. If we had been moving for hours, which was how it felt.

I screamed over my shoulder at Jack, "I think we missed the ship!"

He didn't answer. I turned. He was gone. Lost? Passed out? It didn't matter. I was free!

I tried to crawl forward faster, to put distance between me and Jack, wherever he was. But my feet and hands were so numb that it was like trying to swim with lead flippers.

In my misery, I was enjoying knowing that I had shortened the life of a son of a bitch who didn't deserve to live.

Thunk.

Something struck the top of my head as I crawled forward. No, I had crawled into something. I thrust my face forward, and forced my eyes open in the wind. It was a hull plate, vertical in the snow. Probably just debris, but . . . my heartbeat quickened.

I pressed my numb, mittened hands along the plate until I found its edge. It joined another. I crabbed sideways. Another, then another. I pounded with a mittened fist on the plate and a hollow

276

echo came back. My heart leapt. It was the *Midway*, or what was left of her. Blankets. Shelter. Maybe even things that could make a fire.

But now what? I was probably still going to die, alone in the snow. Or maybe I would be rescued after the storm blew out.

Either way, for the rest of my life, short or long, I would live it knowing that I had abandoned Jack to die, that I was no better than Jack, or Cutler.

Orion always insisted that my parents hadn't abandoned me. I always believed her and always would. And she had spent her life saving the lives of kids like me who somebody said didn't deserve to live.

I sighed. Then I turned around and felt my way back along the hull until I returned to the spot where my tracks butted up against the hull plates. Then I turned into the wind, and crawled back, away from the safety of the wreck, along my own trail. It was already being wiped away by the storm.

Eighty-nine

The grezzen lay atop the stiff water, alongside the bloody carcass of its kill. He was cold. Though he had eaten, he felt no stronger.

He didn't realize that the number of calories required to support his gargantuan metabolism was even greater in the cold. He didn't realize that his body was chemically incapable of extracting nourishment from whale flesh, or from any other flesh on Earth.

He tried to stand, and his legs wobbled beneath him. He collapsed.

For all the things that he did not realize, he suddenly realized one thing. He was dying. Grezzen had no literature, much less a concept of literary irony. But now, contemplative in his weakness, he remarked the inversion of events that had brought him to this. He had been forced to this place by his fear of death by fire. Now the opposite of fire was killing him.

He felt his cousins, faint and inconceivably distant. But they couldn't help him, and, in the grezzen way, would not help him if they could.

Then, through the storm and through his weakness, he heard a thread, strong and close.

"Where are you?"

It could not be his cousins. It was female. In the confusion of his weakness, he thought it could be his mother, and so he reached out. "I am here."

He felt relief and excitement surge back to him along the thread. "I can help you. And you can help me. But I need your help to locate you."

Horrified, he realized that the female he felt was Kit. He had just touched her thread. He had confirmed the capabilities of his race to a human, and worse, to an influential human, who already suspected the truth, who would not dismiss his reply as a fantasy of her own mind.

She thought, "I'm flying as low as I dare in this weather, just above the coast line—the boundary between the land and the water. Are you close to the boundary? Look, there's no possibility that I'll be able to see you through this storm. And you can't see this tilt wing, either. You may be able to hear it though. It has turbine engines, so it will make the same whistling sound as our tank did. If you hear that sound, just think to me."

The grezzen heard and saw nothing, but if he had, he would not have acknowledged it. It was bad enough that now she knew. He wouldn't make things worse. He would lie here silent, and die, first.

"I know you don't want to acknowledge me. And you're so god-damn arrogant that you think you're invincible. But believe this: Your metabolic rate is extraordinarily high. Especially in this cold, you have to eat a lot to stay alive. But your body can't convert the tissue of this world's animals to energy."

He turned his head and stared at the shredded body of the aquatic predator, blood stiffening on its clean-picked vertebrae. He felt his ebbing strength, and knew that Kit was speaking, as a grezzen would of course, truth.

She thought, "No matter how much you may have eaten, you're starving. I have catalytic supplements on board that I think can help you, that can keep you alive. Otherwise, you will die."

If he survived this, he might yet find Cutler and avenge his mother. So Kit's proposition tempted him. But he had already resolved to die rather than risk exposing his intelligence and his ability to feel others' thoughts. Kit would claim that he had touched her thread, but he had learned that humans were profound skeptics. On balance, it was best to lie here and die.

She thought, "There's something else you should know. I damn near stole this aircraft because I figured that if you and Parker were alive, you had come down near the wreck. Now I don't have enough fuel to get back, and I can't land this thing in this crap without help. If you can't help me not only will you die, I will."

Her words helped him recognize the proper course. If he did nothing, he and Kit would die. The secret would be as safe as he could make it under these circumstances. The solution was imperfect. Cutler would escape retribution.

"*Goddamn it! I've bet my life on you! Say something!*"

In the distance, ragged on the wind, he heard the whistle of a human shell. This sound differed from the buzz of the shell of Herbert that he had heard before. It had to be Kit.

The sound came close, closer, passed directly overhead, invisible, then faded.

He lay still, and he felt her despair.

She thought, "*He was never there. This was idiotic. Christ, fuel's down below a hundred pounds.*"

Then he felt her audibilize, softly, though there was clearly no other intelligence nearby. "*I know this is hypocritical. But you must get first prayers like this a lot . . .*"

Suddenly inspiration came to the grezzen. He reached along her thread. "*You just passed directly above me.*"

"*What?*"

"*Moments ago.*"

"*Yeah! I knew it! I knew that was you before! I'm circling back. I'll drop flares. Red lights. If you see them, tell me where you are in relation to them. Then guide me to a flat, solid spot.*"

He heard Kit's flying shell come closer, again.

She thought, "*I only need a space maybe twice as big as you are, okay? Just so I'm not on thin ice. You understand?*"

He understood thin ice only too well, now. He wouldn't direct her to thin ice. He would guide her safely to him, and allow her to feed him. When he had recovered his strength, he would kill her brutally, in a way consistent with the behavior of a simple animal. Then he would find Cutler, and kill him in the same way. Eventually, he would die, but his mother would be avenged, and the secret would remain safe.

Above him in the maelstrom, the whistling sound changed to a cough.

Kit thought, "*Lost one engine. The other's on fumes.*"

She thought to him, "I'm dropping flares. If you don't see them, we'll both be dead soon."

That, the grezzen thought, would be true in any case. He stared upward into the opaque, blowing whiteness and waited.

Ninety

I shoved Jack's limp, unconscious body up against the *Midway*'s hull. I tried to sit him up, to keep his face out of the snow, but my hands and feet were as clumsy as clubs, and my arm and leg muscles refused to move them, anyway.

It had taken hours to find Jack, half-buried and unconscious in the snow, then drag him back to the wreck. Now I was too weak and exhausted to move left and right along the hull until I found a way in.

I tugged my mitten off, then held my bare fingers beneath Jack's nostrils. I thought I could feel a faint flutter as he breathed, but, really, my fingers were too numb to be sure.

I sat back. The hell of this would be if I had dragged Jack's sorry, frozen ass back here just so he could die beside me.

I sighed, then I rummaged in the rucksack until I found the lifeboat's first aid pouch. It proved to be pretty high-powered, more like a platoon medic's pouch. That was unsurprising because it had been packed to serve a lifeboat population of twenty people.

It took me minutes to find the pouch's HTS syrettes. That was partly because they didn't look like the modern versions I knew, mostly because my fingers barely functioned.

A hypothermic treatment syrette, like any good field med, is idiot proof. It's a fat, pressurized stab-and-click hypodermic. It injects a timed cocktail of circulation boosters, depressants and stimulants that will keep a temperature casualty in the big game until real medical help arrives.

I got HTSd during my first tour on Weichsel. The aftereffects suck, but not as bad as the alternative.

The cocktail's so strong that intravenous injection can kill the casualty. The injection has to be done by stabbing a big muscle, preferably the thigh or ass. I chose Jack's ass, in the hope that it would hurt him more, and stabbed harder than necessary. Unfortunately, he didn't seem to notice. By the time I got him bundled up again, I could barely lift my arms, much less feel any fingers at the end of them.

The storm still howled.

I sat beside Jack and rested my aching back against the hull, and hugged myself, just for a minute. A reward to myself, I supposed, for being a good guy.

If I had just left Jack to die in a cold sleep, I could have used my energy to get in out of the weather, inside the hull. Now, I had just prolonged things for us both for a few uncomfortable hours.

It occurred to me that I probably should give myself a thigh stab, too. But I was so tired. My eye lids drooped. Then I drifted off and slept.

Ninety-one

The grezzen lay in the snow, watching Kit as she struggled in the swirling whiteness that surrounded them both. Encased completely within an artificial skin the color of a lemon bug, she reclined ventral side up, then scuttled beneath the shell that had plummeted out of the sky with her in its belly. The shell's tapered form resembled that of the whale, but with spatulate appendages on both sides that apparently functioned like a gort's wings and allowed it to fly.

At least, that was what Kit said. All he had seen it do was fall from the sky, almost on top of him, with such force that it had been crippled.

She muttered, then wriggled back across the ice, out from under the damaged flying shell, and stood staring at the shell's twisted lower appendages, her forelimbs folded across her thorax. "Got the transponder and the antennae, too."

It had been so long since he had communicated with another. And her fate was not in doubt, so how much she knew of him was unimportant. He reached to her, "What does that mean?"

"That I have totaled a very expensive government tilt-wing that I signed for."

"I don't understand."

"It means I'm fucked."

"I thought that meant—"

"It doesn't. At least not in this case. Look, in your world, you know exactly what things mean. But in this one, you only think *that you know. And the difference can kill you. And the rest of your race."*

She reentered the crippled flying shell, and returned dragging a sack like a seed pod as large as her thorax. She slid it across the stiff water until it rested alongside his kill, then straightened up, panting as she stared at the carcass.

She said aloud, "Wow. I would've bought a ticket to watch that fight. Were you injured? Either by the crash or by the whale?"

"Just weak."

"That I can fix." Kit bent forward, tore open the sack with a tiny artificial claw, then sprinkled powdery bits of the exposed contents over an uneaten portion of the carcass.

She said, "We usually use this stuff to clean industrial equipment. But it should catalyze a reaction between your digestive enzymes and this animal's flesh. Try a bite.

He razored off a tissue morsel as small as Kit's head, speared the flesh on a claw, and touched it to his tongue. He growled and thought, "Now it tastes even worse!"

"It's already raw blubber. It can't taste worse. Eat up. It's good for you."

She sounded like his mother. He rumbled a sigh, then forced down a portion, seasoned with her dreadful powder. It was as large as Kit was.

She said, "Lie still. I don't have any more of that stuff if you barf it out. Give it an hour or so. Then we'll see whether it works."

He shuddered, but lay still as instructed. She returned to the crippled tilt wing, then folded her body slowly alongside it, sheltered from the wind by the shell's bulk. Only then did he feel from her intense pain. Her survival had become critical to his own.

He thought, "You are injured."

She said aloud, "Hard landing. Cracked ribs probably."

He nodded, mimicking the human gesture of affirmation that he had learned. He knew this injury. Prey animals often cracked ribs in falls, or as the result of butting attacks, like the attack the sons of this whale had just launched against him. Rib damage impaired mobility. Impaired mobility rendered a weakened animal easier prey. But as for the injury itself, most animals recovered from it. Probably she would, too.

However, sometimes the organs within the cavity that the ribs enclosed ruptured. He had often watched animals far more robust than Kit die when that happened, as their internal cavities flooded with their own blood.

Based on his brief but precarious experience in this unfamiliar world, he needed Kit alive, to assure that he would live long enough to reach and kill Cutler.

He looked closely at her. She breathed shallowly, and tiny beads of moisture leaked from her closed eyes. She was not barfing out blood, as animals bleeding internally often did. But when he felt her pain, it was disproportionate to a mere rib injury. Anxiety sped his heartbeat. He thought to her, "Is your heart broken?"

Her eyes opened wide. "What?" She wiped them with a padded forepaw. "You sarcastic asshole."

Her anger bewildered him. "I asked whether you have suffered internal injuries?"

She said, "Oh. No. At least, I don't think so. I thought you meant because Jazen may be . . . " She stopped speaking, but in her mind she finished, "Dead."

He remained silent.

She said, "You felt my emotional pain just then, didn't you? You can feel us, even if we aren't thinking specifically, can't you? Not just talk to us, feel us."

The grezzen felt hope blossom in her. She continued, "And if you can, you know whether he's alive. Right?"

The grezzen remained so weak that he could no longer separate threads. She was right. He needed to rest. So did she. There would be time enough to sort this out.

He felt the pain of her injuries and the strain of her efforts drag consciousness from her.

Then he slept, himself.

Ninety-two

"Wake up!"

The grezzen opened his center eye. Kit stood a paw stretch in front of him, forelimbs across her thorax. White stiff water encrusted her yellow wrapper, and the wind tugged and flapped it. He heard her as well as felt her, because she was shouting above the gale.

He moved a paw, and it crackled, as a bark of stiff water broke off his fur and was carried away by the wind. However, he felt his old strength returning to the limb.

Kit said, "Are you stronger?"

Before he responded, he drew all his limbs beneath himself, then stood. He lifted each leg in turn, then flexed it. Finally, he thought, "Somewhat."

"Eat more."

He turned his eyes upon the whale carcass. The wind had piled stiff water against it like sand washed down river by a flood. Kit's injured shell was similarly covered.

He stepped to the carcass and picked at it.

Kit shouted, "Can you find Jazen?"

The grezzen felt his acuity was as restored as his physical strength. There was no benefit to him or to his objectives in finding Jazen. Kit possessed the knowledge and skills that he needed.

"Well?" Kit peered up at him through a tiny transparent shield that covered her eyes.

But Jazen had often placed his own welfare behind that of the grezzen. More than that, the grezzen had felt in Jazen feelings, of affection for his mother, of loneliness, of fear, that mirrored his own feelings. It had even occurred to the grezzen that he would have someday liked to knock back a few with Jazen.

"I'll try. But I won't find anything if he is—if he is not close."

The grezzen substituted the last phrase for the word "dead." In fact, he knew full well that close or distant made no difference. He realized that he had just told less than the truth. He had done so without premeditation, and he had done so to spare Kit sadness. It was a very ungrezzenlike reflex, but a very human one.

The truth that he did not tell was that in all probability Jazen was dead. The grezzen felt that Kit knew it, too. Possibly Jazen had been alive after the crash. But as frail as humans were, and as harsh as this world was, it was probable that Jazen now lay stiff and dead and buried in cold whiteness.

He reached out, searching, with scant enthusiasm, and even less hope.

Ninety-three

Somebody poked me.

I opened my eyes, and frost crinkled off the lashes. There was nobody there.

Snow covered me like a blanket, and I couldn't feel my fingers or my toes. I turned my head and saw a mound in the snow beside me. It was somebody, but I couldn't remember who.

The wind still howled, and needled snow into my eyelids.

For some reason, it seemed wrong to go back to sleep. I tried to stand, but my legs wouldn't move. I was so tired, and sleeping was so easy.

So I slept.

Ninety-four

While the wind howled, Kit paced in front of the grezzen. She stopped, then stared up into the grezzen's eyes. "Well?"

"A flicker. No more than that. Scarcely more aware than the walrus was."

"That could be him! If he's hypothermic he can't even add two plus two. He'd be dopey. Can you tell where he is?"

"How can I express distance to you? From the burned tree to the place where I found the fat woog is not meaningful to you."

Kit raised her forelimbs and threw back her head. "I dunno. The Midway. How many times the length of the Midway?"

"The Midway as it was, or as it is?"

She cocked her head to one side. "How the hell would I know how long it is now? As it was!"

The grezzen sat back on his haunches. She was as impatient as his mother could be.

Kit said, "I'm sorry. But I need to reach him quickly. He can't survive long in these conditions. He may already have been exposed for hours. He may be injured, too."

"Seven Midways."

She folded her padded foreclaw and punched the air. "Yes!"

He canted his head. Why had she answered when no question was pending?

"Seven miles. In what direction? Just ballpark."

"Ballpark?"

290

She waved her foreclaw. "Forget it. Can you just point at him?"

The grezzen raised his forepaw toward the wreck of the Midway.

Kit nodded, then scrambled back into the mound of snow that now covered the spoiled shell that had carried her here. When she reemerged she carried a pack, like the one she carried when he had followed her and Jazen back home. She also carried coiled vines of human construction.

She said, "You've seen how quickly this environment can kill you. You can imagine how quickly this storm can kill one of us. I need to get to him pronto."

"I have seen you move. In this storm you will not cross a distance of seven Midways pronto."

"But you can."

"Easily. But I am incapable of assisting him. If I carry him back to you I may break him."

"Right. But what neither of us can do alone the two of us can do if we work together." She held up the coiled vines in a foreclaw, and they flapped in the wind. "I can rig a riding harness with these ropes."

The obscenity of her suggestion caused him to rock back onto his hind legs so violently that his hindquarters plopped into the snow. This misadventure had already forced him to endure confinement, and proximity to other individuals, and human individuals, at that.

No adult grezzen of manners would even approach another within a hundred body lengths. It was not merely vulgar, it was unnecessary.

Actual physical contact with another grezzen was beyond vulgarity. It was unthinkable, except to mate. Actual physical contact with another species was even more abhorrent, unless the animal was food. Now that he had come to regard Kit as a person, he could no more think of her as food than he could think of cannibalizing another grezzen.

"No!" He shook his head at her, as the humans did, to punctuate his refusal.

Kit nodded. "I understand. But I've risked my life for you. You know it won't hurt. Don't be a wuss."

"What is a wuss?"

"Cooperate and I'll tell you."

He sighed, folded his forepaws, then knelt and exposed his back to her. He bowed to her not because he cared to know what a wuss was, but because he cared whether Jazen lived.

Kit spun the end of one of the vines, then hurled it up and across his back. It landed on his fur like a tree snake and he shuddered, but held still. Then she crawled beneath him to retrieve the loose end of the vine.

He felt the first touch of her back against his belly hair, and it made him grit his teeth.

Kit said, "Yippee-eye-yo!"

Shortly thereafter, he bounded through the storm, chafing at the unfamiliar harness that wrapped beneath his forelimbs. Kit sprawled ventral side down against his back, gripping the harness with her foreclaws and straddling his back with her hind legs. She was, in truth, scarcely noticeable. Indeed, he felt that she was suffering far more than he, because her weight pounded her injured ribs against his broad back each time he landed.

Slowed by the lack of visibility in the storm, and by the depth of the snow, his bounds carried them at a rate of progress only equal to fifty Midways per human hour. Still he could feel her exhilaration as she clung to him.

Kit thought, "No wonder I wanted a pony for Christmas."

He had scarcely grown accustomed to her touch before the dark bulk of the Midway's remains loomed ahead in the swirling snows.

Kit said, "The wreck? He's in the wreck? Nobody could survive that crash."

The grezzen said, "I did. Jazen wasn't in the wreck when I was. I would have felt him."

"Then where—?"

"Perhaps he came to the wreck afterward, for shelter. If it was him that I felt, he is close by but he is not inside the wreckage." The grezzen began a slow circle around the base of the wreckage, stepping carefully. It would scarcely do to crush the frail body they were trying to save.

As he walked and probed, the storm abated.

They had come halfway around the wreckage, and the wind had abated, when Kit tugged on his harness. "Stop! Over there!"

As he paused, she slid down his flank into snow that reached the middle joints of her hind limbs. Then she stumbled through *the snow until she reached a mounded area alongside the hull, where a tiny patch of orange was visible.*

He trotted up behind Kit and watched over her shoulder as she pawed snow off of an orange human.

"Oh, God, Parker. Oh, God."

The grezzen could feel no life in the male.

Kit peeled off the coverings on her foreclaws, then dug tiny, shiny implements from her bag. Then she skinned Parker and poked his upper hind leg with one of the implements.

The grezzen thought. "I fear it is useless."

Behind her transparent eye shields, moisture leaked down her cheeks. "Shut up! He's gonna make it. It just takes this stuff a while to work." The grezzen felt that she didn't believe her own words. But that rarely seemed to stop humans from hoping that their words would become true.

Kit huddled close to the still body, then waved a foreclaw at the grezzen. "Get over here and snuggle up to us."

The grezzen rocked back and forth while he plucked at the offensive harness beneath his forelimbs. He looked up and surveyed the now-visible wreckage. The crumpled hull stretched away in both directions, blackened by its fiery passage through this curiously changeable sky. A human-sized cleft in the hull was visible four of his body lengths to their left. Directly above them, he saw the tear he had made in the outer hull when he had cut and burrowed his way out from the cargo bay.

Indeed, Jazen could not have been here when the Midway had first struck this place, or the grezzen would have landed on top of him.

Kit said, "We need your body heat."

The grezzen realized that her words were only part of what she felt. While she indeed felt that the grezzen's great metabolic furnace might reanimate Jazen, she also felt that the grezzen's physical proximity would heal the wound to her spirit.

He had already debased himself by allowing Kit to touch him. So, desensitized to this additional perversion, he stepped forward, then carefully bent his body to cocoon them against the cold.

He realized that he could, by a small shift of his weight, smother them both to death. But he also realized that, regardless of the sense that made, he no longer wanted to.

He settled into the snow and, along with Kit, waited and hoped.

Ninety-five

I remembered that post-HTS shock felt like the Main Battle Tank of Hangovers, combined with lingering paralysis. But I didn't remember that it smelled this bad.

I opened my eyes and saw that a tangled, brown rug covered me. Being a GI, I said what we usually do when confronted with the unknown, "What the fuck?"

It came out through my blubbery lips, "Uf ta fup?"

"Parker? Oh, God! Parker!"

I could barely feel Kit as she brought her face up alongside mine, and squinted into my eyes. "How do you feel?"

"Fupped. Fursty."

Kit sobbed, and hugged me, which I presumed meant that I was off the hook for my outburst on the lifeboat deck about a million years earlier.

The enormous brown rug that was smothering us both moved and I realized that it was the grezzen, which accounted for the smell.

When the grezzen had backed off, and sat watching Kit and me, I saw that I was lying propped against the wrecked hull of the *Midway*, right where I had been the last thing I remembered.

Post-HTS leaves you immobile for maybe an hour, then you're, as the medics say, ambulatory. Frostbitten, grumpy, and dehydrated maybe, but ambulatory. And so insanely thirsty that you think you have a mouth full of cotton balls.

Kit stepped away, then returned with an alloy bottle, from which she poured water onto a gauze pad, then moistened my lips with it.

"More."

Kit laid her palm on my chest. "Slow. You'll just puke it out. How'd you get down? Lifeboat?"

I blinked to clear my bleary eyes, then managed to turn my head side to side and look around. The snow to my left and right and to my front had been trampled and melted by eleven tons and six legs of grezzen. But all that I saw was packed snow.

I said, "Ares dack?"

Ninety-six

The grezzen watched as Kit knelt beside Parker. Her actions had reanimated Parker. That was something no grezzen could do for another. He supposed that, with the storm's abatement, he should be planning how to proceed against Cutler. And against the two humans in front of him.

He reached out casually, as if he might find Cutler.

And he was shocked when he felt another intelligence, neither Jazen nor Kit, close by.

And then it began to rain.

Ninety-seven

"Paugh!" I spit out the soaked gauze that Kit held to my lips. The damned water tasted like kerosene. In fact, everything tasted, no, smelled, like kerosene. The stuff came cascading down out of the clearing sky like a waterfall, drenching Kit and the grezzen and me and pattering down into the snow all around us.

Trueborns bragged a lot about Earth weather. How convenient to never mention the kerosene storms.

Kit leapt up, then back, and stared up at the hull behind me through her snow goggles. "What the hell are you doing?"

I twisted around until I plopped on my back into the snow, just as the kerosene rain stopped.

Thirty feet up the hull it was breached, widely enough to drive a Kodiak through. On a girder that twisted out of the breach like a pulpit stood One-eyed Jack, leaning out above us and laughing his ass off. In one hand he held a dripping utility hose, like the one I had unreeled in the cargo bay, then used to wash puke and crap off the grezzen. In the other hand Jack held his cigarette lighter, its flame flickering in the newly-still air.

Kit drew a pistol from beneath her parka, and aimed it up at Jack two-handed. "Back off with that lighter, asshole!"

Jack called down to her, "Settle down, cutie. Any of you move, or you shoot me, I drop the lighter, and you all fry."

Unfortunately, this all made sense to me. Because I had HSTd him, Jack had recovered while I was out. He had gone exploring inside the wreck. When he returned and saw that Kit and the grezzen had stolen his prize, Jack wanted me back. But he had learned that he couldn't shoot a grezzen, and that he didn't even want to get close to one. So he hooked up a hose and an auxiliary pump from the cargo bay to a kerosene bladder, then dragged the hose up to the hole in the hull that overlooked us. Then he made us all into human fire bombs, for which he could light the fuse any time he wanted to.

I tried to get up, and succeeded only in flopping onto my side in the snow.

Kit, kerosene dripping off her parka's cuffs, flexed her fingers on her pistol's grip. But she kept it trained on Jack. "What the hell do you want?"

"Your boyfriend. I got no beef with you or your big pony. Just toss your gun out into the snow, and you can mount up and ride back the way you came."

In the distance, I heard the whistle of approaching tilt wings.

Kit jerked her head in the direction of the engine sound. "Rescue, inbound. All I have to do is stand here. When those ships get here, you're done."

Jack shook his head. "I don't think so. This is a shipwreck. I can make you three part of an accidental secondary fire. Or you and the animal can leave." He flicked his eyes to the approaching tilt wings, barely visible on the horizon.

Kit said, "Look, no matter what you do with me and Jazen, don't hurt the animal. You have no idea how important he is."

Jack threw back his head and laughed. "This is like a fuckin' game show. If your boyfriend and your dog are hangin' off a cliff, and you can only save one, which one would it be?"

It wouldn't be Jack. I struggled again and got nowhere. This was my reward for saving an asshole's life.

I twisted my head toward the tilt wings. They were too distant to matter.

Knowing Jack, it was all just a game. In a few more seconds, he would drop the lighter and kill us all, no matter which choice Kit made.

Ninety-eight

The grezzen felt the human named Jack and realized that he had no intention of letting either Kit or Jazen live. As for himself, it was likely that if he leapt aside suddenly, he could escape the flames. But Jazen was immobile. He would certainly die, and Kit almost as certainly. And in any event Jack intended to kill Jazen, then trade his body for food and things that humans valued.

It would be the pragmatic act of a grezzen to leap aside and save himself. But at some point in his journey the grezzen had become something else, at least something else in the way that he thought. Not a human, certainly. But no longer simply an arrogant, self-centered loner.

The grezzen's mother would have given herself up for him, but for no other being in the world. Kit or Jazen or Halder or so many others of these peculiar little creatures would sacrifice themselves for another, even for the likes of him.

He could never return to the simplicity of the life he had left behind, even if he could return there physically. And somehow surviving for the purposes of killing Cutler, and of preserving a lie, for that is what the concealment of his race's true nature truly was, no longer seemed necessary. He had grown to trust that humans like Kit would attend to Cutler and to the defense of grezzenkind. Not because Kit was a grezzen, obviously, and not because it would profit her. But because it was right.

There was really only one right thing left to do.

He gathered himself, imperceptibly, while he measured the distance between his forepaws and the upraised foreclaw of Jack that held the small fire.

Then he sprang.

Jack had barely time to widen his eyes before the grezzen swatted the flame from him. It skittered back inside the ship, away from Kit and Jazen.

In the same instant, the grezzen's jaws closed on Jack's torso. The man screamed as his rib cage snapped and his chest ruptured..

As the grezzen felt life drain from the man, he felt him wonder, "What the fuck?"

And then, as the grezzen came to rest within the hull of the Midway, *the kerosene that soaked him from nose to tail burst into flame.*

Ninety-nine

Six days after the tilt wings picked us up and medevaced us to a place called Fairbanks, I lay in a chaise on a beach, watching the warm sun rise out of a glass sea as blue as Kit's eyes. I hadn't noticed much more about the scenery, because I spent most of my time watching Kit.

She, in turn, spent most of our time together in something called a bikini, and looked magnificent. The rest of our time together she spent out of the bikini, and looked even better.

She came out from the house, sat in the sand alongside me, and handed me coffee. "How are the toes this morning?"

"Better every day. Ribs?"

She leaned across me, kissed my forehead, and I smelled flowers. She asked, "Did I complain last night?"

I smiled, sat up, sipped my coffee, then frowned.

The trouble with perfect worlds is that they're surrounded by real ones. Kit's parents' winter place—she was in fact richer even than most Trueborns—actually had garden walls and security that kept the world, and in particular bounty hunters, out.

But I had decided that today I would get real. She only knew that Jack was some psychopathic jerk who had tried to kill me, and I let her keep thinking that. She didn't know that he had every legal right in the world to do it. I would level with her. Then I would leave for Mousetrap and a new life.

Before I could speak, she took both of my hands in hers and looked into my eyes. "Parker, I can't go on like this. After we got to Fairbanks, the people I work for found something out about you."

Crap. Orion always said it was better to admit a lie than be caught in one. "I should have told you." I squeezed her hands. "Kit, please—"

Behind us I heard a tilt wing whistle, low and with the props at landing pitch.

We turned, visoring our hands up, as it shot over the house roof, hovered, and dropped onto the beach forty feet from us. The rear ramp flicked down, and a guy in civvies, machine pistol drawn, sprang down into the landing sandstorm.

Bounty hunter! I should have anticipated that the Trueborn variety would have expensive ways of getting over walls.

I jumped in front of Kit and knocked her flat on the beach while I knelt and scooped a fistful of sand. The first rule of hand to hand combat is get a weapon. And anything can be a weapon.

She spit out sand. "Parker! It's just my boss."

Actually, it was just her boss's security detail.

I dropped the sand.

The tilt wing killed its engines, and when the sand stopped flying, a very old, wrinkled man floated down the rear ramp on a C-drive scooter, then slid across the sand to us. Kit stood, brushed off sand, then looked from him to me. "Howard, this is Jazen Parker."

He stared at me through old-fashioned glasses for longer than he needed to. "Obviously." He extended a bony hand, and I shook it. "You have no idea what a pleasure this is."

Ten minutes later the three of us sat around a table on the house veranda sipping coffee while the breeze off the sea freshened.

Howard frowned. "The only lives lost in the *Midway* crash were the marine platoon and Ted Halder's. That is miraculous. I knew Ted, so it will never be miraculous to me, and certainly not to the families of those marines. But it is miraculous nonetheless. Ted will be decorated posthumously, about which he wouldn't care. The *Midway*'s duties will be assumed by a *Nimitz* class cruiser that will be rechristened HUS *Theodore Halder*. That would please Ted mightily."

Kit said, "There was another casualty."

Howard frowned. "Ah, yes. Jackson Aldecott Poge. Licensed Independent Fugitive Detention Agent. Survived the crash, but perished in the subsequent storm. Regrettable accident. Almost as regrettable as the indictment lodged yesterday against Bartram Cutler. I would describe the government's relationship with Mr. Cutler as one of unfinished business. Your friend the grezzen certainly sees it that way."

I said, "Mr. Hibble,"—Apparently Howard had a rank, but preferred not to use it—"What about the grezzen?"

"The vets in our shop are taking credit for his recovery. But I think we all knew from the start of treatment that it would've taken more than a few gallons of kerosene and a little singed fur to keep a grezzen down." Howard Hibble unwrapped a nicotine lollipop and sucked it, then he said, "He appeared before an expedited ISPA hearing panel yesterday."

I winced. "Did he do very well?"

Howard shrugged. "Every politician in Washington thinks they read minds. A witness who actually can will always do well."

I asked, "Now what?"

"We've offered him a return ticket home on us. In more comfortable accommodations. Or in the alternative, a position with our organization. He's mulling it over. Which brings me to the purpose of my visit—"

I leaned forward, and looked from Howard to Kit. "I gather you've found out that I'm—" I swallowed, "An Illegal."

Howard said, "You mean because you were born on Yavet without a permit?"

I nodded. "That's what an Illegal is." Obviously.

Howard said, "Despicable law."

"But it *is* the law. Even here." I turned to Kit, shaking my head "I'm sorry. I should have told you. I just—"

Howard raised his palm. "Yes, that's what the Full Faith and credit Clause of the Human Union Charter says. The Charter also says that a child born to Trueborn parents is a Trueborn regardless of physical delivery venue. There isn't, never has been, and never will be, a bounty on Trueborns."

I straightened in my chair. "How nice for Trueborns. Not for the rest of us. You don't understand. I have no idea who my parents are."

Howard reached into his pocket, then slid a chip across the table to me. "But I do. Those are the results of a DNA match that was run from samples gathered when your frostbite was treated. Not that I need them. You look more like your father than he did at your age."

My jaw slackened and I shook my head. "No. That's impossible."

"I served with your father during the War. And your mother."

I turned to Kit and stared.

She said, "Jazen, the first time I met you I could see you weren't just a tall Yavi. It takes a Trueborn to know a Trueborn, I suppose. But all the rest of this was new to me, too."

I kept shaking my head. "No. Orion would have known."

Howard said, "The midwife who raised you? With five hundred planets out there, the last thing anybody expects an offworld stranger to be is Trueborn. And page ninety-six of the Human Union Charter is hardly relevant to daily life on Yavet."

"But my parents would have—"

"Your parents wouldn't have advertised their provenance. They were working on a project for me at the time."

"Were? Are they—?"

"Indecently healthy, last I heard. But it's been awhile since I heard. The universe is a big place. I ask very little of my people and they tell me less. Most of our teams prefer it that way."

I sagged back against my chair back, blinking.

Howard leaned forward. "I know it's a lot to absorb, Jazen. But here's the thing. Your pedigree intrigues me. Kit speaks highly of you, to say the least. I'd like you to consider an entry level case officer position with us."

"Entry level."

"You'd be teamed with a senior officer."

"Senior."

Kit smiled at Howard. "I think you can find one who'll take him on."

Howard patted my arm. "Think it over. Our dental plan's terrific."

I wrinkled my forehead. "My parents. They never came back for me."

"I suppose you would think that." Howard settled back in his chair, raised his eyebrows at Kit, and spun his finger at all three of our cups.

While she poured coffee, he steepled his fingers. "But that's a long and interesting story. Fortunately, we have plenty of time. After all, nobody's chasing you."

Afterword

Einstein defined a genius as a plagiarist who is better at concealing his sources.

I'm manifestly no genius, and I'm no plagiarist. But everything is inspired by something, and most authors say that the most frequent question they field is "where do you get your ideas?"

The obvious truth about the idea for *Overkill* is that it springs from the physical and historical universe, the characters, and the voice that were created in the five Jason Wander books, beginning with 2004's *Orphanage*. So if you want to know where the War, and Cavorite drive, and Jazen's parents came from, a voyage through a copy of *Orphanage, et seq* will float your boat.

To quote Ferris Bueller, "If you have the means, I highly recommend picking one up." In fact, I recommend you pick up two.

The Jason Wander books said most of what I wanted to say about being a soldier, in particular a soldier cast into a war against an enemy alien to him and to his world.

But they said very little about alien intelligence. That was unavoidable, because *Orphanage* was written after 9–11 and concerned an indiscriminate attack by an enigmatic, indeed literally faceless, enemy upon a bewildered world. "Who are those guys, and why do they hate us?" The four subsequent volumes chronicled the long, remotely-contested, trial-and-blunder (is there any other kind?) war that followed. The aliens remained enigmatic to support the 9–11/Iraq/Afghanistan allegory. Twitter generation consult Wiktionary under "A."

Overkill doesn't wear the allegorical handcuffs of the world in which it was written. It explores alien intelligence and our reaction to it. But at an accessible depth designed, as Robert Heinlein claimed of his fiction, "to entertain and to buy groceries." If you find more there, I'm flattered.

But *Overkill* has an inspirational seed I want to acknowledge.

In 1940 and 1942, the great A. E. van Vogt wrote for *Astounding Science Fiction Magazine* a couple of short stories pitting mankind against the ezwals, a race of grumpy, six-legged predators who read minds. Van Vogt years later pasted these "shorts" together with other, unrelated, shorts and created a "fixup" novel, a format he is credited both with inventing and naming. In 1959, that novel, *The War Against the Rull*, was finally published.

During the Golden Age of Science Fiction, defined by each generation as whatever it was reading at age thirteen, I read *The War Against the Rull*.

I thought the part about the ezwals was *really cool*, but should have been, you know, longer, and stuff.

Action on this sophisticated literary insight was postponed by puberty, then by four decades that were rewarding, and stuff. But not *really cool*.

Hence, in 2011, *Overkill*. With apologies and sincere appreciation to A. E. van Vogt.

—Robert Buettner

Acknowledgments

Thanks, first, to my publisher, Toni Weisskopf, for the opportunity and encouragement to create *Overkill*, as well as for insights and ideas that helped make it better. Thanks also to Laura Haywood-Cory for wise and patient editing, to Managing Editor Danielle Turner for managing so well, and to copy editor Miranda Barbare for perfection. My appreciation to Hank Davis and Jim Minz for making this a book, and to cover artist Justin Adams, to Twin Typesetting's Deborah Monette, Amazon/Audible.com's Steven Feldberg, and the good folks at Simon & Schuster for making sure it arrived on the shelves looking and sounding great, and to everyone else at Baen books for remarkable support and enthusiasm.

Special thanks to all the soldiers of Third Heavy Brigade Combat Team, Third Infantry Division, the Sledgehammer of the Rock of the Marne, deployed at this writing in the Republic of Iraq, for their service. Even more special thanks to Third HBCT's Captain Charlie Barrett, SFC Stephen Burden and Staff Sargeant Joseph Maughon, for getting an old tanker's son up close and personal with a contemporary Abrams. Thanks also to Harry Sarles and Brenda Donnell of the Department of the Army Office of the Chief of Public Affairs, and to Major Lon Widdicombe, USA, for making it all possible. Any errors regarding tanks and tankers are mine, not theirs.

Thanks, as ever, to my superb agent, Winifred Golden. To date, the battles she has fought on my behalf haven't been against tanks. Fortunately for the tanks.

Finally and forever, thanks to Mary Beth for everything that matters.

About the Author

Robert Buettner's first novel, *Orphanage*, nominated for the Quill Award as best Science Fiction, Fantasy and Horror novel of 2004, was compared favorably to Robert Heinlein's *Starship Troopers* by the *Washington Post*, *Denver Post*, Sci-Fi Channel's *Science Fiction Weekly*, and others. Now in its ninth English-language printing, *Orphanage* has been translated into five languages. *Orphan's Triumph*, the fifth and final book in the Jason Wander series that began with *Orphanage*, was named one of Fandomania's best fifteen science fiction, fantasy, and horror books of 2009–one of only two science fiction books to make the list.

A former Military Intelligence Officer, National Science Foundation Fellow in Paleontology, and Colorado lawyer, Robert Buettner lives in the Blue Ridge foothills north of Atlanta, with his family and more bicycles than a grownup needs. Visit him on the web at www.RobertBuettner.com.